HARDCASTLE'S OBSESSION

Graham Ison

This first world edition published 2011
in Great Britain and the USA by
SEVERN HOUSE PUBLISHERS LTD of
9–15 High Street, Sutton, Surrey, England, SM1 1DF.
Trade paperback edition first published
in Great Britain and the USA 2011 by
SEVERN HOUSE PUBLISHERS LTD.

British Library Cataloguing in Publication Data

Ison, Graham.
  Hardcastle's obsession.
  1. Hardcastle, Ernest (Fictitious character)–Fiction.
  2. Police–England–London–Fiction. 3. World War,
  1914-1918–Casualties–England–London–Fiction.
  4. Great Britain–History–George V, 1910-1936–Fiction.
  5. Detective and mystery stories.
  I. Title
  823.9'14-dc22

ISBN-13: 978-0-7278-8002-4 (cased)
ISBN-13: 978-1-84751-329-8 (trade paper)

Except wher
described for
publication a
is purely coi

All Severn H

Severn Hous   FSC],
the leading ii   es that
are printed o   FSC logo.

Typeset by Palimpsest Book Production Ltd.,
Falkirk, Stirlingshire, Scotland.
Printed and bound in Great Britain by
MPG Books Ltd., Bodmin, Cornwall.

GLOSSARY

ALBERT: a watch chain of the type worn by Albert, Prince Consort (1819–61).
APM: assistant provost marshal (a lieutenant colonel of the military police).

BAILEY, the: Central Criminal Court, Old Bailey, London.
BAILIWICK: area of responsibility.
BEAK: a magistrate.
BEETON, Mrs: famous writer of a widely read cookery book.
BEF: British Expeditionary Force in France and Flanders.
BIRD, to give the: to dismiss.
BLACK ANNIE or BLACK MARIA: a police or prison van.
BLIGHTY ONE: a wound suffered in battle that necessitated repatriation to the United Kingdom.
BLOW, a: police slang for a relief.
BLUEJACKET: a seaman in the navy.
BOB: a shilling (now 5p).
BOCHE: derogatory term for Germans, particularly soldiers.
BOOTNECK: a member of the Royal Marines.
BOOZER: a public house.
BRADSHAW: a timetable giving routes and times of British railway services.
BRIEF, a: a warrant _or_ a police warrant card _or_ a lawyer.

CARPET: three months' imprisonment. Three months was the time it took to weave a carpet in prison workshops.

DABS: fingerprints.
DARTMOOR: a remote prison on Dartmoor in Devon.
DDI: Divisional Detective Inspector.
DEKKO: a look (_ex_ Hindi).
DRUM: a dwelling house, or room therein. Any place of abode.

DUFF, to put up the: to make pregnant.
DUMMY, to throw a: to set a false trail.

FOURPENNY CANNON, a: a steak and kidney pie.
FRONT, The: theatre of WW1 operations in France and
  Flanders.

GAMP: an umbrella (from Sarah Gamp in Charles
  Dickens's *Martin Chuzzlewit*).
GLIM: a look (a foreshortening of 'glimpse').
GLOSTERS: Alternative spelling for the Gloucestershire
  Regiment.
GUNNERS, The: a generic term to encompass the Royal
  Horse Artillery, the Royal Garrison Artillery and the
  Royal Field Artillery. In the singular, a member of such a
  regiment.
GUV *or* **GUV'NOR:** informal alternative to 'sir'.

HALF-COLONEL: a lieutenant colonel.
HAVE IT UP, to: to engage in sexual intercourse.
HAWKING THE MUTTON: leading a life of prostitution.
HOLLOWAY: women's prison in North London.

JIG-A-JIG: sexual intercourse.

KC: King's Counsel: a senior barrister.

MADAM: a brothel keeper.
MATELOT: a sailor, usually of the Royal Navy.

NICK: a police station <u>or</u> prison <u>or</u> to arrest <u>or</u> to steal.
NICKED: arrested <u>or</u> stolen.

OLD BAILEY: Central Criminal Court, in Old Bailey,
  London.
ON THE GAME: leading a life of prostitution.
OX AND BUCKS: Oxfordshire and Buckinghamshire
  Light Infantry.

PICCADILLY WINDOW: a monocle.
PIMP: a prostitute's 'minder'.

POLICE GAZETTE: official nationwide publication listing wanted persons, etc.

PROSS: a prostitute.

PROVOST, the: military police.

QUID: £1 sterling.

RAGTIME GIRL: a sweetheart; a girl with whom one has a joyous time; a harlot.

RECEIVER, The: senior Scotland Yard official responsible for the finances of the Metropolitan Police.

ROSIE: tea (rhyming slang: Rosie Lee).

ROYAL A: informal name for the A or Whitehall Division of the Metropolitan Police.

SALLY ANNE: the Salvation Army.

SAM BROWNE: a military officer's belt with shoulder strap.

SAUSAGE AND MASH: cash (rhyming slang).

SCREWING: engaging in sexual intercourse.

SDI: sub-divisional inspector.

SHILLING: now 5p.

SILK, a: a King's Counsel (a senior barrister) from the silk gowns they wear.

SKIP *or* SKIPPER: an informal police alternative to station-sergeant, clerk-sergeant and sergeant.

SMOKE, The: London.

SOMERSET HOUSE: formerly the records office of births, deaths and marriages for England & Wales.

SOV or SOVEREIGN: one pound sterling.

SPALPEEN: a rascal; a worthless fellow.

SWADDY: a soldier (*ex* Hindi).

TITFER: a hat (rhyming slang: tit for tat).

TOM: a prostitute.

TOMFOOLERY: jewellery (rhyming slang).

TOMMING: pursuing a life of prostitution.

TOMMY or TOMMY ATKINS: a British soldier. The name 'Tommy Atkins' was used as an example on early army forms.

TOPPED: murdered or hanged.

TOPPING: a murder or hanging.
TOUCH OF THE VAPOURS, a: to be overcome with faintness.
TRICK, a: a prostitute's client.
TRICK, to turn a: to engage in sexual intercourse.
TUMBLE, a: sexual intercourse.

UNDERGROUND, The: London Underground railway system.
UP THE SPOUT: pregnant.
UP THE DUFF: pregnant.

WAR HOUSE: army officers' slang for the War Office.
WAR OFFICE: Department of State overseeing the army. (Now a part of the Ministry of Defence.)
WIPERS: Army slang for Ypres in Belgium, scene of several fierce Great War battles.

ONE

A Zeppelin hovered over central London. But the moderate south-east wind was not strong enough to move the clouds, and the visibility was so poor that the huge menacing shape of the giant airship was invisible to the probing searchlights on Apsley Gate. Only the steady throb of its four 210-horse-power Maybach engines could be heard in the streets below. And it was raining.

It was five past ten on the night of Sunday the 24th of September 1916. The Great War had been in progress for just over two years, and the nation was still reeling from the losses on the first day of the Battle of the Somme: 58,000 casualties of which a third were dead.

The maroons, warning of an air raid, had been set off thirty minutes earlier from the nearby fire station in Greycoat Place. At the time, there were thirteen people in the old Victorian house at 143 Washbourne Street; it was perhaps fortunate that there were not more.

When the alert had sounded, a few of the residents had made for the basement of the four-storied dwelling. Others, some in nightclothes with just an overcoat or even a blanket around their shoulders, had fled the short distance to Victoria railway station, there to seek sanctuary in the depths of the Underground railway system. Some were clutching their dearest personal possessions; in their haste others had not bothered. A couple of the women were clasping tiny babies each wrapped in a shawl.

Minutes after the departure of the shelter-seeking inhabitants, the Zeppelin discharged a cluster of bombs intended for the railway station. But they struck the roof of No 143, and penetrated to the third floor before exploding with deadly force. The entire house imploded, sending tons of masonry into the basement. A section of wall fell outwards into the street, and by chance struck a passing telegram delivery boy. He was thrown from his bicycle and died instantly, another casualty of this apparently interminable war.

The fire brigade crew that arrived minutes later could do little but extinguish the flames. If anyone was buried beneath the piles of rubble, it would need more than the slender resources of the firemen to excavate them. They sent for workmen from the City of Westminster depot. But neither they nor the fire crew held out much hope for any survivors.

The search operation had continued all night. But by nine o'clock on the Monday morning, when clerks were hurrying to work at the offices in Victoria, seven bodies had been recovered, two of them small children.

Inspector Jasper Sankey and two constables from Rochester Row police station had been on hand for most of the night to assist in the recovery of the corpses.

A small knot of sightseers watched the grisly task confronting police and rescue workers. Corralled to one side of this crowd were the lucky residents of number 143 who were congratulating themselves on the wisdom of having taken shelter elsewhere. But delight at their salvation from this latest German atrocity was tinged by the sadness of having lost their homes, all their worldly possessions, and in some cases, their friends.

'Is there anyone from this house who's an old soldier?' asked Sankey, addressing the group of survivors. He had a good reason for posing the question.

'Me, sir.' A man of about forty stepped forward. He was wearing an old tweed jacket over a collarless shirt, and thick flannel trousers. The right arm of the jacket was pinned up. 'Lost me arm at Festubert last year, guv'nor,' he explained.

'In that case, you'll have seen a few dead bodies in your time, I imagine,' said Sankey.

'Aye, too many, guv'nor, and that's a fact.'

'What's your name?'

'Albert Jackson, sir. Sergeant in the old Ox and Bucks I was, until I got me Blighty one.' Jackson tapped the stump inside his empty right sleeve.

'The Ox and Bucks?' queried Sankey.

'Yes, sir, the Oxfordshire and Buckinghamshire Light Infantry. Second battalion. Our lot was at Waterloo with the Duke of Wellington, you know.'

'Were they indeed?' Sankey was not greatly interested in the history of Jackson's former regiment. 'Would you be prepared to come with me to the mortuary to identify these people, Mr Jackson?' He pointed at the departing lorry on to which the dead and disfigured bodies from the house had been loaded. And the one body of the telegram boy.

'Might as well,' said Jackson. 'I've got bugger all else to do.' He took a pipe from his jacket pocket, and adroitly filled it from a pouch. 'Learned a few one-handed tricks since Fritz took me arm off, guv'nor,' he added with a grin. 'Case of having to. Still, I was one of the lucky ones, I s'pose. Could've been blinded or lost me legs like some poor buggers.'

'D'you know the people who lived there?' Sankey nodded towards the ruined house. With four floors housing separate families, it suddenly occurred to him that Jackson might not know them all.

'Yes, I do. Most of the menfolk are away at the Front, see, and I try to keep an eye open for the wives and their bairns. In case there's anything I can do, like. Amazing, ain't it? The wives are expecting to hear their husbands have copped it, but now it's the other way round.'

'How many people were living in the house, Mr Jackson?'

'Thirteen all up, Inspector.'

'We've recovered seven bodies from the basement,' said Sankey. 'Plus the telegram lad, but he wasn't in the house.'

'That don't add up, guv'nor,' said Jackson.

'What doesn't add up? What d'you mean by that?' Sankey turned to face the old soldier.

Jackson waved his hand at the small crowd of survivors. 'There's seven of us here what lived there, so that makes fourteen in all. One too many, if you see what I mean.'

'Perhaps one of them was staying with a relative who lived there,' suggested Sankey.

'Who'd want to come up to the bloody Smoke with all this going on?' queried Jackson, shaking his head. 'They'd have to be raving mad.'

'Anyway, I dare say we'll sort it out.' Sankey beckoned to a passing cab, and directed the driver to take him and Jackson to Horseferry Road mortuary. He hoped that he would be able to claim reimbursement of the fare on the grounds that he was escorting a disabled ex-soldier on official business.

The Metropolitan Police was extremely parsimonious when it came to expenses.

As befitted an old soldier who had seen too many dead bodies, Albert Jackson displayed no emotion as he surveyed the victims of the air raid. For a moment or two, he just stood silently, wondering, yet again, what was to be achieved by such a pointless loss.

One by one he put names to each of them. Except for one. The exception was a young woman, probably in her twenties and who, compared with the others, was almost unscathed.

'Dunno who she is,' said Jackson, 'but I reckon she died of the shock. It happens, you know, guv'nor. I've seen it in the trenches.'

'Yes, I know,' said Sankey, who had dealt with air raid victims on all too many occasions. 'And you're sure you've no idea who she is.'

'Positive, guv'nor. Never set eyes on her till now. She certainly don't live at one-forty-three.'

Inspector Sankey was now faced with a problem. If the dead woman had been a visitor to the ruined house, and had been staying with a family that had been killed, the chances of identifying her were considerably lessened. And that meant it would not be possible to inform her family. Not that it would be the first time that an air raid victim had been buried in an unmarked grave.

It was now eleven o'clock on the Monday morning, and Sankey had been on duty for thirteen hours. But there was still work to be done.

He made his way to the Royal Horticultural Society hall in Vincent Square where the newly homeless of the Washbourne Street bombing were being given temporary shelter.

He found the disconsolate group in a corner of the large hall. Those who had made for the railway station in their nightclothes were now dressed in a variety of clothing provided for them by the Salvation Army.

'I'm Inspector Sankey of Rochester Row police station,' he announced.

Seeing the policeman's drawn face, and his torn and dust-covered uniform, a young woman in 'Sally Ann' uniform handed him a cup of tea. 'I reckon you could do with that, Inspector,' she said.

'Thank you, miss.' Sankey took a sip of the scalding liquid, and returned his gaze to the Washbourne Street survivors. 'We found the body of a young woman in the basement of your house,' he began, 'but Mr Jackson couldn't identify her.'

'Never seen her before,' said Jackson.

'She appeared to be in her early twenties with long brown hair. She was wearing a fancy red cotton blouse, a black skirt to about mid-calf, and high, black, laced boots. Do any of you know this woman? Or had any of you seen her at all?'

There was a brief babble of conversation among the survivors, but eventually it was obvious that none of them was able to help.

Sankey decided that he had done enough, and could safely leave it to others to find out the name of the young female victim.

At eight o'clock on Thursday morning, Divisional Detective Inspector Ernest Hardcastle walked into the front office of Cannon Row police station. Built to the plans of Norman Shaw, the station and the daunting structure of New Scotland Yard opposite had been built of granite quarried from Dartmoor by prisoners from the nearby prison.

'All correct, sir,' said the station officer, his four-bar chevrons indicating that he was a station-sergeant.

Hardcastle grunted an acknowledgement. He was always irritated that the regulations required junior officers to report thus, whether all was correct or not.

The station officer placed the crime book on the desk, opened it and stood back to allow Hardcastle to sit down. The DDI put on his spectacles, and glanced quickly through the night's entries. Two pickpockets had been detained outside Buckingham Palace the previous evening, a burglar had been arrested during the night in Grosvenor Place, and a man had been caught stealing a bicycle in Waterloo Place.

Deciding that none of these crimes required his immediate attention, Hardcastle stood up and walked upstairs to his office.

'Good morning, sir.' Detective Sergeant Charles Marriott stood at the door of the detectives' office. As the first-class sergeant, he was in charge of the junior Cannon Row detectives, and was the officer that Hardcastle favoured to assist him in any investigation that was assigned to him. 'Mr Hudson wishes to see you straight away, sir.'

'Oh?' Hardcastle paused. 'What's that all about, then?'

'I don't know, sir,' said Marriott.

'No, I didn't expect you to, Marriott. I was wondering aloud, so to speak. Superintendents don't usually tell sergeants why they want DDIs.' Hardcastle entered his office and placed his bowler hat and umbrella on the hatstand. It had been a mild autumn so far, and he had not deemed it necessary to bring his chesterfield overcoat into use. 'Well, I'd better see what it's all about, I suppose.' He walked along the corridor and tapped lightly on Superintendent Arthur Hudson's door before entering.

'Ah, Ernie, good morning.' Hudson, the officer in command of the A or Whitehall Division of the Metropolitan Police was standing behind his desk reading a file.

'Good morning, sir.'

'Sit yourself down, Ernie. I've got a tricky murder for you here.' Hudson flourished the file.

'All my murders are tricky ones, sir.'

'Yes, but I think this one just might test you more than a little,' said Hudson with a smile, as he seated himself behind his desk. 'Do light up, Ernie.' The superintendent knew it to be Hardcastle's invariable habit to start his working day by smoking a pipe.

'Thank you, sir.' Hardcastle filled his pipe with his favourite St Bruno tobacco, and accepted the box of Swan Vestas matches that Hudson pushed towards him.

'There was a bomb at a hundred and forty-three Washbourne Street on Sunday night,' Hudson began.

'Yes, I know, sir.' Hardcastle expelled smoke towards the nicotine-stained ceiling; Hudson, too, was an inveterate pipe smoker, perhaps smoking more often than even Hardcastle.

'Inspector Sankey of Rochester Row was in charge of the incident,' began Hudson, reading from the inspector's report. 'Apart from a telegram boy who was killed in the street, there were seven fatalities in the house itself. However, the body of a young woman was found in the basement, but Sankey was unable to discover her identity. A man called Jackson assisted Sankey at the scene, but swore he'd never seen the woman before. Sankey is fairly satisfied that she wasn't a resident.'

'Could've been a visitor, I suppose, sir,' said Hardcastle.

'Possibly,' said Hudson, 'but there's a complication. The doctor who examined her, only in order to certify death, was of the opinion that she might've been strangled.' The superintendent glanced at Hardcastle, a half smile on his face.

'Who was this doctor, sir?'

'A Doctor Thomas, a local GP.'

'Not a pathologist, then,' said Hardcastle dismissively.

'No, but the Home Office can't spare a forensic pathologist to examine every victim of a bombing, Ernie. No doubt you'll want Spilsbury to take a look.'

Dr Bernard Spilsbury was an eminent specialist in the field of murder, and his reputation was such that the likelihood of his appearance in the witness box caused many a defence counsel to work into the small hours preparing his cross-examination. One of Spilsbury's most recent *causes célèbres* was the Brides-in-the-Bath case when his evidence of the method by which George Joseph Smith had murdered his several wives was instrumental in sending Smith to the gallows just over a year ago.

'Indeed, I shall, sir. Dr Spilsbury will tell us whether the woman had been strangled or not. Frankly, I don't trust a local GP to be certain of the cause of death, and I'd hate to have to put him in the witness box. Defence counsel would make mincemeat of him, particularly if it were someone like Marshall Hall.' Sir Edward Marshall Hall, scourge of prosecution witnesses, was regarded as the foremost defence counsel of the day. But even he, when defending Smith, had been bettered by Spilsbury. 'Where's this here body now, sir?'

Hudson referred to the report again. 'Horseferry Road mortuary.'

'I dare say Dr Spilsbury will want the body moved to St Mary's at Paddington. It's where he always does his post-mortem examinations.'

'I'll leave you to speak to Spilsbury about that, Ernie. And the best of luck.'

Hardcastle walked back down the corridor, shouting for Marriott on the way.

'Yes, sir?' said Marriott, as he followed the DDI into his office.

'We've got a suspicious death to deal with, Marriott.'

'Yes, sir, I know,' said Marriott.

Hardcastle frowned. 'How did you know that?' he demanded.

'It's the job of the first-class sergeant to know all that's happening on his subdivision, sir.' Marriott risked a smile.

'Yes, well as you're so clever, Marriott, perhaps you can tell me who this young woman is.'

'I'm not that clever, sir.'

'No, I didn't think so. Get on that telephone thing, and ask Doctor Spilsbury if he'd be so good as to examine a body for us.' Although conversant with its use, Hardcastle disliked the telephone and in common with many of his contemporaries, regarded it as a newfangled invention that would not last.

Marriott returned ten minutes later. 'Doctor Spilsbury asked that the body be removed to St Mary's at Paddington, sir, and he'll examine it at two o'clock this afternoon.'

'Yes, well, I thought he'd want it there. See to it, Marriott.'

'Manual strangulation, Hardcastle, without a doubt,' said Spilsbury. 'There were bruise marks on the young woman's neck, and when I opened her up I found that the thyroid cartilage had been broken. I would say that considerable force was applied by the thumb of the right hand, or even by both thumbs. It might even have been a chopping action with the heel of the hand, but it was no accidental killing.'

'Is it possible that the injury was caused by the falling masonry on the night of the bomb?' asked Hardcastle, wondering if, even yet, he might avoid a murder enquiry.

'Maybe,' said Spilsbury, 'although I very much doubt it. There was nothing to indicate that to be the case. I would definitely say that deliberate pressure was applied with the intention of killing the victim, or, as I said just now, a lethal blow.'

'Well, that's murder, then,' said Hardcastle phlegmatically. 'Anything else I should know, Doctor?'

'It's not possible in the circumstances to say how recently she had indulged in sexual intercourse, my dear Hardcastle, but I can tell you that she was about two months pregnant.' Spilsbury paused to turn the body on its side. 'There is a birthmark here behind the left knee,' he said, pointing with a pair of forceps. 'That might help. I understand that the cadaver has yet to be identified.'

'That's correct, Doctor. We don't know who she is at the moment, but I'll find out, you may rest assured of that.'

Spilsbury smiled, and took off his rubber apron. 'I'm sure you will, Hardcastle.'

'Let's have a look at the clobber she was wearing, Marriott,' said Hardcastle when, once again, the two detectives were back at Cannon Row police station.

Marriott opened the large paper bag in which he had carried the unknown woman's clothing from the hospital, and emptied it on to a table in the detectives' office.

Using a pencil, Hardcastle poked at the various items, paying particular attention to the woman's underwear. 'That's the sort of stuff a tart would wear, Marriott,' he said eventually. 'My girls wouldn't be seen dead in that sort of clobber.'

'No, sir,' said Marriott, forbearing from saying that the unknown woman *had* been found dead in that sort of clobber. The DDI did not appreciate such humour, unless he was the one practising it.

'I wouldn't be surprised to find that she's a prostitute. Where's the nearest whores' beat to Washbourne Street, Marriott?'

'These days it's mainly Victoria station, sir, and the girls usually congregate when a troop train's due in. They seem to know that the two things a swaddy wants when he gets home on leave is a pint and a tumble. They tend to gather near the buffets, but the railway coppers move them on. So they just shift to the street outside, usually near the pub on the corner of Wilton Road. Then they get moved on again by our men.'

Hardcastle glanced, in turn, at each of the four detective constables who were standing around the table in the centre of the room. 'Catto.'

'Sir?' said Detective Constable Henry Catto, stepping across to the DDI.

'Take your three colleagues down to Victoria station and start asking questions among the prostitutes who hang about there. I want to know if any one of them is missing.' That done, Hardcastle addressed himself to DS Herbert Wood. 'Get a message off to surrounding stations, Wood, asking them to check reports of any missing persons who fit the description of our body.'

'Anything for me, sir?' asked Marriott.

'Yes. Ask Mrs Cartwright if she can rustle up a couple of cups of tea, Marriott. Then we'll sit down and put our thinking caps on.'

TWO

'How's your boy Jack, Mrs Cartwright?' asked Hardcastle, as the station matron set down her tray and placed two cups of tea on the DDI's desk.

'He was all right the last time I heard from him, sir, thank you. He's a lance-bombardier now.' Mrs Cartwright was proud of her son who had been serving with the Royal Garrison Artillery since the outbreak of the war. 'I managed to get some of your favourites,' she added, putting a plate of ginger snaps on the desk.

'Well done, Mrs C,' said Hardcastle, and dropped three pennies on the tray.

'Thank you, sir.' Mrs Cartwright scooped up the coins and put them in the pocket of her overall coat.

'Where's your lad stationed now, Mrs C?'

'I don't rightly know, sir, except that he's somewhere in France or Belgium, I suppose. He's not allowed to say exactly where in his letters. I know he tries to tell me, but sometimes they arrive with whole bits blacked out.'

'That'll be the censor's work,' said Hardcastle. 'It's in case old Fritz happens to read the lad's letters, so the censor's making sure your boy doesn't accidentally tell the enemy anything.'

'I s'pose so, sir,' said Mrs Cartwright, failing to understand how the Germans could possibly read her son's letters home. Picking up the tray she went on her way.

'Well now, Marriott,' said Hardcastle, dunking a ginger snap in his tea. 'What are we going to do about this here murder of ours?'

Marriott was tempted say 'Wait and see', but he knew that was not the answer his chief wanted. 'Is it possible that she was staying with one of the deceased, sir?' he asked tentatively.

'It's possible, Marriott, but I doubt we'll ever know now. Anyway, that don't help us to identify her. She could've come from anywhere.' Hardcastle found the prospect of investigating the unknown's murder a daunting task, but he was not about to admit it to his sergeant.

'I suppose the birthmark on her leg might help, sir.'

Hardcastle shook his head. 'It's a dog's dinner, Marriott,' he said, using one of his favourite expressions to describe a difficult enquiry, although this was sometimes varied to 'a dog's breakfast'. 'We'd better see what Catto and his colleagues turn up, I suppose, if anything. There are times when I think that Catto needs a squib up his arse, Marriott. You really need to get a hold of him.'

'Yes, sir,' said Marriott, but forbore from further comment. He knew that DC Henry Catto was a good detective, and it was only when he was in the DDI's presence that he seemed to become bereft of his confidence.

For the remainder of the morning, Hardcastle toyed with his detectives' reports. Some he accepted, some he sent back with acerbic pencilled comments in the margin for alteration, and others he rejected outright.

At one o'clock, he again summoned Marriott. 'Time you bought me a pint, Marriott,' he said, and together they adjourned to the downstairs bar of the Red Lion. That Marriott should pay was one of the DDI's jokes; Hardcastle never paid for his beer in the Red Lion.

The public house was conveniently situated on the corner of Parliament Street and Derby Gate, just outside the Whitehall entrance to New Scotland Yard. As usual, their lunch consisted of a fourpenny cannon and two pints of best bitter.

'And now, Marriott, we'll go round to Washbourne Street, and have a dekko at the scene of this here crime.'

The pavement and part of the road in front of 143 Washbourne Street had been barricaded, and a policeman stood guard.

'All correct, sir.' The PC saluted as he recognized the DDI.

'Doesn't look like it,' muttered Hardcastle, gazing at the ruins of the house. 'What are you doing here, anyway?'

'Mr Marsh says we're to keep an eye open for looters, sir.' Marsh was the sub-divisional inspector in charge of the Rochester Row station.

'Safe to go in there, is it, lad?' Hardcastle always called PCs 'lad' regardless of their age or service.

'I think so, sir. The men from the council depot have been round tidying up and making safe.'

'Oh, you *think* it's safe, do you? Well, I hope you're right, lad, because if I fall arse over tit, I'll come after you.'

Ducking beneath the barrier, Hardcastle and Marriott stepped across the rubble. Eventually finding the cellar steps, they descended warily into the basement. Much of the debris had been cleared away by council workmen, and the detectives were able to see reasonably well.

'Have a look around, Marriott, and see if you can find anything that might shed some light on this poor girl's death.' Hardcastle began poking about with his umbrella, but held out little hope of finding anything that might further his investigation, but in that he was wrong.

Marriott caught sight of something glinting in the light that had penetrated that part of the basement. Stooping, he picked up a piece of jewellery.

'What have you got there, Marriott?' asked Hardcastle.

'It's a necklace, sir. Lucky one of the workmen didn't nick it.'

'Let me have a look.' Hardcastle put on his spectacles, took the necklace and examined it closely. 'That's called a dog collar necklet, Marriott. Looks like silver, and unless I'm much mistaken, they're diamonds. I wonder who it belongs to.' He handed it back. 'Have a word with one of the jewellers on the ground, and see what he has to say about it. Might lead us somewhere, I suppose.'

'It looks as though the clip's been broken, sir,' said Marriott, examining the necklace afresh.

'Could've been torn off the victim's neck in the struggle, I suppose,' said Hardcastle. 'Not that I think a tom could've afforded a piece like that. Of course, it might've been given to her by a grateful client, or she might've nicked it.'

'Maybe so, sir,' said Marriott, slipping the necklace into his pocket. 'But I don't think there's anything else here to interest us.'

Leaving Hardcastle to return to the police station alone, Marriott made for a jeweller of his acquaintance in Victoria Street.

'Good afternoon, Mr Marriott. Won't keep you a moment.' Gilbert Parfitt was dealing with a customer, a well-dressed man, who was examining a tray of rings.

The man eventually decided against a purchase, and left the shop.

'We've had today's list, Mr Marriott,' said Parfitt, turning his attention to the detective. The list to which he referred was circulated daily to jewellers and pawnbrokers, and detailed stolen items of jewellery and valuable metals that thieves might have attempted to sell.

'Yes, I know, Mr Parfitt.' Marriott withdrew the necklet from his pocket. 'I wonder if you'd have a look at this silver and stones piece,' he said, and handed it to the jeweller.

Parfitt spread a baize cloth on the counter, placed the necklet on it, and screwed a jeweller's glass into his eye. He spent some minutes studying the piece before looking up. 'A very nice setting, Mr Marriott.' He put aside his glass. 'Is it stolen?'

'Not as far as I know,' said Marriott. 'It was found at the scene of a murder. We're not sure who it belongs to, but we're fairly certain it's too expensive to have belonged to the prostitute who was murdered.'

'Unless she stole it,' said Parfitt with a smile.

Marriott nodded. 'It's a possibility we have to consider, of course. But can you tell me what it would be worth?'

'The stones are diamonds set in platinum, not silver.' For a moment or two Parfitt gave the matter some thought, and then referred to a large book that he withdrew from beneath counter. 'At a reasonable estimate,' he said eventually, 'I doubt you'd get much change out of three hundred and fifty pounds, Mr Marriott.'

Marriott emitted a low whistle. 'As much as that?'

'I would say that it belonged to a woman of some wealth, Mr Marriott.'

'I suppose there's no way of tracing who it belonged to originally, is there?'

Parfitt looked doubtful. 'I can take a description, Mr Marriott, and circulate the details among the trade. It may take some time, and even then I might not discover the owner. But I'm willing to try.'

'Very good of you, Mr Parfitt,' said Marriott. 'I'm much

obliged.' And with that, he returned to Cannon Row, and told the DDI what he had learned.

'Don't get us much further, Marriott,' grunted Hardcastle.

It was not until six o'clock that evening that Henry Catto returned to the police station. He tapped on the DDI's door and waited for the barked command to enter.

'Yes, Catto?'

'Er, it's about the prostitutes, sir,' said Catto nervously.

'Well, what about them? And don't stand there hovering in my doorway like a dying duck in a thunderstorm. Come in, lad.'

'Yes, sir.' Catto took a pace or two towards Hardcastle's desk. 'We talked to the women who frequent the Victoria station area, sir, and—'

'I should hope you did, Catto. That's what I sent you up there for. What did you find out?'

'We spoke to several of the women, sir, and Gordon Lipton found out that the one woman they haven't seen for a few days is called Queenie Douglas.'

'Where's Lipton now?'

'Er, in the office, sir.'

'Well, I want to hear it from him. I won't have any truck with hearsay or sloppy reporting, Catto. You should know that. Fetch him in here at once.'

'Yes, sir.' Catto fled, reappearing seconds later with DC Lipton.

'Now, what's all this about a missing tom, Lipton?'

'I spoke to several of the women, sir, and one of them, a Polly Brewer, knew her quite well. She told me that Queenie Douglas hasn't been seen around since last Sunday. That'd be the twenty-fourth, sir.'

'And our anonymous body was found in the rubble of the house in Washbourne Street early on the Monday morning,' said Hardcastle. 'Did this Polly Brewer know where Queenie Douglas lived?'

'Apparently she dossed down in Strutton Ground in a room over a chandler's shop, sir. At least, that's where she said Queenie turned her tricks.'

'Right, carry on, and tell Sergeant Marriott I want him.'

Hardcastle buckled on his spats, seized his hat and umbrella and met Marriott in the corridor. 'We're going to Strutton Ground, Marriott. Get your titfer and gamp. Looks like it might rain.' The pessimistic Hardcastle always thought it was about to rain.

'Very good, sir.' Marriott crossed the corridor to the detectives' office and collected his bowler hat and umbrella, and he and the DDI set off for Victoria Street.

'Well, Marriott, there seems to be only the one chandler's shop here.' Hardcastle stared up and down Strutton Ground.

'Nice juicy apples, guv'nor,' yelled a market trader from the other side of the road. 'Fresh up from Kent today.' He held up a large Cox's Orange Pippin.

Hardcastle glared at the vendor. 'I hope you've got a licence, lad,' he said. 'And when were your scales last checked?'

'Bloody coppers,' muttered the fruiterer, and replaced the apple on the carefully constructed pyramid of fruit on his costermonger's barrow.

Hardcastle pushed open the door of the chandler's shop. 'Police,' he announced tersely. 'Who are you?'

'Fred Watson, guv'nor, and I've been here twenty years and never had any trouble with the law.'

'Well, you might have now,' said Hardcastle. 'What can you tell me about this prostitute who lives over your shop?'

'D'you mean young Queenie Douglas, sir?' The chandler sounded shocked at the suggestion that one of his tenants could be a prostitute. The apprehension showed in his face; he knew the allegation to be true.

'Yes, I do.'

'She ain't no pross, guv'nor,' protested Watson. 'Nice young lady she is. I wouldn't have no loose women in my lodgings.' But the nervous twitching of Watson's hands told the DDI otherwise.

'Really?' Hardcastle sounded sceptical. 'You own these premises, do you?'

'Not exactly,' said Watson. 'I rent the shop and the three rooms upstairs, but now our boy's off to sea with the Royal Navy, we don't need all three, so I thought as how I'd sort of sublet the spare room.'

'Did you indeed, well, we'll need to have a look at this here room that you've sort of sublet to Queenie Douglas.'

'Is young Queenie in some kind of trouble, guv'nor?' The chandler appeared anguished by Hardcastle's request.

'We think she might've been murdered,' said Marriott.

'Oh my Gawd!' exclaimed Watson, but his shock was more likely the result of a loss of rent, than sorrow at the fate of the dead woman. 'You'd better come this way.' He led the detectives through his shop to a staircase at the rear. On the way he shouted to someone called Reginald.

An acne-stricken youth of about fifteen appeared from a storeroom. 'Yes, Mr Watson?'

'Take over the shop, Reginald. I've got to take these gents up to Queenie's room.'

The room into which Watson showed the two CID officers was obviously the room to which Queenie Douglas took her clients. There was a bed, a wash-hand basin, and a small rug covering the centre of the bare-boarded floor. But there appeared to be no personal possessions.

'It doesn't look as though Queenie Douglas lives here,' Hardcastle announced, in a tone of voice that brooked no argument. Although in that, he was wrong.

'I thought she did,' said Watson, looking extremely concerned at the DDI's abrasive attitude, and at once contriving an expression of mystification.

'Mr Watson, it's as plain as the nose on my face that this here Queenie Douglas uses this place for plying her trade as a common prostitute. How much rent does she pay you? And don't even think of lying because I'll check.'

The chandler paused for a moment. 'Seven bob a week,' he said.

'That seems to be a great deal of money for renting this room, Mr Watson,' said Marriott. 'I suggest that you knew how she made her money, and decided that you'd have some of it. And that, my friend, makes you guilty of living on immoral earnings.'

'I never knew that's what she was up to, so help me,' protested the anguished Watson.

'How many other girls use this room, Watson?' demanded Hardcastle. That the DDI had omitted the honorific of 'mister' indicated that he had moved Watson from the status of helpful informant to one of culpable lessor.

'None, guv'nor, honestly,' exclaimed Watson.

'I hope so, for your sake,' said Hardcastle, 'because if I find that there are other whores using this accommodation you'll be doing a carpet for keeping a brothel.'

'I never knew nothing about any of that, guv'nor, so help me,' whimpered Watson, wringing his hands. 'And seven bob seemed a reasonable rent for central London. What with the war being on.'

'I don't see what the war has to do with you fleecing a young girl, Watson,' said Hardcastle brutally. 'Anyway, you can get on with your chandelling, or whatever you call it, while Sergeant Marriott and me has a look round this drum. But you haven't seen the last of me.'

The chastened Watson fled downstairs; Hardcastle's threat of imprisonment had terrified him.

'D'you think that Mr Collins might have any luck here, sir,' suggested Marriott. Detective Inspector Charles Stockley Collins was head of the Yard's fingerprint bureau, and the leading expert in this comparatively new field of criminal investigation.

'Doubt it, Marriott,' said Hardcastle gloomily. 'If this here Queenie Douglas picked up a Tommy every night, or even more than one, Mr Collins wouldn't know where to start.' But having thought about Marriott's suggestion, he added, 'But it wouldn't do any harm for him to have a go, I suppose.'

'I'll get on to him, sir,' said Marriott.

'I don't think we're going to learn very much here,' said Hardcastle. 'I wonder where she lived when she wasn't whoring.'

'That Polly Brewer that Lipton spoke to might know, sir.'

'Yes, I think we'll have a word with those women. In the meantime, I'll have another go at Watson. I'm sure he knows more than he's telling.'

When Hardcastle and Marriott returned to the ground floor, the chandler was selling a woman customer two candles. Waiting until she had paid her sixpence and left the shop, the DDI adopted a more conciliatory approach.

'Now then, Mr Watson, I'm prepared to overlook you having accommodated a prostitute if you're willing to assist me.' Hardcastle knew very well that he would need far more evidence than he currently possessed in order to convict Watson for living on immoral earnings. Apart from which, with a murder enquiry to resolve, he had no time for such comparatively trivial offences.

'I honestly didn't know what she was up to, sir, and that's a fact.'

'Maybe . . .' said Hardcastle, deliberately injecting a tone of doubt into his voice, 'but it rather depends on how helpful you are.'

'Anything I can do, just say the word, guv'nor,' said Watson, now sycophantically desperate to please.

'I suppose that Miss Douglas used that door at the side of your premises in order to get to her room. She wouldn't have come through the shop, would she?'

'No, sir. Any road, I close at nine o'clock of an evening.'

'And does that door make a noise whenever anyone comes in?'

'It squeaks something cruel, guv'nor. I keep meaning to oil it, but I never seem to get round to it.'

'Odd that,' said Hardcastle, 'seeing as how you've got a shop full of oil.' He turned to his sergeant. 'Not surprising though, Marriott. Have you ever noticed that men who sell shoes always seem to be down at heel?'

Watson appeared bemused by this aside of Hardcastle's, but kept silent.

'And did the door bang when this Queenie came in, Mr Watson?' Much to the chandler's concern, Hardcastle kept belabouring the question of the noisy door.

'Yes, it does. I kept telling Queenie to shut it quietly, but she never took no notice.' Watson sighed at the apparent selfishness of his tenant. But Hardcastle was convinced that the chandler liked to keep a check on how many clients the girl brought back with her, and had deliberately left the door so that its hinges squeaked. Probably with a view to extracting a little more money from the girl.

'Did you ever see any of the men she brought back?'

'No, I didn't.'

'Did anyone come here asking after her?'

Watson thought about that. 'There was a soldier who called in here a couple of times.'

'Any idea of his name?'

'No, he never said. But there was something funny about his uniform. Apart from the two stripes on it.'

'Oh? What was that?'

'He had a badge on the back of his cap as well as on the front.'

'I've never heard anything like it,' exclaimed Hardcastle. 'I hope you're not trying to sell me a dummy, Watson.'

'No, guv'nor, honest. I thought it was a bit odd meself.'

'Well, if this here swaddy returns, you're to let me know *tout de suite* at Cannon Row police station. Got that, have you?' said Hardcastle, as he and Marriott turned to leave.

'You can rely on me, guv'nor,' said Watson, delighted that the detectives were leaving.

'I'd like to think so, Mr Watson.'

Followed by a hurrying Marriott, Hardcastle strode back along Strutton Ground towards Victoria Street on his way back to the police station. 'A soldier with a badge on the back of his cap, Marriott,' he muttered irritably. 'I've never heard the like of it.'

'There is a regiment that wears two badges, sir,' said Marriott.

Hardcastle stopped and stared at his sergeant. 'I hope you're not taking the piss, Marriott,' he said.

'No, sir. It's the Gloucestershire Regiment. When they were the 28th of Foot they won the distinction of wearing Sphinx badges on the front and the back of their headdress to commemorate the rearguard action they fought at the battle of Alexandria in 1801.'

'You're a bloody know-all, Marriott,' said Hardcastle, 'but that might just come in useful,' he added, ever one to turn his sergeant's knowledge of military matters to his own advantage.

'There's a lot of them though, sir,' said Marriott. 'It'll not help much until we've got a name.'

'Let's hope that Watson's so terrified of having his collar felt that he'll let us know if this here front-and-back badge soldier comes around looking for Queenie, then.'

As Hardcastle strode down the corridor leading to his office, he bellowed for DC Lipton.

Gordon Lipton appeared immediately. 'Sir?'

'This Polly Brewer woman you spoke to, Lipton, the one who said that Queenie Douglas had been adrift for a few days . . .'

'Yes, sir?'

'Get hold of her, not literally, of course,' said Hardcastle, smiling at his own little joke, 'and take her round to the mortuary at Horseferry Road. Get her to have a glim at the body there and tell us if it's Queenie Douglas. Then come back here and report. Got that?' The DDI wondered why he had not thought of it before. 'I'm surprised you didn't suggest it.'

'Yes, sir,' said Lipton, thinking that it was not his place to advise Hardcastle on how he should conduct a murder enquiry.

THREE

Hardcastle always claimed to be unwilling to go to work on an empty stomach. On Friday morning, as he did every other morning, he had enjoyed a breakfast of fried eggs, bacon, two pieces of fried bread and a couple of sausages followed by two slices of toast and marmalade. Finally, he washed down the meal with three cups of tea.

He caught his usual tram from the stop in Westminster Bridge Road at the corner of Kennington Road where he lived at number 27. It was the house in which he and his wife Alice had lived since their marriage 23 years ago, and was just a few yards along the road from where the famous Charlie Chaplin had once resided.

The tram crossed Westminster Bridge and deposited Hardcastle at the stop opposite the entrance to the Houses of Parliament. Known to A Division's policemen as the Clock Tower entrance, it was at the foot of the world famous Big Ben. A policeman had been assigned to the post some years ago to facilitate the turning of Members' hansom cabs in the face of trams crossing the centre of Westminster Bridge. The policeman there this morning saluted, and reported that all was correct.

Grunting an acknowledgement, Hardcastle crossed Bridge Street and strode down Cannon Row to the police station that bore its name.

'Good morning, sir. All correct, sir,' intoned the station officer. 'There's a gent waiting in the interview room, sir, name of Watson. He's the chandler from Strutton Ground, and he says it's important.'

'I hope for his sake it is,' growled Hardcastle.

'Will you be wanting to see the books, sir?' The station officer had already laid the large volumes on his desk.

'Anything to interest me, Skipper?'

'No entries in the crime book since the last time you initialled it yesterday morning, sir.'

'I can see my detectives need a squib up their arses, Skipper,' said Hardcastle. 'Get someone to bring this Watson up to my office, then,' he added curtly, as he mounted the stairs.

Within seconds, a PC knocked on Hardcastle's office door, and ushered in Fred Watson.

'I'm told you have something important to tell me, Watson,' said the DDI as he slowly filled his pipe.

'Yes, sir. That soldier I told you about.'

'What about him?'

'He come by yesterday evening, guv'nor, not long before I'd shut up shop. But the funny thing about it was that Queenie turned up a few minutes later.'

Hardcastle took the pipe from his mouth and stared at the luckless chandler. 'Where is she now?'

'In her room, as far as I know.'

'Thank you, Watson,' said Hardcastle. 'It's a great shame you didn't see fit to tell me this last night,' he added acidly. 'It would have saved me a great deal of trouble.'

'I thought you might've gone home, guv'nor,' whined Watson.

'*Gone home?* I'm not a bloody chandler, Watson. I'm a senior detective investigating a murder, and I don't pack it in at nine o'clock and put my feet up.'

'I'm sorry, guv'nor.'

'You can go, Watson.' Hardcastle dismissed the chandler with a wave of his hand.

In fact, it would have made very little difference if Watson had told him the previous evening about Queenie Douglas's reappearance, but Hardcastle saw no reason to say so.

For a few moments after Watson's departure, Hardcastle pondered whether there would be any profit in interviewing Queenie Douglas. Eventually he decided that there might be some merit in talking to the soldier that had asked for her, and Queenie could lead the DDI to him. If the Gloucestershire Regiment corporal was in the habit of consorting with prostitutes, it was possible that he might have known the dead woman.

'Marriott,' bellowed the DDI.

'Yes, sir?' said Marriott, appearing in Hardcastle's doorway.

'We're going back to Strutton Ground,' said Hardcastle, and told Marriott what he had just learned from Watson.

Fred Watson was surprised, and not a little alarmed, to see Hardcastle and Marriott enter his shop. It was only a matter of twenty minutes or so since Watson himself had left the police station.

'Is she in?' demanded Hardcastle.

'Yes, guv'nor, she's up there now.'

'Good.' Hardcastle marched through the shop, bounded up the uncarpeted staircase with an agility that belied his bulk, and hammered on Queenie Douglas's door.

'What d'you want?' demanded a shrill voice from within.

Hardcastle threw open the door to find Queenie lying on the bed reading a romantic penny magazine called *My Paper*. 'Are you Queenie Douglas?'

'Yeah. What of it?'

'I'm Divisional Detective Inspector Hardcastle of the Whitehall Division, and I'm investigating a murder.' It was a blunt statement intended immediately to concentrate the woman's mind.

In some alarm, Queenie swung her legs to the floor and stood up. She was barefooted and clad only in a shift. 'I ain't had nothing to do with no murder, mister,' she protested.

'I didn't say you had, my girl. But one of your sisters of the street was found strangled last Monday in the basement of a bombed house in Washbourne Street not half a mile from here.'

'Well, I don't know nothing about that.'

'Who's this soldier you've been seeing, Miss Douglas?' asked Marriott.

'Soldier? What soldier?'

'That's what I'm asking,' said Marriott patiently. 'He's a corporal in the Glosters.'

'That's Harry Waldren. We're going to get wed.'

'God Almighty!' muttered Hardcastle. 'And where can we find this Corporal Waldren?'

'What d'you want him for?'

'Now, just you listen to me, my girl,' thundered Hardcastle. 'Like I said, I'm investigating a murder, and I don't have time to be buggered about by the likes of you. So, unless you want to spend the night in the nick, tell me where he is.'

'I don't rightly know. Not now, like. He was staying at the Union Jack Club, so he said.'

'When did you last see him?' asked Marriott. His policeman's instinct told him that Waldren might be a deserter, and would not be found at the club near Waterloo railway station that provided accommodation for soldiers on leave, and which was visited frequently by the military police in search of absentees.

'Last night.'

'And did he stay with you the night?'

'What bleedin' business is that of yours?' demanded Queenie, placing her hands on her hips in an attitude of defiance.

'Every business,' snapped Hardcastle.

'Yeah, he did as it happens. So what?'

'When are you seeing him again?'

'Dunno,' said Queenie churlishly.

'If I take you down the nick, lass, you won't be seeing him at all,' threatened Hardcastle. 'So, when are you seeing him again?'

Queenie gave a loud sniff and tossed her head defiantly. 'Tonight.'

'Where?'

'Down the Elephant boozer, other end of Perkins Rents. Why?'

'What time?'

'He reckoned as how he'd be there come seven o'clock.'

'One other thing, lass . . .' Hardcastle turned to Marriott. 'Have you got that necklace we found?'

'Yes, sir.' Marriott produced the platinum and diamond necklet that had been discovered in the basement of the bombed-out Washbourne Street house.

'Have a look at that, Queenie,' said Hardcastle. 'Did you ever see any of the girls wearing that?'

Queenie Douglas glanced at the piece of jewellery. 'Nah, never.'

'Didn't think so,' muttered Hardcastle, and without another word, he swept down the stairs and out into Strutton Ground.

'That'll give us time to make a few enquiries, Marriott,' Hardcastle said mysteriously, as he and his sergeant turned into Victoria Street.

With Marriott beside him, Hardcastle marched confidently through the maze of streets that led to Horse Guards Road, and crossed the parade ground into Horse Guards Arch.

The dismounted Life Guards sentry, since the outbreak of war clad in drab khaki rather than the ceremonial dress of the Household Cavalry, dutifully brought his sword to the salute. Hardcastle, accustomed to being mistaken for an army officer, doffed his bowler hat in acknowledgement of a compliment to which he was not entitled, and pushed open the door leading to the office of the Assistant Provost Marshal of London District.

'Good morning, Inspector,' said the APM's chief clerk, a military police sergeant named Glover. 'You'll be wanting to see Colonel Frobisher, no doubt.'

'Maybe not, Sergeant Glover. I've always found that military police sergeants usually know more about what's going on than their officers do,' said Hardcastle with uncharacteristic flattery. 'But don't tell the colonel I said so.'

'Always happy to help, Inspector,' said Glover, preening himself slightly at Hardcastle's empty blandishment. 'What can I do for you?'

'D'you know anything about a Corporal Harry Waldren of the Gloucestershire Regiment, Sergeant Glover?' Hardcastle's sensitive antennae had told him that Waldren might have come to the notice of the Provost Branch, a conclusion to which Marriott had already arrived.

'Ah, The Slashers,' said Glover.

'The Slashers?' repeated a puzzled Hardcastle.

'It's a nickname, sir,' said Marriott. 'When the regiment was in Canada in 1764 they acquired—'

Hardcastle held up a hand. 'Enough, Marriott. I don't want another of your damned history lessons.'

'Bear with me, Inspector,' said Glover, smothering a laugh as he crossed to a filing cabinet and took out a file. 'Here we are. Corporal Harry Waldren. I thought the name rang a bell. He's adrift.'

'Thought as much,' said Hardcastle. 'How long's he been on the run?'

'About five weeks,' said Glover. 'He was sent on leave from the First-Fourth Battalion up near Albert, but he never went back. D'you know something about him, then?'

'Yes, and you can tell the APM that I'll likely lay hands on him before the day's out.'

'Perhaps you'll let us know when you nick him, Inspector, and we'll send an escort to collect him.'

'Not before I've asked him a few questions about a murdered prostitute,' said Hardcastle. 'Thank you for you assistance, Sergeant Glover, and I'll let you know when you can have him back.' The DDI paused at the doorway. 'As a matter of interest, is this Waldren married?'

Glover glanced at the file again. 'Yes, he is, Inspector. His wife's called Mabel, and she lives with their three kids in Barnstaple. We've had patrols call there several times, but she said she'd not seen hair nor hide of him for over a year.'

'Well, that don't come as a surprise,' said Hardcastle.

When the two detectives returned to Cannon Row police station, DC Lipton was waiting for the DDI.

'Got a positive identification, sir.'

'About time,' muttered Hardcastle. 'Come in the office.'

'I eventually found Polly Brewer at Victoria station last night, sir,' said Lipton, 'but I had to hang about until half past nine before she turned up.'

'I'm sure your devotion to duty is commendable,' observed Hardcastle drily. 'Get on with it.'

'Yes, sir. Any road, she was talking to a soldier, but I intervened, and the soldier scarpered. I took her round to the mortuary, and I had to wake up the night watchman. He weren't too pleased and said as how he shouldn't—'

'For God's sake, Lipton,' growled Hardcastle, 'there's no need to make a book out of a short story. Just tell me what you found out.'

'Yes, sir. Well, Polly had a good look at the body, and after she'd had a touch of the vapours, she told me that the dead woman was Annie Kelly, a single woman twenty-three years of age.'

'That's more like it. And where did this Annie Kelly turn her tricks? Did this here Polly Brewer tell you that?'

'Yes, sir. Annie had a room in Ebury Street, next door to the school on the corner of Belgrave Street.'

'Good,' said Hardcastle.

Lipton took that single word as both a commendation and a dismissal, and returned to the detectives' office.

'This evening,' said Hardcastle, as he took the head off his lunchtime pint of bitter in the downstairs bar of the Red Lion, 'we'll get ourselves round to the Elephant pub at about six o'clock, and lay in wait for our Corporal Waldren. I've a shrewd suspicion he might turn up earlier than Queenie suggested. Then we'll lift him and have a cosy chat back at the nick. He might just have had his wicked way with Annie Kelly. When he wasn't having a tumble with Queenie, that is.'

The public bar of the Elephant public house in the street bearing the apt name of Perkins Rents was crowded. Cigarette and pipe smoke hung in the air, and a sailor was managing to conjure a popular tune from a piano that badly needed tuning.

'Hello, Mr Hardcastle,' said the landlord, a jovial red-faced individual. 'Don't often see you in here. You'll be a bit busy, I s'pose,' he added, nodding a greeting at Marriott.

'You could say that, Arthur.'

'A couple of pints of the best, is it? On the house, of course.'

'Very kind,' murmured Hardcastle, who had not expected to pay anyway, 'but you can do me a favour.'

'Just say the word, guv'nor.' Arthur, sensing that the DDI was about to impart a confidence, leaned closer to him.

'I don't want to be seen in here because I'm waiting for a swaddy who might have some information that'd help me out with a murder. If he spots me he might just run. In fact, he's sure to because he's adrift from the army.'

'You'd best come in the parlour, then, guv'nor,' said Arthur, opening the flap in the bar and leading the two detectives into a room at the back. 'Who's this soldier you're after, Mr Hardcastle?' he added, placing their beer on the table.

'He's a corporal in the Gloucestershire Regiment, Arthur. Harry Waldren, he's called, and he's got badges on the front and back of his cap.'

'Shouldn't be too difficult to spot, then. I'll tip you the wink when he shows. On his tod, d'you reckon?'

'He will be when he comes in,' said Hardcastle. 'But he's supposed to be meeting a tom in here, name of Queenie Douglas.'

'What, Queenie from Strutton Ground?'

'D'you know her, Arthur?' asked Marriott.

'I do that, Mr Marriott,' said Arthur, 'but I never knew she was on the game. Well, that's her barred, and no mistake. I've got me licence to think of.'

'Well, don't bar her tonight, Arthur. You might frighten her soldier boy away.'

Ten minutes later, the landlord appeared in the parlour with two fresh pints of beer. 'Young Queenie's turned up, Mr Hardcastle,' he said, 'and she keeps eyeing the door like she's waiting for someone. Seems a bit on edge.'

'That don't surprise me, Arthur,' said Hardcastle. 'I've got an idea that she knows me and Sergeant Marriott are anxious to lay hands on her beau.'

'Right. I'll let you know when he shows up.'

But neither Hardcastle nor Marriott had a chance to start on his second pint of beer before the landlord reappeared.

'He's just come in the public, guv'nor,' said Arthur in a stage whisper.

'Is there a way out of here so that we can get into that bar from the street, Arthur?' asked Hardcastle. 'If we approach him from this side he'll likely take to his heels, and I'm getting a bit old in the tooth for chasing after villains.'

'Come this way, guv'nor.' Arthur led Hardcastle and Marriott out of the parlour door and along a short narrow passage. 'If you go through here into the private bar,' he said, indicating another door, 'you can go out into the street, and back into the public.'

Eventually the two detectives were outside again. Hardcastle pushed open the door of the public bar just as Queenie and her soldier were making for the exit.

'Corporal Harry Waldren?' queried Hardcastle.

Sensing that the two men confronting him were police officers, the soldier looked over his shoulder, a hunted expression on his face, but seeing there was no way of escape, yielded. 'Yeah, what of it?'

'I'm a police officer, Waldren, and I'm arresting you for being a deserter from His Majesty's armed forces.'

'Dunno what you're talking about,' responded Waldren predictably.

'And I want to talk to you about a murder that took place locally last Sunday.'

'I don't know nothing about no murder.' Waldren's face reflected his panic.

'And your wife's complaining that she hasn't heard from you for over a year,' the DDI added.

Hardcastle's statement brought about a fierce reaction from Queenie Douglas. Reeking of stale, cheap scent, and dressed in a garish, red stuff dress with a feather boa and velvet hat with a purple ostrich feather, she was the epitome of a low-class whore.

'Wife?' screeched Queenie. 'Are you bloody married?' Without waiting for a reply, she swung her handbag and dealt Waldren a heavy blow on the side of the head, causing him to lose his cap and stagger backwards. 'You two-timing lying little sod, Harry Waldren. If you've put me up the duff, I'll find you and cut your balls off.' She closed with Waldren and delivered what was known in wrestling circles as a forearm smash.

''Ere, bloody leave off, Queenie,' shouted Waldren, shaking his head and rubbing his chin.

Queenie's fisticuffs and her loud, coarse tirade had caused the pianist to stop playing, and there was a round of applause from the clientele who had quickly gathered close to the warring pair, delighted that this domestic exchange was providing a little light relief to their mundane lives.

'That'll do,' said Marriott, stepping between the couple, 'unless you want to join him at the nick, Queenie.'

'For Gawd's sake get me out of here,' beseeched Waldren as he attempted to distance himself from Queenie Douglas.

'Get a cab, Marriott,' said Hardcastle as he took a firm grip on the errant soldier's arm.

A minute later Marriott returned to the public bar. 'Waiting outside, sir,' he said.

Hardcastle stared at the figure of Corporal Harry Waldren, now slouched in a chair in the interview room at Cannon Row police station.

'You're a deserter from your battalion in Albert,' said Hardcastle.

'No, I ain't. You've got that wrong. I'm on leave.'

Having paused to light his pipe, Hardcastle leaned towards the corporal. 'Only this morning I was talking to the military police at Horse Guards, Waldren,' he said quietly, 'and they told me that you're on the run. And that's good enough for me. Now then, we can do this one of two ways. I can tell the provost that you surrendered to the police, which'll go in your favour at your court martial, or I can tell 'em that you denied it. In that case, you'll cause me a great deal of trouble because I'll have to take you in front of the Bow Street magistrate tomorrow morning. And I won't hesitate to tell him you resisted arrest and had to be restrained by Sergeant Marriott and me.'

'All right, all right,' said Waldren churlishly. 'Have it your own way.'

'Mind you,' continued Hardcastle, 'that still might change unless you help me out over this murder I'm looking into.'

'I told you in the boozer, I don't know nothing about no murder,' protested Waldren.

'The murdered woman was Annie Kelly, and she was a mate of your ex-fiancée Queenie Douglas.'

'You didn't have to tell the girl I was wed,' complained Waldren. 'If she'd known, she wouldn't have let me have it for nothing.'

'Did you know Annie Kelly, Waldren?' asked Marriott.

'Met her a couple of times. When I was picking up Queenie.'

'Did you know any of the men she went with?'

'There was a matelot who took her off once or twice.'

'What ship was he from?' asked Hardcastle.

'Dunno,' said Waldren. 'He was a petty officer.'

'What's that got to do with it?' demanded Hardcastle testily. 'Don't they have the name of their ship on their hats?'

'Not petty officers, they wear peaked caps,' said Waldren. 'Weird lot, the navy.'

'To hell with it,' muttered an exasperated Hardcastle as he stood up. 'Lock him up, Marriott, and send word to Sergeant Glover at Horse Guards and tell him that he can have Corporal Waldren as soon as he likes.'

'Very good, sir,' said Marriott. 'By the way, sir, sailors haven't worn the name of their ship on their cap ribbons since December 1914. It was an order designed to prevent enemy spies discovering which ships were in port and which were at sea.'

'Thank you for that useless piece of information, Marriott,' said Hardcastle acidly, and returned to his office, shouting for Lipton on the way.

'Yes, sir? Lipton hurried into the DDI's office.

'Get up to Victoria station, Lipton, and bring Queenie Douglas here. I should've brought her in when I nicked Waldren. And take a cab.'

Surprised at Hardcastle's free-handedness with the Commissioner's money, Lipton raced away to do the DDI's bidding.

DC Gordon Lipton alighted from his cab outside the Victoria Palace Theatre, and made his way across the street towards the railway station. A small group of women was gathered outside the public house in Wilton Road opposite the entrance to the station.

At the sight of Lipton, who many of them knew was a policeman, some of the women started moving away.

Lipton spotted Queenie Douglas and broke into a run. 'My guv'nor wants a word with you, Queenie,' he said breathlessly as he caught up with her.

'Ain't you lot done enough damage for one night,' shouted Queenie.

'Now then, don't you give me any trouble, Queenie,' said Lipton. 'We'll just take a ride to the nick in a cab, unless you want me to send for a Black Annie. Then I'll take all your mates with you.'

The threat of being carried off in a prison van was enough for Queenie Douglas, and she waited while Lipton called a taxi.

'Pulled a copper, have you, Queenie?' shouted a raucous young trollop with a décolletage that appeared to defy gravity. 'Lucky you! Make sure you see the colour of his money before you get your drawers off,' she added from a safe distance.

FOUR

It was approaching nine o'clock when DC Gordon Lipton brought Queenie Douglas into the interview room at the police station. Leaving the duty constable to keep a watch on the girl, Lipton went up to the DDI's office.

'Queenie Douglas is downstairs, sir. She wasn't any trouble.'

'*Any trouble?*' scoffed Hardcastle, raising an eyebrow as he appraised Lipton's stocky six-foot-tall figure. 'I should bloody hope not. All right, lad, you can get about your duties.'

Shouting for Marriott on his way downstairs, Hardcastle threw open the door of the interview room, and dismissed the attendant PC.

'I wanna know what I've been nicked for,' demanded a truculent Queenie.

'Soliciting prostitution contrary to Section Three of the Vagrancy Act 1824 if you want to go to court,' said Hardcastle. 'If you don't, just answer my questions. Now then, about Annie Kelly.'

'What about her?'

'Your *betrothed* Harry Waldren—' began Hardcastle sarcastically.

'Don't bloody talk to me about that lying little bastard,' said Queenie angrily. 'How was I to know he was wed? What's going to happen to him, anyway?'

'He'll probably be shot at dawn for desertion,' said Marriott mildly.

'Bloody hell!' exclaimed Queenie, staring at Hardcastle's assistant. 'Serve the sod right.'

'Harry Waldren told me that a sailor was in the habit of picking up Annie Kelly,' continued Hardcastle. 'What d'you know about that?'

'Yeah, I seem to remember a bluejacket hanging round her. Handsome big bloke, he was. I wouldn't've minded having him across me.'

'And did they go off together?'

'Yeah, I think they did. Once or twice.'

'And they went to Annie's place in Ebury Street, I suppose,' suggested Hardcastle.

'Well, he never looked like he'd got enough sausage and mash to fork out for a hotel,' said Queenie with a cheeky grin.

'Any idea of his name, Queenie?' asked Marriott.

'I think she called him Jimmy, but I never heard his other name.'

'When did you last see him and Annie Kelly together, Queenie?' asked Marriott.

'Must've been about a week ago, I s'pose, but he might've been with her since,' said Queenie. 'I never kept a tally of

how many tricks she turned,' she added sarcastically. 'I had
me own tricks to look after.'

'And he went with Annie two or three times?'

'Yeah, like I said. He seemed quite sweet on her,' said
Queenie. 'But I suppose he was married an' all,' she added,
with the typical cynicism of a prostitute whose knowledge of
men had been acquired rapidly and at an early age.

'All right, you can go,' said Hardcastle, having decided that
he would get no more out of the young woman.

'Is that it, then?' Queenie stood up and put her hands on
her hips in an attitude of defiance. 'You going to pay for me
cab back to Victoria, then?'

'No, you can walk,' said Hardcastle. 'The exercise will do
you good.'

'Bleedin' hell,' exclaimed Queenie. 'You've cost me a few
bob already.'

'Thank your lucky stars that's all it's cost you,' commented
Marriott. 'Annie Kelly got topped.'

Despite the fact that it had gone half past nine, Hardcastle
decided that it would be an apposite time to call at the late
Annie Kelly's lodgings in Ebury Street.

A hatchet-faced harridan answered the door to Hardcastle's
persistent knocking. Dressed in black bombazine, her greying
hair was drawn back into a tight bun.

'What's all the bleedin' racket about?' demanded the woman.
'Disturbing honest folk at this time of night.'

'Police,' said Hardcastle. 'What's your name?'

'Clara Foskett. And it's *Mrs* Foskett to you.'

'Are you the owner of this property?'

'Nah, it's rented, not that it's got anything to do with you.
Any road, what do the police want with me, might I ask?'
Mrs Foskett stood four-square in the doorway, arms akimbo.
'I ain't done nothing wrong.'

'D'you let a room to Annie Kelly?'

'What if I do?'

'I'm not going to stand on your doorstep bandying words
with you, missus,' said Hardcastle, and he and Marriott pushed
past the woman into the hall.

'Oh, come in do,' said Mrs Foskett caustically.

'When did you last see Annie Kelly?' asked Hardcastle.

'Last Saturday,' said Mrs Foskett promptly. 'Why all the questions about her? She's my niece, and she's a good girl. Never gives no trouble.'

'Is that a fact?' Hardcastle did not for one moment believe that Annie Kelly was the landlady's niece. 'Well, Mrs Foskett, I'm sorry to have to tell you that your *niece* is dead.'

'Oh my Gawd and heavens above!' exclaimed Clara Foskett and took hold of the banister post at the bottom of the staircase. 'What happened? Get run over by a tram, did she?'

'No, Mrs Foskett, she was murdered.'

This further news caused Clara to sit down on the second stair, her legs spread in an ungainly fashion. 'Who could've done such a thing?' she asked, and looked up at the DDI with an imploring look on her face, as though he would come up with an answer.

'That's what we're trying to find out,' said Marriott. 'But it's not going to be easy, seeing as how she was a whore.'

'What d'you mean, a whore?' snapped Mrs Foskett, recovering her composure sufficiently to fix Marriott with an accusing gaze.

'We know that she was plying her trade outside Victoria station, and was in the habit of picking up soldiers and sailors who paid her for her favours,' continued Marriott. 'Did she bring her tricks back here?'

'She sometimes brought a gentleman friend back here, yes,' said Mrs Foskett defensively.

It did not escape Hardcastle's notice that she was familiar with the term 'trick' for a prostitute's client.

'Anyone called Jimmy, a sailor?'

'I think there was a nice young gent in navy uniform what come once or twice. A petty officer, Annie said he was. Quite high up in the navy.'

'The crow's nest is about the highest he'll get,' muttered Hardcastle.

'Did Annie tell you his surname?' asked Marriott.

Mrs Foskett gave the question some thought. 'Yes, it was Nelson. We had a bit of a laugh about that, and asked him if he was related to the admiral what was killed at Trafalgar.'

'And where did Annie and Nelson go, once they were here?'

'Up to Annie's room, of course. I don't have a decent sitting room, not for visitors. There's only my private one

where I occasionally entertain, and I don't like to be disturbed
by any ragtag and bobtail.'

'We'll have a look in Annie's room, then,' said Hardcastle.
'Perhaps you'd show us the way, Mrs Foskett.'

'What d'you want to go up there for?'

'Because your nice young sailor might just have been the
one who strangled her,' said Hardcastle.

'I s'pose I might get to my bed before midnight,' complained
Mrs Foskett, as she struggled into an upright position and led
the way to the first floor.

'Thank you, *madam*,' said Hardcastle, as the landlady
hovered at the door of Annie's room. 'You can go now.'

Without a word, Mrs Foskett tossed her head, and returned
to the ground floor muttering, yet again, about police disturbing
honest folk late at night.

Hardcastle and Marriott searched Annie Kelly's room thoroughly. Surprisingly it was neat and tidy. The bed was made,
and the articles on the dressing table, including a hairbrush,
a comb, and several pots of cream and other women's neces-
sities, were laid out in an orderly fashion.

There were a few items of flashy cheap clothing in a
cupboard, and one or two trashy magazines, but nothing that
might lead them to her killer.

'Well?' Mrs Foskett was waiting in the hall when the two
detectives came downstairs.

'That'll be all, Mrs Foskett,' said Hardcastle. 'For the
moment.'

'Charmed, I'm sure,' said Clara Foskett. 'You wouldn't like
to turn the house inside out while you're here, I s'pose?' she
asked sarcastically.

Hardcastle opened the front door. On the doorstep were a
man and a young girl, probably no older than twenty. The girl
had a key in her hand.

'D'you live here?' demanded Hardcastle.

'Yes, I do. And who might you be?'

'Police,' said Hardcastle.

'Christ!' exclaimed the man who was with the young
woman, and promptly turned and ran down the street.

'Oh, thanks a bleedin' lot,' said the girl as she watched her
trick escaping.

'What's your name, miss?' asked Marriott.

'Fanny Booth. Why?'

'How well d'you know Mrs Foskett?'

'She's my niece,' said Clara Foskett from the foot of the stairs, before Fanny could reply.

'Is that true?' asked Marriott of the young girl.

'Er, yes, of course.' But Fanny had paused long enough for the detectives to know she was lying.

'How well d'you know Annie Kelly?' asked Hardcastle, once Fanny had stepped into the hall and closed the front door.

'Not all that well.' Fanny glanced at her 'aunt' in much the same way that a faltering actress glances at the prompt box for help with the next line.

'But if you're Mrs Foskett's niece, you and Annie must be sisters, or at least cousins.'

'We're a big family,' put in Mrs Foskett.

'Be quiet, Mrs Foskett,' snapped Hardcastle.

'Why are you asking about Annie?' asked Fanny.

'Because she's been murdered, Miss Booth,' said Marriott.

'Murdered?' Fanny's face drained of colour. 'What happened?'

'She was found strangled in the basement of a bombed-out house in Washbourne Street last Monday morning,' said Hardcastle. 'What d'you know about that?'

'Nothing, as God's my witness,' protested Fanny Booth.

'Did you ever see her coming in with a sailor?' queried Marriott. 'Petty Officer Jimmy Nelson of the Royal Navy.'

'She did come in with a sailor once or twice, yes.'

'When was the last time?'

'Must've been about a week ago, I s'pose.'

'And you've not seen him since?'

'No, I never.'

'Where did she pick him up? Victoria station, was it?'

'I dunno. Maybe.'

'Are you one of the girls who pick up soldiers coming off the trains at Victoria station, Fanny?' asked Marriott.

'No, I ain't.' Fanny contrived outrage. 'What d'you take me for?'

'A common prostitute,' said Hardcastle harshly. 'And if I was in your shoes, I'd pack it in. At least until we find out who topped your mate. You never know who he might pick on next. It might be you. I suppose you've heard of Jack the Ripper.'

And with that dire warning Hardcastle dismissed Fanny Booth, and turned his attention, once more, to Mrs Foskett. 'I want details of where I can find Annie Kelly's family,' he said.

'I don't know nothing about her family,' responded Clara Foskett truculently.

'Really? But you said she's your niece. That means that either her father or her mother is either your brother or sister.'

'Well, she's not exactly a niece,' said Clara Foskett. 'More of a distant relative.'

'D'you have a telephone here, Mrs Foskett?' asked Hardcastle.

'Can't afford such luxuries, unlike some. What d'you want a telephone for, anyway?'

'To send for a Black Annie to take you to the police station,' said Hardcastle. 'Unless you come up with an answer now.'

'All right, all right,' said Mrs Foskett, now thoroughly alarmed. 'She was just renting a room here, but I never knew what she was up to.'

'I'll take that with a pinch of salt,' said Hardcastle. 'So, what *do* you know about her?'

'Only her name.' Clara Foskett paused. 'But a letter come for her yesterday.'

'Fetch it,' commanded Hardcastle, his patience shortening by the second.

Mrs Foskett scuttled into her sitting room, returning moments later clutching a letter.

Hardcastle snatched the missive and put it in his pocket. 'You'll be hearing from the police again, Mrs Foskett,' he said. 'Running a brothel can get you locked up for quite a long time. I should think you'll settle in at Holloway prison quite happily.' And with that parting sally, he and Marriott left Mrs Foskett to contemplate a future incarcerated in the notorious North London women's prison.

'At least we've got a name of someone Annie Kelly was seeing regularly, sir,' said Marriott, as he and Hardcastle strode down Ebury Street in search of a cab.

'Yes, for what good that'll do us. But I suppose we'll have to pay a visit to the Admiralty,' said Hardcastle, stopping to light his pipe.

'Are you going to do anything about Mrs Foskett running a brothel, sir?'

'Haven't got the time, Marriott, but remind me to have a word with the sub-divisional inspector at Gerald Road. He'll likely want to nick Mrs Foskett in the fullness of time.' Hardcastle glanced at his watch. 'There won't be anyone at the Admiralty at this time of night, so it'll have to be tomorrow.'

'Tomorrow's Saturday, sir,' observed Marriott.

Hardcastle stopped again. 'Are you suggesting that the Royal Navy takes the weekend off in wartime, Marriott?'

'I don't know, sir, but we might have a wasted journey.'

'Find out, Marriott. Anyway, the Admiralty's only down the road from the nick.'

Hardcastle eventually spotted a cab. 'Scotland Yard, cabbie,' he said to the driver. 'Tell 'em Cannon Row, Marriott,' he added in an aside, 'and half the time you'll finish up at Cannon Street in the City.'

'Yes, sir,' said Marriott wearily, who had been given this advice on almost every occasion that he and Hardcastle had returned to their police station by taxi.

Once in his office, Hardcastle donned his spectacles and tore open the letter addressed to Annie Kelly.

'This letter addressed to Annie Kelly comes from an address in Greenwich, Marriott. It don't say much: just the usual stuff about the family. But here's the interesting bit. "I hope you've settled in your new job as a housemaid in Ebury Street, Annie dear. Do let your pa and me know how you're getting on. And come and see us when you've got a day off." It's signed "Your loving mother."' Hardcastle placed the letter in the centre of his desk. 'It looks like it'll be us breaking the news to Annie's loving mother, Marriott.'

'Yes, sir. When d'you propose to do that?'

'As soon as we can fit it in, Marriott,' said Hardcastle, 'but that'll be after we've tracked down Petty Officer Nelson.'

When Hardcastle arrived at Cannon Row at his usual time of half past eight on Saturday morning, Marriott was waiting for him.

'I've spoken to the Admiralty, sir. The custodian there told me that a Lieutenant de Courcy is the duty officer this weekend, and will be arriving at about ten o'clock this morning.'

'Ten o'clock?' echoed Hardcastle. 'You wouldn't think there was a war on, would you, Marriott? Or doesn't Fritz come out to play earlier than that on a Saturday?'

Marriott remained silent, knowing from previous experience that it would be unwise to encourage one of Hardcastle's acerbic diatribes about the armed forces and the war.

At five minutes to ten, Hardcastle seized his bowler hat and umbrella, shouted for Marriott, and together they made their way down Whitehall.

As the two policemen passed through the gate of the Admiralty, an armed sailor, assuming Hardcastle to be an officer, sloped arms and gave him a butt salute.

The DDI solemnly acknowledged the compliment by raising his bowler hat. 'For all the good he is, Marriott,' he said in an aside, 'we could be a couple of German spies.' He waved his umbrella at Admiralty House to the left of the main building. 'Admiral Nelson lay in state there in 1806 after they'd brought his body home from Gibraltar in a cask of spirits of wine, Marriott.'

'Is that so, sir?' Marriott had always been surprised by Hardcastle's occasional flashes of historical knowledge, even though he had heard of Nelson's lying in state every time he and the DDI had passed through the gates of the Admiralty. Apart from the snippet about the liquid in the cask. 'But I thought his body was brought home in a barrel of brandy, sir,' he said.

'Only as far as Gibraltar, Marriott. Then it was put into a cask of spirits of wine for the voyage back to London.'

A uniformed custodian opened the door. 'Can I help you, gentlemen?' he asked.

'Police officers,' said Hardcastle, and produced his warrant card. 'We're here to see a Lieutenant de Courcy. I understand he's the duty officer.'

'Very good, sir.' The custodian beckoned to a messenger. 'Take these police officers to Lieutenant de Courcy's office, Charlie.' That done, the custodian turned to a telephone to alert de Courcy of the detectives' arrival.

The tall naval officer rounded his desk with hand outstretched. 'Hugo de Courcy, gentlemen.' He paused, appraising the two detectives. 'I've a feeling we've met before,' he said.

'Indeed we have,' said Hardcastle. 'A couple of years ago; just around the outbreak of war, I believe.'

'Yes, of course. Inspector Hardcastle, is it not?'

'That's so.'

'Please take a seat, gentlemen, and tell me how I may be of service to you,' said de Courcy.

'I'm investigating the murder of a prostitute,' said Hardcastle, and recounted brief details of the circumstances under which Annie Kelly's body had been found. 'We've reason to believe that a petty officer by the name of Nelson was seen in the woman's company on several occasions. I'm very anxious to trace this man, Lieutenant de Courcy. He's known as Jimmy, but I suppose his first name is James.'

'I'll see what I can do,' murmured de Courcy, and made a few notes on a foolscap pad. Replacing the cap on his fountain pen, he put it down beside the pad. 'It will take a few minutes to get the appropriate documents, Inspector,' he said. 'They're kept in the vaults, you see. But in the meantime, may I offer you a cup of tea?'

'Thank you,' murmured Hardcastle, and settled down for what he imagined would be a long wait.

De Courcy struck a brass bell on his desk and a clerk appeared. 'Perhaps you'd order some tea for these two gentlemen, Rawlings. Oh, and a cup for me. Once you've arranged that, go down to the records section and draw the service history of this man.' He quickly wrote Nelson's name and details on a slip of paper and handed it to the clerk. 'He's a petty officer, not a dead admiral,' he added with a wry smile.

To Hardcastle's surprise, the tea arrived within minutes, and a pile of files containing records of service shortly afterwards.

'It'll probably come as no surprise to you, Inspector, that there is more than one Petty Officer James Nelson in the Royal Navy,' said de Courcy, stirring his tea with one hand while sifting through the files with the other. 'Have you any idea when this petty officer was here in England?'

'All I can tell you is that witnesses spoke of seeing him a week ago.'

De Courcy examined his files once more. 'Two Nelsons were killed in action at Jutland in June of this year,' he said. 'Another is serving on HMS *Royal Oak* at sea, and then . . . ah, here we are: a PO James Nelson is in HMS *Epsom* currently undergoing a refit at Chatham. He could be your man, Inspector.'

'How do we find him, Lieutenant?'

De Courcy smiled, and arranged the files into a neat pile. 'Go down to Chatham and ask the ship's captain, I should think.'

It was three o'clock that afternoon when Hardcastle and Marriott arrived at Chatham Dockyard. A Metropolitan Police constable of the Dockyard Division and a sailor armed with rifle and fixed bayonet stood in front of the closed dockyard gates.

'All correct, sir.' As the two detectives approached, the policeman saluted even before Hardcastle had spoken a word.

'How d'you know who I am?' asked Hardcastle suspiciously.

'You're DDI Hardcastle of the Royal A, sir,' said the PC with a grin. The informal name for the Whitehall Division was a recognition that five royal palaces fell within its area of responsibility. 'I'm PC Ledger, sir, and I served at Rochester Row up to a couple of months ago.'

'Well, Ledger, as you're such a clever officer you can tell me where I can find HMS *Epsom*.'

'Certainly, sir. I'll just get my mate to relieve me, and I'll show you the way.' Ledger shouted to another constable in the gate office. 'Harry, give us a blow while I show Mr Hardcastle the way to *Epsom*.'

PC Ledger pushed open the huge gate, and led Hardcastle and Marriott confidently through the labyrinthine dockyard, eventually arriving at the gangway to HMS *Epsom*. A khaki-clad Royal Marine stood guard.

'This Bootneck will want to have a glim at your brief, sir. Suspicious lot, the Bootnecks,' said Ledger, nodding towards the Royal Marines sentry. 'Couple of police officers to see your skipper, mate.'

FIVE

The officer of the day, a youthful sub-lieutenant with a telescope tucked beneath his left arm, stood at the top of HMS *Epsom*'s gangway. Hardcastle and Marriott, having been alerted to naval traditions by Ledger, the dockyard PC, raised their hats as they stepped on board. The DDI explained who he wished to see, and the two detectives were conducted to the captain's cabin.

'Henry Cobbold, Inspector. I'm *Epsom*'s skipper,' said the young lieutenant-commander, once Hardcastle had introduced himself and Marriott. 'How can I help you?' He stepped across the cabin and shook hands with each of the detectives.

'I understand from Lieutenant de Courcy at the Admiralty that a Petty Officer James Nelson is a member of your crew, Captain,' said Hardcastle.

'Yes, he is,' said Cobbold. 'The Admiralty sent me a signal saying that you'd be coming. De Courcy said that you think Nelson might know something about a murder.'

'Indeed.' Hardcastle told the captain about the murder of Annie Kelly that he was investigating, and that Petty Officer Nelson might be able to assist him. 'But first, Captain, can you tell me where Nelson was on the night of Sunday the twenty-fourth of September?'

'Certainly.' *Epsom*'s captain stepped across the cabin and referred to a duty state displayed on a bulkhead. 'He was here, Inspector,' he said, glancing back at Hardcastle. 'He returned from shore leave on Tuesday the nineteenth of September. He's been aboard ever since then.'

'Is there any chance he could have slipped ashore and gone to London? Last weekend, say.'

'Certainly not, Inspector,' said the captain firmly. 'In fact, I saw him several times over that weekend.'

'That rules him out, then,' muttered Hardcastle. 'Would it be possible to have a word with Nelson, Captain?'

'Of course.' Cobbold opened the curtain at the entrance to his cabin. 'Pass the word for Petty Officer Nelson,' he said to the marine sentry.

'You sent for me, sir?' Minutes later a smartly dressed, well-built rating appeared in the entrance of the cabin, his cap tucked beneath his left arm.

'Come in, Nelson,' said the captain. 'These two gentlemen are police officers from London, and they want to ask you a few questions. At ease.'

'Aye, aye, sir,' said Nelson, adopting a more relaxed stance.

'When did you last see Annie Kelly, Nelson?' asked Hardcastle, deciding to get straight to the point.

Nelson glanced at his captain and back at Hardcastle. 'I

don't know who you're talking about, sir,' he said. 'I don't know anyone of that name.'

'Are you married, Nelson?' Hardcastle immediately sensed the reason for the young petty officer's reticence.

'Yes, sir.'

'Well, I shan't go running to your wife to tell her you've been shagging a Pimlico whore, lad.'

'Is this true, Nelson?' demanded Cobbold, whose immediate concern was that Nelson might have contracted a venereal disease. 'You'll need to see the ship's surgeon straight away. And that's an order.'

'If you don't mind, Captain,' said Hardcastle mildly, 'I'd rather you left this to me.'

'I've disrated men for less,' muttered Cobbold, half to himself.

'Maybe,' said Hardcastle, 'but the matter I'm dealing with is far more serious than the consequences of a sailor consorting with a prostitute.' He turned back to Nelson. 'Annie Kelly's been murdered. Her body was found in the basement of a house in Washbourne Street, Westminster, on the morning of Monday the twenty-fifth of September.'

'Oh my oath!' exclaimed Nelson, clearly shocked by this news. 'Who could've done such a thing? She was a sweet kid was Annie.'

'So you do know her,' said Marriott irritably. 'So, rather than wasting any more of our time, can you tell me if she ever told you about anyone else she was seeing?'

Nelson ran a hand around his chin, and shot a worried glance at his captain. 'There was some bloke Annie reckoned was making a nuisance of himself, so she said. Mind you, sir, I took that with a pinch of salt. These girls tend to say things like that to make you jealous.'

'Did you ever see this man, Nelson?' asked Hardcastle.

'Annie pointed him out to me once, sir, when I was chatting to her on the corner of Wilton Road. He was going into the Victoria Palace. That's the music hall in Victoria Street.'

'Yes, I know where the Vic is,' commented Hardcastle.

'Anyway, this bloke had some common sort of woman with him, his wife, I suppose,' Nelson continued, 'and he never acknowledged Annie. But you wouldn't've expected him to, would you, sir? Any road, I told Annie that if she ever had any bother with him, I'd tell him to sling his hook in a way that'd make sure he never come back again. If you get my drift, sir.'

Hardcastle permitted himself a brief smile. 'I think I do, Petty Officer.' Appraising Nelson's stocky build, the DDI thought that any man who picked a fight with him would probably regret it. 'Did Annie tell you who this man was?'

'No, sir. All she said was that he had a "sir" in front of his name, and was something to do with making uniforms for the pongos . . . er, soldiers, sir.'

'Excellent,' exclaimed Hardcastle, and turned to the captain. 'I think that's all that Petty Officer Nelson can assist me with, Captain.'

'Very well, Nelson, carry on,' said Cobbold. 'And see the surgeon immediately,' he added.

'Aye, aye, sir.' Nelson drew himself to attention, turned smartly and left the cabin.

'I hope that's been of some assistance to you, Inspector,' said Cobbold.

'It might be another piece of the jigsaw, Captain,' said Hardcastle. 'On the other hand it might come to nothing. There's always a lot of work to be done before I have a man standing on the scaffold. But rest assured, I will. Sooner or later.'

'Yes,' said Cobbold pensively, 'I'm sure you will.' He had quickly assessed the DDI as a man with whom it would be unwise to trifle.

It was almost seven o'clock by the time that Hardcastle and Marriott returned to Cannon Row police station.

Hardcastle sat down in his office and contemplated what to do next.

'Well, Marriott, all we've got to do now is find a "Sir Somebody" who manufactures army uniforms.'

'Yes, sir.'

'But there's nothing we can do until Monday. Get yourself off home. I dare say your good lady's wondering what's happened to you. How is your family, by the way?'

'All right, sir, thank you. Young James is doing well at school, but little Doreen's proving to be a bit of a handful. She's six now.'

'Girls always are difficult, Marriott, and it only gets worse,' commented Hardcastle gloomily. 'And I should know: I've got two of them. But our Kitty's the problem; she insists on working on the buses. It's no job for a young girl, but I can't persuade her to change her mind. Maud's all right though, she's nursing. Proper job for a girl is that. Anyway, get off with you, Marriott, and give my regards to Mrs Marriott.'

'Thank you, sir, and mine to Mrs H.' Marriott had been surprised at Hardcastle's brief insight into the problem of his eldest daughter. It was a rarity for the DDI to discuss his family.

It was eight o'clock when Hardcastle opened the door of his house in Kennington Road, Lambeth and hung his hat and umbrella on the hooks in the hall. Taking out his chrome hunter, he glanced at the clock next to the mirror. Satisfied that the hall clock was keeping good time, he wound his watch and dropped it back into his waistcoat pocket.

'Is that you, Ernie?' called Hardcastle's wife from the kitchen. 'I'd almost given up on you.'

'Yes, it's me, Alice.' Hardcastle walked into the kitchen and pecked his wife on the cheek. 'What's for supper, love?'

'Chops, mashed potato and cabbage, Ernie,' said Alice over her shoulder. 'And a glass of sherry wouldn't go amiss. I'm fair parched.' It was Alice's custom always to have a glass of sherry on a Saturday evening.

'I think I'll join you,' said Hardcastle, which is what he always said when Alice asked for a drink. He went into the parlour and poured a glass of sherry for his wife and a substantial measure of whisky for himself. Taking the drinks back to the kitchen, he put Alice's glass on the flap of the kitchen dresser, and crossed to the wall by the cooker where he had pinned the war map provided by the *Daily Mail*.

'For goodness' sake don't get under my feet, Ernest,' said Alice testily. Her use of Hardcastle's full name was an indication of her frustration. 'Not while I'm cooking supper. You can make sure the war's progressing all right when I'm done,' she added, with a hint of sarcasm.

Hardcastle moved away. 'Where are the children?' he asked. Even though they were young adults, he still referred to them as children.

'Kitty's on the back shift, home at ten, but Maud will be in shortly. And young Wally should be in from the post office very soon.'

As Hardcastle had explained to Marriott earlier, Kitty Hardcastle was a constant source of worry to her parents, but more so to her father than to her mother. He was always concerned for her safety, travelling home alone at night from the bus depot. But his main concern was the constant danger of bombs dropped by Zeppelins, or from the new menace, the giant Gotha bombers. Young Walter, Wally to his family, was a telegram boy and spent most of his working day delivering the sinister little yellow envelopes that would tell of the death or wounding of a husband, son or brother at the Front. But he was mindful that even that occupation had its dangers; he recalled the death of the young telegram boy who was hit by falling masonry outside the bombed house in Washbourne Street.

No sooner had the Hardcastles sat down to supper than Maud appeared. She walked into the dining room and threw her cape and cap on to a vacant chair. Although only nineteen, her nurse's uniform gave her the appearance of being much older; she had matured quickly tending the victims of the war at one of the big houses in Park Lane that had been given over to the care of wounded officers.

She crossed the room and kissed each of her parents lightly on the cheek. 'Is my supper in the oven, Ma?' she asked.

'Sit down, love,' said Alice, setting down her knife and fork and standing up. 'I'll get it for you. You look worn out. Busy day?' she asked, as she made her way to the kitchen.

'Nine in today,' said Maud, 'all Sherwood Foresters' officers from the Somme. And three of them died before the day was out, one of them while I was holding his hand. He was only twenty.' Suddenly the cumulative stress of her job overcame her and she burst into tears, weeping uncontrollably.

Hardcastle was always at a loss when confronted by a sobbing woman, and did the only thing he could think of: he poured his daughter a glass of Scotch. 'There, love, drink that,' he said.

Maud took a tentative sip of the whisky, the unfamiliar fiery spirit catching the back of her throat.

'What on earth are you doing, Ernest Hardcastle?' exclaimed Alice, returning with her daughter's supper. 'Is that whisky you've given the girl?'

'If she's old enough to look after dying officers, Alice,' said Hardcastle, 'she's old enough to have a drop of whisky when she needs it.' And in an attempt to divert his wife's criticism, he added, 'By the way, Marriott sends you his regards.'

'Marriott?' exclaimed Alice. 'Doesn't your poor sergeant have a Christian name?'

'Probably,' muttered Hardcastle, and lapsed into silence.

Ten minutes later, Wally arrived, still in his Post Office uniform.

'Hello, Pa, Ma,' he said cheerfully. 'You're home early, Maud,' he added, glancing at his sister, 'and drinking the hard stuff, too. I don't know what the world's coming to.'

'Oh for peacetime again when everyone came in for meals at the same time,' complained Alice. Once more, she disappeared to the kitchen, returning seconds later with her son's supper.

'Five KIAs, two MIAs, and three wounded today, all in this area,' said Wally as he began to devour his chops. 'All Sherwood Foresters from the Somme.'

'And what might KIAs and MIAs be, Wally?' demanded Hardcastle. He knew perfectly well what the abbreviations meant, but tried to discourage the use of such military argot by his son.

'Killed in action, and missing in action, Pa,' mumbled Wally through the forkful of mashed potato he had put into his mouth.

'Don't talk with your mouth full, Wally,' cautioned his mother.

As was his custom on a Sunday, Hardcastle checked the accuracy of the eight-day clock on the mantelpiece in the sitting room, and wound it. It was a wedding present from Alice's parents, and had kept good time for the whole of the 23 years it had stood above the fireplace.

Hardcastle spent Sunday morning reading the *News of the World*. He was particularly interested in an account of the British Army's recent capture of Thiepval, a village that the Germans had held since the first day of the Battle of the Somme. Now, however, it had fallen to an attack by eight of the new Mark I tanks that had first been used only eleven days previously at that infamous battle. He walked into the kitchen, took a German flag from the war map, and, with some satisfaction, replaced it with a Union flag.

'We could go for a walk, Ernie,' suggested Alice after lunch, sensing that her husband was at a loose end.

'I do quite enough walking when I'm at work,' said Hardcastle grumpily, and began to read a copy of *John Bull*. But he soon tired of it. 'Scurrilous rag,' he muttered, tossing aside Horatio Bottomley's magazine. He was fretting about his murder enquiry, but knew that there was nothing he could do until the following day. Nevertheless, he regretted wasting time sitting around at home.

Hardcastle was pleased to get back to work on Monday morning. He examined the crime book, but found nothing of pressing interest. The internment of so many aliens under the provisions of the Defence of the Realm Act seemed to have reduced the volume of crime in the capital. And that, Hardcastle frequently said, was about the only advantage of the war.

He shouted for Marriott, entered his office and lit his pipe.

'Good morning, sir,' said Marriott.

'Sit down, Marriott. We've got to put our thinking caps on if we're going to find this toff who's been consorting with Annie Kelly. I've no doubt that there are quite a few firms making uniforms for the army, and I dare say a fair number of their bosses have got knighthoods. God knows why you get made a "sir" just for staying out of the firing line and making a lot of money.'

'I suppose we could rule out those firms that are out of London, sir,' suggested Marriott. 'I believe there are quite a few of these factories in Birmingham, and even further north.'

'That's very helpful, Marriott,' said Hardcastle acidly. 'But what about those here in London?'

'I'll get a couple of DCs on to it straight away, sir.'

'When you've arranged that, come back. I've had an idea.'

It took Marriott only a few minutes to set DCs Catto and Lipton to searching for manufacturers of army uniforms in the London area, before returning to discover what his DDI had in mind. It always unnerved him a little when Hardcastle professed to having had an idea.

'I want all the prostitutes in the Victoria area brought into the nick, Marriott,' said Hardcastle. 'Today. And at the same time.'

'All of them, sir?' Marriott was aghast at yet another of Hardcastle's bizarre suggestions. He was aware, however, that his DDI often achieved the right result by way of the wrong route.

'Every one of them,' said Hardcastle. 'I'll need to arrange for the sub-divisional inspectors here at Cannon Row and at Rochester Row to parade sufficient men to carry it out. I'll have a word with Mr Tunnicliffe here, and get Mr Rhodes to speak to Mr Marsh at Rochester Row.'

'What time were you thinking of doing it, sir?' asked Marriott, wondering how this plan would help in furthering the discovery of Annie Kelly's murderer.

'I think nine o'clock tonight would be a good time. That should catch most of the regular tarts.' Hardcastle refilled his pipe, lit it and walked down the corridor to the office of his deputy, DI Edgar Rhodes.

'Good morning, sir.' Rhodes took his pipe out of his mouth and stood up.

'Mr Rhodes, I'd be obliged if you'd make your way to Rochester Row and ask Mr Marsh if he would arrange for a number of officers to be available at Victoria railway station at nine o'clock this evening. I want all the prostitutes there to be arrested and brought to Cannon Row. Be so good as to tell him that I shall make similar arrangements for Mr Tunnicliffe to assist him. Once you've done that, have a word with the inspector in charge of the railway police at Victoria station, and ask for his co-operation in the matter. I dare say he'll be pleased to have something to occupy his time.' Hardcastle's harsh opinion of the railway police was that they had a good conceit of themselves, but had very little to do other than playing at being policemen.

'Very good, sir. Might Mr Marsh and the railway inspector be told the purpose?'

'I intend to question all these whores, Mr Rhodes,' said Hardcastle. 'One of them must know who was seeing Annie Kelly. And if we're lucky, she might be able to put a finger on the girl's killer.'

Hardcastle next made his way to the office of the sub-divisional inspector in charge of Cannon Row's uniformed police.

Frank Tunnicliffe looked up from the file he was studying. 'Morning, Ernie. Don't tell me, you need help from the Uniform Branch.'

Hardcastle took a seat and re-lit his pipe. 'Victoria station, Frank. There are a load of toms who congregate there to pick up swaddies coming off the troop trains.'

'I know, Ernie, and one of them got topped a week ago. What d'you want from me?'

'Enough officers to arrest the bloody lot of them at nine o'clock tonight, Frank. I'm going to give them a talking-to. One of them must know something. Once you've got 'em rounded up, I'd be obliged if you'd have 'em put in the yard here at Cannon Row. I'm arranging for Harry Marsh at Rochester Row to lend a hand, so there should be enough men to make sure we catch the bloody lot of 'em.'

'I'll do my best, Ernie,' said Tunnicliffe, and turned to examine the duty state on his desk.

Finally, as a matter of courtesy, Hardcastle reported to Superintendent Arthur Hudson, A Division's commander, and explained what he was doing.

'Seems a bit drastic, Ernie,' said Hudson, 'but if you think it's the only way, so be it.' The superintendent had great faith in his head of detectives and, although his methods were at times unorthodox, they frequently achieved the desired result.

Hardcastle downed his second lunchtime pint of beer, and wiped his moustache with the back of his hand.

'I think that now would be a good time to pay Annie Kelly's parents a visit, Marriott, and give them the sad news about their daughter.'

'Have we got time, sir?'

'Of course we have, Marriott. The uniforms won't round up our toms until nine o'clock, and Greenwich ain't that far.'

'I thought I recognized this place,' said Hardcastle, as the cab stopped in Nelson Street. 'We came looking for Albert North here about three or four months ago. It was there,' he added, pointing at the gap in the houses where once number 12 had stood.

'It was the night we nearly copped it by the land mine that destroyed it, sir,' said Marriott. 'Lucky we were in the Goose and Duck,' he added, naming the pub at the corner of the street.

Hardcastle rapped loudly on the door of number 27.

'Yes, what is it?' A careworn woman wearing an apron opened the door, and stared suspiciously at the two men on her doorstep. 'If it's the rent you're after, I ain't got it.' She spoke with a distinct Irish accent.

'We're police officers, madam.' Hardcastle raised his hat. 'Mrs Kelly, is it?'

'Yes, I'm Mrs Kelly. Whatever's wrong?'

'Perhaps we could come in, madam,' said Hardcastle.

After a moment's hesitation, Mrs Kelly opened the door wide to admit the two detectives, and conducted them into the parlour.

'I'm afraid we've got bad news for you, Mrs Kelly,' Hardcastle began. He was not good at telling relatives of the death of a loved one. 'It's your daughter Annie. I'm afraid she's dead.'

'Holy Mary, Mother of God!' exclaimed Mrs Kelly, and collapsed into a chair.

The door of the parlour was flung open, and a large man stood on the threshold. 'What's going on here?' he demanded aggressively. 'And who might you be?' He glared at the two policemen.

'I'm Divisional Detective Inspector Hardcastle of the Whitehall Division, sir. I take it you're Mr Kelly.'

'I'm Patrick Kelly, yes.' Kelly stepped across to his wife. 'Maureen, whatever is it?'

But it was Hardcastle who provided the answer. 'I'm afraid your daughter's dead, Mr Kelly,' he said.

'Glory be to God! May the Lord have mercy on her soul. What happened, Inspector?'

As briefly as possible, Hardcastle summarized what the police knew of the death of the Kellys' daughter.

'What was she doing in the basement of a house in . . . where was it you said?'

'Washbourne Street, sir,' said Marriott. 'It's in Victoria, not far from the railway station.'

'But what was she doing there? She had good post as a housemaid with a family in Ebury Street.'

This, Hardcastle knew, was going to be the difficult part. 'I'm sorry to have to tell you, Mr Kelly, that your daughter had been soliciting prostitution in the Victoria area, and she'd been murdered.'

'Are you telling me my daughter was a common tart, Inspector?' Kelly took a step closer, his fists clenched, and for a moment Hardcastle thought that the Irishman was about to strike him.

'Oh, my Lord!' exclaimed Mrs Kelly, who had recovered

from the initial shock of learning of Annie's death, but now lapsed once more into a state of partial collapse.

'I'm afraid there's no doubt of it, Mr Kelly,' said Marriott.

'I'll just get a drop of water,' said Kelly, and left the room. He returned moments later, and handed the glass to his wife. 'Drink that, dear, and you'll be feeling better.' He turned to Hardcastle. 'This has been a terrible shock, Inspector,' he said.

'I imagine so,' said Hardcastle.

'Have you caught the spalpeen who killed the poor wee thing?' asked Kelly.

'Not yet, Mr Kelly, but rest assured I shall,' said Hardcastle. 'Are you in work?'

'I'm on the night shift at Woolwich Arsenal, Inspector. Making shells for our lads at the Front. And if you're thinking that's a strange job for an Irishman, I can tell you that me and Maureen are Protestants from Derry, and true to King and Country.'

'How long had your daughter been at Ebury Street, sir?' asked Marriott.

'Not more than six months,' said Kelly. 'We thought she'd settled into a good house, but now you tell me she was nothing more than a whore. Oh God, the shame of it.'

'Was she walking out with anyone before she left home?' Marriott was not convinced that the uniform manufacturer mentioned by PO Nelson was responsible for Annie Kelly's death and wondered if her murderer might be closer to home.

'There was a young fellow, name of Seamus Riley who she was seeing up till the time she left home.'

'What can you tell me about him, Mr Kelly?'

'He was a milkman, working out of the dairy in the High Street.'

'Is he still there, d'you know?'

'I don't know. We don't have our milk delivered, you see. I take the can when I go on the night shift and get it filled in the morning on my way home. Why? D'you think he might have something to with poor Annie's death?'

'I don't know,' said Hardcastle, 'but it's something we'll look into.'

'Where's my dear girl now?' asked Maureen Kelly, at last recovering sufficiently to take part in the conversation.

'In the mortuary at St Mary's hospital in Paddington, Mrs Kelly,' said Marriott.

'You can remove her whenever you like, Mr Kelly,' said
Hardcastle. 'I'll arrange it with the coroner.'

Kelly nodded slowly. 'At least we can give her a decent
Christian burial, and ask the good Lord to forgive her all her
sins,' he said.

SIX

The arrival, from three different directions, of the police
vans outside Victoria railway station caused something
akin to panic among the gathering of prostitutes. And
their alarm was heightened when the A Division policemen
leaped from the vans, and began to detain them.

'Here, what's this all about?' screeched one woman, her
hat becoming dislodged as a policeman seized her by the arm.

'You're nicked, my lovely,' said the PC, 'and you'll find
out what it's all about down at the station.'

Inspectors Tunnicliffe and Marsh, having arranged for a
cordon to be thrown around the women to ensure that none
escaped, stood to one side, ostensibly supervising the operation. However, the sergeants and constables needed no
guidance in dealing with the unruly collection of whores,
and within minutes had herded them all into the vans.
Moments later they were joined by a struggling group of
prostitutes who were hurling abuse at the railway police
officers who had just arrested them.

Predictably enough there were clamorous protests from the
women, and the jocular comment of one PC that they were
being conscripted and sent to Woolwich Arsenal to make muni-
tions for the war effort did nothing to allay their fears.

Sub-Divisional Inspector Tunnicliffe appeared in Hardcastle's
doorway.

'Your ladies of the night are all assembled in the station
yard, Ernie.'

'I'm much obliged, Frank. How many did you round up?'

'Twenty-one including those from the forecourt of the
railway station.'

'Excellent.' Hardcastle shouted for Marriott, and together they made their way downstairs, through the back door of the station, and into the yard.

'There he is,' shouted one woman as she sighted Hardcastle. 'It's a bleedin' liberty, so it is. What's going on, mister?'

'What's this all about, copper?' shouted another cheeky tart.

Hardcastle stood on an upturned beer crate that he took from among those that the canteen manager had left for collection by the brewers. He held up a hand for silence. 'For those of you who don't know me, I'm Divisional Detective Inspector Hardcastle,' he began. 'Last Sunday night a house in Washbourne Street was bombed and the body of Annie Kelly was found in the basement the following morning, but we know she didn't live there. She'd been strangled, and my job is to find out who did it.'

The DDI's statement was met with a dignified silence; news of the murder had spread quickly among the women. Two or three of them crossed themselves, and called upon the Almighty to bless Annie's soul.

'I've spoken to one of the men who'd been with Annie,' continued Hardcastle, 'and he told me that she'd also been with a man who had a "sir" in front of his name. I want to trace this man urgently, ladies, because until I catch Annie's killer you're all in danger.' He forbore from saying that, by the very nature of their profession, they were at risk all the time, but these women were well aware of the dangers they faced daily. 'Some of you must have seen this man, perhaps even know his name. If any of you have, I want to know, sooner rather than later.' He allowed his eyes to pass quickly over the group of women in a questioning manner. 'I don't expect you to shout it out, but if any of you have any information, come and see me here at Cannon Row, or you can tell Inspector Marsh at Rochester Row,' he added, indicating the sub-divisional commander with a wave of his hand, 'and it'll get to me.'

'One other thing, sir,' said Marriott. 'The necklace.'

'Ah, yes,' said Hardcastle. 'Show it to these ladies.'

Marriott put a hand in his pocket and took out the platinum and diamond necklet that he had found at Washbourne Street, and displayed it to the assembled women. 'Did any of you ever see Annie Kelly wearing this necklace?' he asked. 'It was found at the scene of her murder.'

The women gathered round and peered closely at the item of jewellery. One by one each shook her head; none of them appeared to recognize it.

'Very well, ladies,' said Hardcastle, 'now you can get back to work, and thank you for coming to see me.' The implication that the women had come voluntarily did nothing to assuage their annoyance at the manner in which they had been detained.

'Ain't we being nicked for whoring, then, guv'nor?' asked one saucy young trollop.

'Not this time,' said Hardcastle, and stepped down from his beer crate.

'D'you think we'll get anything out of them, sir?' asked Marriott, once he and the DDI were back in Hardcastle's office.

'Maybe, Marriott, maybe,' said Hardcastle cautiously. 'They're a strange lot are toms and they don't much care for talking to the police, but when one of their own gets topped, they'll likely come forward if they know something. What's more, they'll be the first to call the law if they ever see a copper getting the wrong end of a fight. Now, what about Catto and Lipton? Have they come up with anything yet?'

'Yes, sir. It seems there are four main factories in the London area that make uniforms for the army.' Marriott handed Hardcastle a list of the addresses. 'All of them on the outskirts.'

'But there's one here with offices in Vauxhall Bridge Road, Marriott,' said Hardcastle, jabbing a finger at one of the entries.

'Yes, sir, I noticed that. Easy walking distance from Washbourne Street *and* Victoria station. But the factory's in Edmonton.'

'Might be worth making a few discreet enquiries,' said Hardcastle. 'Put Wood on to it.' Detective Sergeant Herbert Wood was one of those officers that the DDI regarded as 'more reliable', a rare compliment for him to bestow.

There was a knock on the DDI's door, and the station officer appeared.

'What is it, Skipper?' asked Hardcastle.

'One of them tarts you had nicked is downstairs, sir, name of Ruby Hoskins. Says she might have some information for you.'

'Bring her up,' said Hardcastle.

The woman who was shown into the DDI's office was in her early twenties. She had heavily rouged lips and cheeks and had applied kohl to her eyes to make herself more attractive. She wore a bright, low-cut red velvet dress, and like many of the other

women of her calling, had a feather boa around her neck. A large
white ostrich quill dominated her black straw hat.

'So, you're Ruby Hoskins, are you?'

'That's me, guv'nor.' With an audacious grin, the girl placed
her hands on her hips and pushed one leg forward in a provoca-
tive pose.

'Stop acting and sit down, lass.' Hardcastle recognized her
as the young woman who had enquired if she was being
charged with soliciting prostitution. 'Have you got something
to tell me, Ruby?'

'I don't know if it'll help, Mr 'Ardcastle,' said Ruby, 'but
I did see poor Annie with a toff one time.'

'Did Annie tell you his name?'

'Nah, she never said.'

'What did he look like, this man?' Hardcastle took his half-
smoked pipe from the ashtray, and lit it.

'I don't s'pose you've got a fag, have you, Mr H?'

'No, I haven't, but I dare say Sergeant Marriott will give
you one of his coffin nails,' said Hardcastle with a smile.

Marriott produced his packet of Gold Flake and gave one
to the girl. Hardcastle slid his box of Swan Vestas across the
desk, and waited while the girl lit her cigarette.

Ruby puffed smoke into the air. 'I reckon this trick was about
fifty, maybe a bit older,' she said, leaning back in her chair and
crossing one leg over the other. 'He had a fancy suit on, and
an albert with a funny design on the medal, and a bowler hat.
Oh, and he had grey spats an' all, and a walking stick with the
head of a dog on the knob. Nasty looking thing it was.'

'Did he have a moustache or a beard, Ruby?' asked Marriott,
who had started to make notes.

'He had a moustache, bit like that Lord Kitchener, him in
the poster what got drowned a couple of months back, but he
never had no beard. Least I don't think he had. No, I'm sure.
He never had no beard.'

'Has he been with any of the other women, d'you know?'

'He might've, but I . . . oh, hang on though. I think he had
a screw with Sarah a couple of times.'

'Sarah who?' asked Hardcastle.

'Sarah Cotton. I think she last went off with him about a
week ago. Leastways, that's when I saw 'em together. He
might've had her more often, o'course.'

'Where can I find this Sarah Cotton, Ruby?' asked Marriott.

'Down Victoria, I s'pose. She's back hanging about with us again now, but not that often. I know she tried Shepherd Market up Soho for a spell, but I think she got warned off by one of the other girl's pimps.'

'Was Sarah Cotton one of the girls who were brought in tonight, Ruby?'

'Nah, she was picked up by a swell just before the rozzers got there, and went off in a taxi with him.'

'Was that the man you mentioned just now?' asked Marriott.

'Nah! This one was a different geezer. Bit of a toff, though. Sarah seems to go in for toffs.'

'When did you last see Annie Kelly, Ruby?' asked Hardcastle.

'The Friday afore she got topped, guv'nor, poor bitch,' said Ruby promptly. 'About a quarter to nine.'

'And did she go off with this other man, then? The one with the cane with a dog's head on it.'

'She might've, 'cos I caught a glim of him chatting to her. But just then I had a trick of me own to do a bit of business with, and I never saw the going of her, nor him. When I got back to me pitch, about ten that would have been, Annie had gone and I never saw her again, poor little cow.' Ruby emitted a compulsive sob, sniffed loudly and wiped away a tear with the back of her hand.

Hardcastle took the necklace from a drawer and pushed it across the desk. 'I know Sergeant Marriott showed you this earlier on, but are you quite sure you've never seen it before, Ruby?'

Ruby Hoskins picked up the necklace, running it lovingly through her fingers. 'Not that I can recall,' she said.

'You didn't see Annie Kelly ever wearing it?'

'No, I didn't. I wouldn't mind having that round me neck and that's a fact, but it looks too bloody expensive for the likes of us. What's it worth.'

'About three hundred and fifty sovs,' volunteered Marriott.

'Cor blimey!' exclaimed Ruby. 'D'you reckon some trick give it her, like this toff what she was seeing?'

'I doubt it,' said Marriott.

'So do I,' scoffed Ruby. 'I'd love to find a trick what'd give me something like that. Some hopes.'

'All right, Ruby,' said Hardcastle, taking back the necklace.

'As soon as you see Sarah Cotton, tell her I want a word with her. I don't want to go looking for her, but let her know she's not in any trouble.'

'Righto, Mr H.' Ruby turned to the handsome Marriott and winked. 'Ta for the fag, mister,' she said.

'One other thing, Ruby. Did you ever hear Annie mention a man called Seamus Riley?'

Ruby frowned. 'No, I don't think so. Why? D'you think it was him what done for her?'

'I don't know, Ruby. I'm afraid he could be one of many she went with.' Hardcastle glanced at his watch as Ruby Hoskins swept out of the office. 'It's gone ten o'clock, Marriott,' he said. 'I think we'll call it a day. See you first thing tomorrow.'

'Very good, sir,' said the grateful Marriott as he rose to leave. He had thought that Hardcastle was about to embark on what Parliament called an all-night sitting. Not that it would have been the first time.

At nine o'clock on Tuesday morning Detective Sergeant Wood was keeping observation in Vauxhall Bridge Road. He had stationed himself by a tram stop on the opposite side of the road from the offices of Naylor Clothiers Ltd, and, trying to look nonchalant, was reading a newspaper.

At ten o'clock precisely a yellow Rolls Royce Silver Ghost drew up outside the offices. For a moment or two, Wood admired the beautiful vehicle and knew, from his interest in motor cars, that it would have cost somewhere in the order of twelve hundred pounds. It was a sum that the detective sergeant could not even begin to visualize, equal as it was to at least ten years of his pay.

A chauffeur leaped from the driving seat, opened the passenger door of the limousine, and doffed his cap, all in one practised movement.

The man who alighted from the car had a moustache similar to that of the late Earl Kitchener, and carried a cane. Although Wood was able to see that he wore an albert, it was not possible for him to see any device that might have been attached to it, but overall the man fitted the description given to Hardcastle by Ruby Hoskins.

Waiting until the man had entered the offices, Wood folded his newspaper and strolled across the road.

'Lovely car,' he said to the chauffeur, surveying the vehicle with an admiring gaze. 'Must be a pleasure to drive.'

'It is, mate. Unfortunately it doesn't get to be driven far. Needs a good blow out up somewhere like the Great North Road. Not that the boss likes me going too fast.'

'Don't you have to drive your guv'nor far, then?'

'Far?' The chauffeur scoffed. 'I don't call bringing him from Grosvenor Gardens to Vauxhall Bridge Road every morning and back again every night much of a journey. And of course, he goes to the Carlton Club for lunch. Every bloody day,' he added with a sigh. 'But on Wednesdays he tells me to clear off of a night. He says he's going somewhere and he'll take a taxi home because he don't know what time he'll finish. Then every weekend it's down to Kingsley Hall of a Friday and back again Monday, regular as clockwork. Oh, but he did go to Brighton once for a dirty weekend.'

'Could be worse, mate,' said Wood with a laugh. 'You could be driving a bus up to the front line in Flanders.'

'Yeah, true enough,' said the chauffeur. 'Got to be grateful for small mercies, I suppose. Anyhow, better go and fill her up,' he added, starting the engine. 'This old lady drinks more petrol than my old man drank beer, and that's saying something, believe me.'

As the Rolls Royce drove away, Wood took a note of the registration mark, and made his way back to Cannon Row.

Hardcastle listened carefully to Wood's report. 'You've checked the registration, I suppose.'

'Yes, sir. The car is registered to Sir Royston Naylor at this address in Grosvenor Gardens,' said Wood, handing a piece of paper to the DDI.

'Right. Get one of the DCs down to Victoria to find this here Sarah Cotton, and bring her back here. I told that Ruby Hoskins I wanted to see her, but nothing's come of it; I suppose she hasn't been about. I've hatched a little plan to get Sir Royston Naylor into my police station so that I can have a little chat with him.'

'D'you reckon Naylor's your man, sir?'

'He sounds like what I call a promising runner, Wood.'

'D'you think this Sarah Cotton will be there at this time

of day, sir?' asked Wood. 'It's a bit early. In my experience tarts don't usually start work before about eight in the evening.'

'That used to be the case before this scrap with Fritz started, but not any more. If there's a troop train in the offing these trollops won't miss a chance to make a few bob, morning, noon or night. And well done, Wood,' said Hardcastle, for him a rare word of praise.

It had gone two o'clock that same afternoon before DC Catto entered the DDI's office.

'I've got Sarah Cotton outside, sir.'

'I'll see her directly, Catto, but when I've finished talking to her I want you to follow her. Find out where she goes, who she meets and where she lives. Stick to her like glue, but be careful not to let her spot you because she knows what you look like. Understood?'

'Yes, sir. But what if she picks up a trick, sir?'

'You still follow her, lad. I thought I'd made that perfectly clear.' Hardcastle sighed with exasperation. 'Everywhere she goes, you go. That don't mean you have to go into her room and watch her at work, of course.' The DDI smiled wryly. 'That's one occasion you can use your discretion. If you've got any,' he added caustically. 'Now send her in. And send in Sergeant Marriott, too.'

'Sit down, Miss Cotton,' said Hardcastle, once Marriott had joined them.

Undoubtedly in her twenties, Sarah Cotton had the unmistakable bearing of being superior to the average prostitute, although she had affected apparel suited to her role of streetwalker. Furthermore, Hardcastle subsequently learned that Sarah Cotton was not her real name.

'What d'you want with me, Inspector?' Sarah raised her head in an attitude of defiance. Although she contrived a cockney accent there was an underlying suggestion that such a mode of speech was alien to her natural way of talking.

'How well d'you know Sir Royston Naylor?' asked Hardcastle, seeing no point in wasting time.

The DDI's direct approach disconcerted the young prostitute, and for a moment or two she said nothing. 'I, er, I've met him once or twice,' she said eventually.

'You mean he's one of your tricks, Sarah.'

'If you like. Why d'you want to know?'

'And it's usually on a Wednesday that he picks you up,' said Hardcastle, making another direct statement based on what Naylor's chauffeur had told DS Wood.

'Yes, it 'as been the case in the past,' replied Sarah cautiously. 'But why d'you want to know about 'im? And why 'ave you brung me in 'ere?' she asked, deliberately dropping an aspirate or two.

Hardcastle smiled at Sarah's attempt to do what character actresses called a 'common'. 'To give you a word of warning, Sarah,' he said. 'Be careful who you go with.' And with that enigmatic word of advice, he told Marriott to see Sarah Cotton out of the station.

'By the way, sir,' said Marriott when he had seen Sarah Cotton on her way. 'I showed her the necklace, but she said she'd never seen it before.'

'No more than I expected, Marriott,' said Hardcastle. 'But it's got to belong to someone.'

'Perhaps it was the property of one of the victims of the bomb, sir, rather than our murder victim.'

'Maybe, Marriott, maybe,' said Hardcastle, 'but I don't think any of them living at Washbourne Street could've afforded a bit of tomfoolery worth three hundred and fifty quid. And now,' he added, pulling out his watch and staring at it, 'I think it's time we took a turn down to Greenwich High Street, and see what this milkman friend of Annie Kelly's has to say for himself. What was his name?'

'Seamus Riley, sir.'

'So it was. Sounds Irish.' Hardcastle grabbed his coat, hat and umbrella and made for the door. 'Well, come along, Marriott, don't dally.'

Marriott rushed into the detectives' office, seized his hat and coat, and followed Hardcastle down the stairs.

A man dressed in a blue and white striped apron and a straw boater was standing behind the counter of the dairy when Hardcastle and Marriott entered.

'A very good afternoon to you, gentlemen, and what can I do for you today?'

'We're looking for Seamus Riley,' said Hardcastle.

'Oh, are you indeed, and what might you be wanting with him?'

'We're police officers,' said Hardcastle. 'Who are you?'

'Cyril Underwood, sir, but I'm afraid you're out of luck. He's gone and joined the Riffs.'

'That's a tribe in Morocco,' said Hardcastle, displaying another aspect of his randomly gathered historical knowledge. 'What's he doing there, Mr Underwood?'

'I don't know if that's where he is, sir, but it's what he called the Royal Irish Fusiliers. It seems that Riffs is their nickname, so he said.'

'I see,' said Hardcastle, irritated that he had been caught out. 'And when did he join these here Riffs?'

Underwood thought about that. 'Must've been all of five or six months ago, sir.'

'And where did he live, before he joined the army?'

'Now that I can't tell you, sir. I do know he was a bachelor gay, but I've no idea where he was staying. I do remember him telling me that his mother and father were both dead. And he used to tell a story about a brother in the Royal Flying Corps who won the Victoria Cross, but was later shot down by the Red Baron. But I reckon he was bragging. You know what the Irish are like for spinning a yarn.'

'Thank you, Mr Underwood,' said Hardcastle, furious at having wasted a journey. 'It looks like we're on our way back to Colonel Frobisher at Horse Guards again,' he added, turning to Marriott.

Hardcastle and Marriott arrived at Horse Guards just as the assistant provost marshal was about to leave.

'You've just caught me, Inspector,' said Frobisher. 'What can I do for you?'

'I'm interested in a man called Seamus Riley, Colonel. I'm told he joined the Royal Irish Fusiliers about six months ago.'

Frobisher burst out laughing. 'Given that it's an Irish regiment, Mr Hardcastle, there must be a hundred Seamus Rileys in the Riffs, but I'll see what I can do for you. Have you any idea where he lived before he enlisted?'

'I'm afraid not, Colonel. All I can tell you is that he was a delivery man at a dairy in Greenwich before joining the army, and he claimed that his mother and father were both dead.'

'I see. Well, I'm sorry to have to tell you that it might take

some time. The regimental records are kept in Dublin and, as
I suggested, it won't be easy to track down this particular
Seamus Riley. I'll let you know as soon as I have something.'

'There was one other thing, Colonel,' said Hardcastle. 'The
dairyman who employed Riley said that Riley claimed to have
a brother who won the Victoria Cross while serving with the
RFC, but was later shot down by the Red Baron.'

'Ah, Manfred von Richtofen, the scourge of the Royal Flying
Corps,' said Frobisher. 'That'll be easy to check, but I have
to say that I've not heard of a Riley who got the VC.'

At nine o'clock the following morning, Catto knocked on
Hardcastle's open door and hovered.

'Don't stand there like you're waiting for a tram, Catto. For
God's sake come in.'

'Yes, sir.' Catto moved closer to Hardcastle's desk.

'Well?' barked the DDI.

'It's about Sarah Cotton, sir.'

'Well, of course it is, Catto. Get on with it.'

'Yes, sir. I followed her as directed—'

'Just cut to the chase, Catto.' Hardcastle took his pipe out
of his mouth and stared at the luckless DC.

Catto took a deep breath. 'She hung about on the forecourt
of Victoria station until ten o'clock, sir, but she didn't pick up
any tricks. One or two swaddies approached her, but she sent
them packing. She seems to be a bit choosy for a tom.' Sensing
that the DDI was about to utter a word of criticism, Catto hurried
on. 'Then she took a taxi, sir, and I followed in another cab.
She let herself into a house in Cadogan Place with her own key.'

'Did she, indeed?' Hardcastle re-lit his pipe, and sat back in
his chair, a satisfied smile on his face. 'And did she go in by
the front door, or down the area steps into the servants' hall?'

'In the front door, sir,' replied Catto, failing to understand
why Hardcastle had posed the question.

'And presumably you've checked the voters' register to see
who lives there.'

Catto knew that would be the DDI's next question. 'Yes, sir.
It's a Lady Sarah Millard and Lieutenant Colonel Hugo Millard.
He's shown as an absentee voter, sir. I suppose he's at the Front.'

'All right, lad. Ask Sergeant Marriott to see me. And well
done.'

'Yes, sir, thank you, sir.' Catto grinned at this rare word of praise and hurried back to the detectives' office, delighted his ordeal was over.

'There's more to Sarah Cotton than meets the eye,' said Hardcastle when Marriott entered. 'From what Catto's found out it looks as though she ain't Sarah Cotton at all, but Lady Sarah Millard.' And he went on to relate what Catto had discovered.

'But surely a titled lady wouldn't be hawking her mutton round Victoria, sir.' Marriott was astounded at the possibility.

'Nothing would surprise me these days, Marriott. It's this damned war,' said Hardcastle. 'Fetch Wood and Wilmot in here. I've a job for them, seeing as how it's Wednesday.'

'You wanted us, sir?' DS Wood and DC Wilmot stood in front of Hardcastle's desk.

'Yes. First of all, I want Ruby Hoskins brought in here as soon as possible. Once you've done that you can stand by for further orders.'

'Very good, sir,' said Wood who, as a sergeant, was the senior of the two.

At seven o'clock, Wood showed Ruby Hoskins into Hardcastle's office.

'You want me to catch whoever murdered Annie Kelly, don't you, Ruby?' said Hardcastle as the young prostitute was about to protest at being brought to the police station yet again.

'Course I do, Mr 'Ardcastle,' said the girl.

'Then listen carefully, lass. This is what I want you to do.'

When Hardcastle had finished, Ruby Hoskins grinned broadly. 'It'll be a pleasure, Mr 'Ardcastle, and that's no error,' she said.

'D'you reckon the other girls will be willing to play along?'

'You can bet your last brass farthing on it, guv'nor. In fact, it'll be a job stopping them. They can be very nasty when the mood takes a hold of 'em.'

'Good. Well, I'm relying on you, Ruby.'

Hardcastle sent for Wood and Wilmot again.

'Get yourselves down to Victoria station and keep an eye on the toms there. With any luck, Sir Royston Naylor will show up and proposition Sarah Cotton. Once that happens,

this is what I want you to do.' The DDI went on to explain
what he had arranged with Ruby Hoskins, and what he required
of Wood and Wilmot. 'You'd better take Catto with you, Wood.
He knows what Sarah Cotton looks like. But once he's pointed
her out to you, send him back here. I don't want him hanging
about and making a Mons of things.'

SEVEN

D etective Sergeant Wood and Detective Constable
Wilmot had been standing beneath the portico of the
Victoria Palace Theatre since eight o'clock. It was
a vantage point from which they had a good view of the
prostitutes gathered on the corner of Wilton Road.

Most of the women were chatting noisily among themselves, and from time to time glancing expectantly towards
the railway station. Presumably they had heard of the immi-
nent arrival of a troop train. But DS Wood, being a resourceful
officer, had checked with the railway police, and learned that
one was due to come in at nine o'clock. He hoped that Naylor
would arrive on the scene before then, otherwise there was a
danger that the women would scatter in search of soldiers.

He need not have worried, however. At a quarter to nine
the two detectives' patience was rewarded. With his cane tap-
tapping the pavement, the figure of Sir Royston Naylor strolled
nonchalantly towards the assembled women from the direction of St James's Park. Without further ado, he made straight
for Sarah Cotton and began to talk to her. From what the
chauffeur had told him yesterday morning, Wood guessed
that Naylor had probably dined at the Carlton Club; that was
certainly the direction from which he had come. Not that it
mattered where he had been.

There was an immediate uproar as the prostitutes surrounded
Naylor and Sarah Cotton and began shouting abuse.
Completely taken aback by the sudden onslaught, Naylor
dropped his walking stick – it bore a knob shaped like the
head of a dog – and attempted to distance himself from the
coarse screaming of the aggressive women encircling him.

As Hardcastle had hoped, Ruby Hoskins appointed herself ringleader. ''Ere, you leave her alone, mate. Sarah don't want no truck with you,' she cried, and started to belabour Naylor with her umbrella. Sarah Cotton, who had not been made privy to Hardcastle's plan, appeared utterly bemused by the sudden furore that had developed around her. She took a step back intent upon removing herself from the unseemly fracas, but a couple of the other girls made sure she did not escape, and pushed her back towards the centre of the contrived disturbance.

'Get away from me, you whore,' yelled Naylor in panic, as he tried to defend himself against Ruby's blows. He then made the mistake of pushing her away, accidentally putting his hand on her breast as he did so.

''Ere, did you see that?' screeched Ruby to her mates. 'He tried to touch me up. It's an assault, that's what it is. Fetch a copper; I want 'im nicked.' She poked Naylor in the chest. 'You're a bloody pervert, mate, that's what you are.'

Seven or eight of the prostitutes encircled Naylor and began to pummel him with their fists, while others shouted at him to leave Ruby alone.

'I think it's time we broke it up, Fred,' said Wood, smothering a laugh, and he and DC Wilmot ran across the road. 'We're police officers,' he shouted, as he and his partner drew closer to the warring crowd. 'Now then, now then, what's going on?' he demanded.

'All right, ladies, leave him be. It's the law. They'll take care of him,' shouted Ruby, who knew what was to happen next. 'This man assaulted me, officer,' she said as the policemen drew within earshot. 'He grabbed hold of me tits.'

'I did nothing of the sort,' protested Naylor loudly. 'It was the other way round. That common little tart attacked me.'

It was a statement that brought forth a further battery of insults directed at Naylor.

'Common little tarts, are we?' shouted one girl. 'But you couldn't wait to have it up with one of us, could you?'

'I'm a police officer,' Wood repeated, seizing hold of Naylor's arm. 'I'm arresting you for making an affray.'

Naylor's face became suffused with rage. 'I hope you know what you're doing,' he exclaimed. 'I'll have you know that I happen to be a personal friend of Sir Edward Henry.'

'I'll make sure he knows you've been arrested,' said Wood

mildly. As an officer stationed in the centre of the capital, he had frequently encountered such veiled threats. 'He's very keen to maintain public order is the Commissioner. I'll probably get a pat on the back.'

'It was that woman who started it,' shouted Naylor as he looked around for Ruby Hoskins, but following Hardcastle's instructions she had fled.

'Pick up that gentleman's cane,' said Wood to a constable, and signalled to the police van that he had arranged to have waiting. Wilmot bundled the still protesting Naylor into it, and Wood arrested Sarah Cotton telling her that she had been a part of the affray.

But neither she nor Naylor was to know that Hardcastle had carefully orchestrated the entire operation.

'Sir Royston Naylor is in the charge room, sir,' said DS Wood, 'and Sarah Cotton is being looked after in the matron's office.'

'Did Naylor give any trouble, Wood?'

'No, sir, apart from screeching like a banshee,' said Wood, with a grin, 'and claiming that the Commissioner is a personal friend of his.'

'Aren't they all?' said Hardcastle phlegmatically, and calling for Marriott, he descended to the charge room.

Naylor leaped to his feet the moment the DDI entered. 'What's the meaning of this?' he demanded. 'And I want to know your name.'

'I'm Divisional Detective Inspector Hardcastle, head of the CID for this division. And this is Detective Sergeant Marriott.' Hardcastle indicated his assistant with a casual wave of one hand while dismissing the attendant constable with the other.

'Well, Inspector, it might interest you to know that I happen to be a personal friend of—'

'If you're going to say Sir Edward Henry, I've just been on the phone to him and he said he'd never heard of you.' Hardcastle had done no such thing of course, but took a chance on the Commissioner not knowing Sir Royston Naylor. Although accustomed to Hardcastle's frequent outrageous statements, Marriott was, nonetheless, flabbergasted at the enormity of his DDI's latest fabrication.

'That still doesn't explain why I was hauled down here in a police van like a common criminal.' The exposure of his lie about knowing the Commissioner did nothing to deflect Naylor's rage at having been arrested.

'My officers tell me that you were engaged in an unseemly brawl with several prostitutes in Wilton Road, Sir Royston,' said Hardcastle mildly. 'And that *makes* you a common criminal in my book.'

'I was trying to defend myself. I was set upon by those damned women for no reason at all.'

'Be that as it may, Sir Royston, I understand that one young woman complained that you'd indecently assaulted her.'

'Poppycock!' exclaimed Naylor. 'It was she who attacked me when all I was doing was having a private conversation with a young woman.'

'You were speaking to a common prostitute,' said Hardcastle brutally, 'presumably in an attempt to arrange for a quick screw?'

Naylor's faced turned scarlet, and he huffed and puffed, and for a moment Hardcastle wondered if the clothing manufacturer was about to have a heart attack. 'What if I was?' he demanded eventually. 'It's not against the law.'

'No, but engaging in a fight in a public thoroughfare, that amounted to an affray, most certainly is an offence. And I see no reason why you should not appear before the Bow Street magistrate tomorrow morning. I've of a mind to charge you with making an affray, and indecently assaulting a female.'

'I suppose there's no way around this, is there, Inspector?' asked Naylor, suddenly adopting a tone of reason as he realized the predicament in which he found himself. He fingered the medallion on his albert and displayed it so that Hardcastle could not fail to see the square and compass device.

'I'm not a Freemason, Sir Royston,' said Hardcastle coldly, as he recognized that Naylor was attempting to seek preferential treatment, 'but I am sworn to uphold the law.' He paused and gazed at Naylor. 'However, I might be able to persuade the complainant to drop the charge.' He paused. 'If you are willing to assist me, that is,' he added.

'In any way I can, Inspector.' Naylor suddenly realized that this brash and irascible detective was offering him a way out. If he were to be taken to court, with all its attendant publicity, the scandal of engaging in fisticuffs with a prostitute whom he was soliciting, would ruin his reputation, and would certainly put paid to the peerage that had been hinted at in certain quarters.

'When did you last have it away with Annie Kelly?'

'Who?' Naylor affected ignorance of the name, but the expression on his face indicated otherwise.

'Let's not beat about the bush, Sir Royston,' said Hardcastle. 'I'm investigating her murder, and I've received information that you knew the woman, and furthermore that you had sexual intercourse with her.'

'D'you mind if I smoke, Inspector?' Naylor began playing for time.

'Not at all.' Hardcastle took out his pipe, and waited while Naylor took an Abdulla cigarette from a gold case.

'It's true that I saw the girl on a couple of occasions, but that was before I met Sarah.' Naylor lit his cigarette with a gold lighter.

'Which brings me to my next question, Sir Royston. Where were you on the night of Sunday the twenty-fourth of last month?'

'I was in the country for the whole of that weekend,' said Naylor promptly, almost as if he had been anticipating the question. 'I didn't return to London until midday on Monday.'

'And where in the country were you, Sir Royston?' asked Marriott, as he opened his pocketbook on the table.

'At my country estate in Buckinghamshire.' Naylor frowned, seemingly offended that a mere sergeant should have the audacity to pose a question to a person of his standing. 'Together with my wife and a number of house guests. Influential house guests, I may say.'

If that were true, Naylor was unlikely to have murdered Annie Kelly, but Hardcastle was not about to accept the word of a suspect. 'Perhaps you'd be so good as to give my sergeant the address,' he said.

'Certainly.' Naylor took a card from his waistcoat pocket and handed it to the DDI who, in turn, gave it to Marriott. 'Both my addresses are on there,' he said, 'and the address of my club. It's the Carlton.'

'Thank you, Sir Royston,' said Hardcastle, somewhat surprised at the man's readiness to provide the information. 'That'll be all. You can go.'

Naylor stood up, and some of his original hostility returned. 'I assume that you have no evidence to support those trumped-up charges, Inspector, and I have to warn you that I am seriously considering a civil action for wrongful arrest and unlawful imprisonment.'

'That's your privilege, Sir Royston,' said Hardcastle, unconcerned at a threat that had been levelled against him many times before. 'But in order to defend such a civil action my officers will be obliged to give evidence that they saw you fighting with a number of prostitutes. The Commissioner is always keen to deny any suggestion that his officers acted in any way incorrectly, and he would strongly defend such an action.'

Without another word, Sir Royston Naylor snatched up his silk hat and cane, left the room and slammed the door.

'I intend to check that story of his, Marriott,' said Hardcastle. 'We'll have to make a few enquiries at this here Buckinghamshire estate to see if this alibi of his holds water. Now fetch Sarah Cotton in here. She's in the matron's office.'

'What the 'ell 'ave I bin arrested for?' demanded Sarah the moment Marriott escorted her into the interview room.

'Sit down, Cotton,' said Hardcastle. 'You've been arrested for making an affray, and soliciting prostitution.'

'That fight wasn't nothing to do with me,' protested Sarah. 'It was them other girls what suddenly decided to set about poor old Charles. I dunno what they started it for.'

'Charles?' Hardcastle smiled. 'I think you mean Sir Royston Naylor, don't you?'

Sarah shrugged. 'He prefers not to use his real name.' Suddenly all pretence at a cockney accent had vanished, and Sarah spoke in well-educated modular tones.

'And while we're on the subject of assumed names,' continued Hardcastle, 'I gather that you're really Lady Sarah Millard.'

Sarah blushed scarlet and placed a hand on her daringly exposed cleavage. 'How on earth did you discover that?' she blurted out.

'Quite simply, Lady Sarah,' said Hardcastle, deliberately using the woman's title. 'I had you followed by one of my best officers who then checked the voters' register.' He did not mention that he had had other enquiries made into the woman's background. His next question, however, revealed that he knew more about her. 'As a matter of interest, what does Colonel Millard think of your shenanigans?'

Sarah blushed and looked down at the rough wooden table

that separated her from Hardcastle. 'He doesn't know,' she
said softly.

'I presume he's fighting for King and Country somewhere,
is he?' Hardcastle's tone of voice implied what he thought of
women who prostituted themselves, literally, while their
husbands were away at the war.

'Yes, he's in Flanders somewhere. I don't know exactly
where.' Lady Sarah Millard looked up in panic. 'He doesn't
have to know about this, does he?' she asked again, an
imploring look on her face.

'I shan't tell him,' said Hardcastle, 'but I doubt you'll keep
it a secret for long. Presumably your servants have seen you
returning home dressed like a common tart.' He waved a
nonchalant hand at the harlot's apparel that Sarah had affected.

'They wouldn't dare to ask questions,' said Sarah imperiously. 'Anyway,' she added, softening her tone, 'if they were
to be so impertinent, I'd tell them that I'd taken up acting.
That it was a part that needed me to dress like this.'

'Well, there's no arguing with that,' commented Hardcastle
drily, although it was common knowledge that actresses always
changed into their day clothes before leaving the theatre.

'Am I to be charged over this silly business this evening,
Inspector? I really had nothing to do with it. It came as much
of a surprise to me as it obviously did to Charles . . . er,
Royston, that is.'

'I'm willing to let it go on this occasion,' said Hardcastle,
giving the impression of great magnanimity, 'but I don't expect
to hear that you're hawking your body around my division in
future. You can go.'

'Oh, thank you, Inspector. I've been a rather naughty girl,
haven't I?' Sarah stood up, and shot a relieved smile at Hardcastle.

'It's not a case of being naughty, Lady Sarah. I'm investigating
the murder of a prostitute who plied her trade on the same pitch
as yours. And it could just as easily have been your body we
found, or any of the other women. I suppose that silly little bored
girls like you think it's a bit of an adventure, going out on the
streets and pretending to be a tart. Well, young lady, I can tell
you that you're playing a dangerous game. For one thing, you're
not able to take care of yourself like the other women. You
should've stayed at home and embroidered a sampler, or whatever it is that women of your class are supposed to do.'

'I'm sorry. I didn't realize,' said Sarah, now thoroughly contrite.

'Just think what Colonel Millard would've thought were he to have received a telegram telling him that his wife's strangled body, dressed like a tart, had been found in a basement in Washbourne Street. I doubt that your father, the Earl Rankin, would've been too impressed, either.' Disgusted, Hardcastle turned to Marriott. 'Show Lady Sarah out, Marriott, and then come up to my office.'

'It looks as though we'll have to start all over again, sir,' said Marriott. 'Naylor seems to be ruled out.'

'Not necessarily, Marriott. You should know me better than that. I think we'll have a trip down to Buckinghamshire tomorrow and check his alibi. Just because he says that's where he was don't mean it's true. What was that address again?'

'Kingsley Hall, sir. It's just outside the small village of Kingsley, five miles from Wendover.'

'How do we get there?'

'Train from Waterloo, sir. It's about an hour and half's journey.' Marriott knew that the DDI would pose that question, and had consulted Bradshaw's railway guide to discover the route and the times of the services. 'There's a train at nine thirty that'll get us there at ten fifty-two.'

Hardcastle took out his watch. 'Great heavens, it's half past ten,' he said, even though it was one of his foibles that he always knew the exact time. 'I'll see you here at eight o'clock tomorrow morning, then, Marriott.' He wound his watch and dropped it back into his waistcoat pocket.

Once Marriott had departed, Hardcastle donned his chesterfield overcoat, which he had now taken into use, gathered up his hat and umbrella, and walked down to the front office.

'The maroons have just gone off, sir,' said the station officer. 'Another air raid. Gotha bombers this time, I'm told.'

'Bugger the air raid, and bugger Fritz,' said Hardcastle testily. 'So long as they don't leave another dead prostitute for me to deal with.' And with that, he walked out into the fresh night air of Cannon Row and on to Bridge Street where the only sound was the popping of the street gas lamps.

It was a clear night, and the searchlights on Apsley Gate were criss-crossing the sky in search of the deadly bombers.

There was a tram waiting at the stop on Victoria Embankment.

'Glad to see that Fritz don't frighten you,' said Hardcastle to the driver.

'It'll take more than those German bastards to rattle me, guv'nor,' said the driver, and swinging the brass control handle, set his tram in motion.

It was an uneventful journey home, and Hardcastle concluded that the observers at Great Yarmouth had, as usual, informed London of the arrival of the bombers the moment they had crossed the coast. London had, also as usual, immediately sounded the alert, but Hardcastle would be indoors before any Gothas reached the capital.

Hardcastle's house was in darkness when he arrived. He hung up his overcoat, bowler hat and umbrella, walked into the parlour and poured himself a whisky. He spent a few minutes scanning the late edition of the *Star*, which he had purchased on the way home, and noted, with a measure of grim satisfaction, that a Zeppelin had been shot down at Potters Bar by Lieutenant Tempest of the Royal Flying Corps. He finished his whisky and made his way upstairs, hoping not to disturb his wife, but she was reading a magazine.

'You're home late, Ernie,' said Alice.

'It's being a detective that does it,' said Hardcastle, quickly undressing and sliding into bed beside his wife. 'The maroons have gone off.'

'Yes, I heard them,' said Alice, and carried on reading *Woman's Weekly*. In common with most of the other residents of London, she had become fatalistic about air raids, and had adopted a similar view to that of troops on the Western Front: If your name's on it, there's not much you can do about it.

EIGHT

There was a solitary taxi on the rank outside Wendover railway station. The driver, an elderly grey-haired man, was reading a copy of the *Daily Chronicle* that he had spread out on his steering wheel, apparently absorbed in catching up on the war news.

'D'you know where Kingsley Hall is?' asked Hardcastle.

'Yeah, of course I do, guv'nor.' The cabbie looked up, irritated at the interruption. 'It's about five miles from here,' he said, and carried on reading his newspaper.

'If it's not troubling you too much perhaps you'd take me there, then,' said Hardcastle acidly. 'And my detective sergeant, too.'

Hardcastle's throwaway line galvanized the driver into action. He leaped from his seat and opened the rear door of his taxi.

'Anything to oblige the law, guv'nor,' he said, half bowing as Hardcastle and Marriott got in.

The cab drove through the open gates of Sir Royston Naylor's estate and wound its way up a long driveway until the house came into view.

Kingsley Hall was an eighteenth-century parsonage set in generous grounds and had been built in 1790 by the Reverend Dr Barnard. The house, which looked out over rolling countryside, had a typical Georgian symmetry about it, its facade decorated, and to a certain extent spoiled, by baroque frills, as though a later owner had tried to lessen the severity of its design.

'Good afternoon, sir.' The door was opened by a butler of forbidding countenance. He was dressed, as befitted his station, in tailcoat and striped trousers.

'I'm Divisional Detective Inspector Hardcastle of the Whitehall Division of the Metropolitan Police, and this is Detective Sergeant Marriott.' The DDI, expecting the usual disdainful reaction that was common among such flunkeys, was surprised by the butler's response.

'Please come in, gentlemen. I'm afraid Sir Royston is in London, if that's who you were hoping to see. But Her Ladyship's here.' The butler smiled and opened the door wide.

'No, as a matter of fact it was you I wanted to speak to,' said Hardcastle, aware that butlers tended to know more about what went on in a household than anyone else there.

'Very well, sir. If you'd care to follow me, I dare say Her Ladyship wouldn't object to my using the withdrawing room.'

'No need for all that sort of fuss,' said Hardcastle. 'I'd find it more comfortable to have a chat in your pantry, if it's all the same to you.'

'Of course, sir. If you'll allow me to take your coats, gentlemen, I'll show you the way. By the by, my name is Drake, sir. Edward Drake.'

Waiting until the butler had deposited their hats, coats and umbrellas on the hall table, the two detectives followed him down the backstairs and into his private quarters.

'You'll have come direct from London, then, gentlemen,' said Drake, once Hardcastle and Marriott were seated in his pantry.

'Yes, we have.'

'In that case, and on account of there being a bit of a nip in the air, I dare say you could do justice to a drop of Scotch.' It was a somewhat untenable excuse; the weather had been mild all week, and today was no exception. Without waiting for a reply, Drake set out tumblers and dispensed substantial measures of Buchanan's Royal Household whisky. 'Five shillings and sixpence a bottle,' he said. 'Sir Royston insists on it and has it sent down especially from Messrs Harrods in Brompton Road. He'll not drink anything else.'

'Good for Sir Royston,' said Hardcastle, taking a sip.

'Well now, sir, what was it you wanted to talk to me about?'

Hardcastle told Drake that he was investigating Annie Kelly's murder, but gave him only as much detail as he needed to know. 'I've spoken to Sir Royston,' he continued, 'and he assured me that he spent the weekend of the twenty-third to the twenty-fifth of last month down here.'

Drake hesitated. 'Well, sir, I—'

'If you're concerned about breaching a confidence, Mr Drake, I can assure you that Sir Royston is aware that I'll be checking his story. In fact, he went further: he insisted upon it.' That was not quite true, but Hardcastle was not above exaggerating when he thought the occasion demanded it. 'Anyway, it's something I have to do; my guv'nor is very particular that I tie up all the loose ends. It's a nuisance, but there we are.' He smiled and spread his hands. 'I'm sure you know that when the boss wants something, you just get on and do it.' As far as Hardcastle was concerned, though, it was nothing of the sort; the DDI was a stickler for conducting a thorough investigation, and had no need of a senior officer to tell him how to do it.

'Ah, yes, I do understand that, sir.' Drake appeared relieved by Hardcastle's assurance, and took a sip of whisky. 'Sir

Royston was here from the Friday evening, sir. That'd be the twenty-second. He was driven down from London and arrived here in time for dinner with Lady Henrietta at nine.'

'Lady Henrietta? Is she an earl's daughter?' As a senior A Division officer, Hardcastle was familiar with the correct manner of address for the titled, often a trap for the unwary.

'No, sir. Being the wife of a knight she should rightly be known as Lady Naylor. What's more, her name's really Hilda, but Sir Royston always calls her Lady Henrietta, and insists that we refer to Her Ladyship in like manner. I know it's not correct, of course. Any butler worth his salt would know that. But people don't seem to worry about things like that any more. It must be something to do with the war.' In common with many other people, the butler blamed almost everything on the war.

'Lady Henrietta, indeed.' Hardcastle scoffed at such disregard for correct form. 'And Sir Royston remained here for the whole weekend, did he?'

'Yes, sir, him and Lady Henrietta. He took a shooting party out on Saturday afternoon. Altogether they bagged twenty-four brace of grouse, and Sir Royston got ten brace of them himself. He's a very good shot, is the guv'nor.'

'I presume that the members of this shooting party were house guests, then.'

'Yes, sir, four couples, all titled they were, but they left on the Sunday about mid-morning.' Drake poured more whisky into the detectives' glasses. 'Surely you can't think that Sir Royston had anything to do with this murder, can you, sir?'

'Good heavens, no, Mr Drake,' exclaimed Hardcastle confidently. 'It's what we in the police call a process of elimination. But he may have witnessed something of importance.' The DDI had no intention of telling Drake the real reason for his suspicion of Naylor. He took out his pipe. 'D'you mind?' he asked, holding it aloft.

'Of course not, sir.' Drake reached across to a ledge and took down an ashtray that he placed in front of Hardcastle.

'A good boss is he, this Sir Royston?' asked Hardcastle casually, as he waved away pipe smoke.

'One of the best, sir, and Lady Henrietta is an absolute peach, a lady in her own right if you take my meaning. More than I can say for some I've worked for, and I've been in service forty-four years all told.'

'Sir Royston must be a busy man. Doesn't get down here too often, I imagine.'

'Oh, very busy, sir. He's involved in making uniforms for the army. Not him personally, of course,' Drake said with a smile. 'It's the company he owns. It takes up most of his time, and I sometimes wonder how he manages to get away for the occasional weekend break.'

'But Lady Naylor stays here all the time, does she?'

'Yes, she does. It's the air raids, you see, sir. Between you and me, Her Ladyship's of a nervous disposition, and . . . well, not to put too fine a point on it, she's terrified of them there Zeppelins. I find that surprising really, because she's only a young woman and not the wilting violet type at all. Odd really because she's quite a fine horsewoman, and quite fearless when it comes to riding. You should see her riding to hounds. The stallion she rides is a proper handful.'

'How old is she, then?' asked Marriott.

'Twenty-five, sir.' Drake lowered his voice, even though there were only the three of them in the room, and the door was firmly closed. 'She's Sir Royston's second wife; his first died of the consumption some four years back.'

'Are there any children, Mr Drake?'

'No, Mr Marriott. It's one of Sir Royston's great disappointments. And it'll be a greater sadness if he gets the peerage that's being spoken of in some circles. There'll be no heir, you see, and the title would die out with Sir Royston, there not being any male relatives either.'

'You seem well informed, Mr Drake,' observed Marriott.

Drake afforded himself a brief smile. 'There's not a great deal that gets past a butler, sir, and that's a fact. And what one butler doesn't know another will. The butlership profession's a bit like a secret society.'

There was a knock at the door, and a plump cheerful woman entered the room. 'I was wondering if these gentlemen would like a bite to eat, Ted,' she said, gazing at the two detectives with a quizzical expression on her face.

'This is my wife Gladys, sir,' said Drake. 'She's the cook general. There used to be a lot more staff here, but now there's only the two of us, apart from Jesse Paxton who's the general handyman. The three parlour maids are off nursing the wounded, the kitchen maid's gone off to make shells, and both the footmen are serving, one in the navy, and the other in the Flying Corps. Not that it matters much, seeing as how there's only Her Ladyship and ourselves to worry about most of the time. But I dare say you'd like some lunch, seeing that you've come all the way from London. These gentlemen are from the police up there, Glad,' he added.

'Very nice,' said Mrs Drake. 'Have them poachers been about again, then? Now there's no permanent gamekeeper, they're running riot, in a manner of speaking.'

'Lunch would be most acceptable, Mrs Drake, thank you,' said Hardcastle, addressing himself to the butler's wife, 'but we don't want to put you to any trouble. And no, we're not interested in poachers.'

'It's no trouble at all, sir. To tell the truth, Ted and I are always glad of a bit of company. It gets a touch lonely down here.'

'You said that Sir Royston hosted a shooting party the weekend before last, Mr Drake,' said Marriott.

'That's correct, Mr Marriott.'

'Sir Royston must employ beaters and a gamekeeper, then.'

'That he does, sir, but like Glad said they're not what you'd call regular staff. They're resident in the village, and come up here as and when they're required. They're farm people mostly, but, as I explained, things are different now there's a war on.'

Having been treated to a splendid lunch of roast lamb – Sir Royston had his own flock of sheep, Drake explained – Hardcastle and Marriott announced their departure.

'Would it be possible for you to telephone for a taxi, Mr Drake?' asked Hardcastle.

'No need for that, sir,' said the butler. 'I'll run you to the station in one of the estate cars.'

The two detectives arrived at Waterloo at four o'clock, and Hardcastle engaged a taxi on the station forecourt. 'Scotland Yard, cabbie,' he said, and in an aside to Marriott, added, 'Tell 'em Cannon Row and half the time you'll finish up at Cannon Street in the City.'

'So I believe, sir,' said Marriott wearily.

Once in his office, Hardcastle sat down, removed his spats and shoes, and began to massage his feet.

'I think we've had enough walking about for one day, Marriott.'

Marriott did not believe that he and the DDI had walked any more than usual, perhaps even less, but he kept his counsel. 'Bit of a waste of time, wasn't it, sir?' he suggested. 'Seems as though Sir Royston didn't have anything to do with it.'

'Not necessarily, Marriott,' said Hardcastle, reaching across his desk for his pipe. 'That Drake was a bit too obliging for my liking. In my experience butlers are usually hoity-toity and completely loyal to their masters. Frankly, I wouldn't be at all surprised to learn that the minute Naylor left the nick last night he was on the telephone to Drake telling him what to say to us. For instance, Drake said that Naylor was there on the Friday night in time for dinner at nine, but Ruby Hoskins reckoned she saw Naylor talking to Annie Kelly at nine o'clock that night in Victoria. No, Marriott, it don't hang together. What's more, I think that Naylor told his butler to give us the soft-soap treatment.'

'There's not much we can do about that, is there, sir?'

'Not for the moment, Marriott, but the bird might yet come home to roost,' said Hardcastle mysteriously. 'Sit yourself down, m'boy, and smoke if you want.'

'Thank you, guv'nor.' Recognizing that Hardcastle was about to embark on one of his informal little chats, Marriott lapsed into the more familiar form of address. He took out a packet of Gold Flake cigarettes and lit one.

'You should take up a pipe, m'boy,' said Hardcastle. 'Those things you smoke won't do you any good.'

'I tried it once, guv'nor, but I couldn't take to it.' It was the reply that Marriott always gave to the question that Hardcastle invariably posed whenever he saw his sergeant smoking a cigarette.

'I've had an idea, m'boy,' said Hardcastle, as he replaced his shoes and spats.

'You have, guv'nor?' Marriott's response was apprehensive. He knew that Hardcastle was prone to steering the investigation in an unrelated direction whenever an enquiry seemed to be stalling, and Marriott frequently had difficulty in following the reasoning behind the DDI's proposed course of action. Nevertheless, his chief seemed to possess an unerring ability to get to the nub of the matter.

'Have a word with Inspector Sankey at Rochester Row, Marriott. I seem to recall something about him having got an old soldier to identify them that was killed in that Washbourne Street bomb.'

'How will he help, sir?' Marriott reverted to formality, realizing that Hardcastle had done so.

'He might've seen Naylor hanging about Washbourne Street on the Sunday night.'

'You still fancy Naylor for this topping, then, sir.' Marriott had believed Drake, the butler, when he had said that Sir Royston was at Kingsley Hall for the whole of the weekend in question. That apart, a few questions to the titled folk that Drake had said comprised the shooting party would confirm Naylor's alibi. Marriott thought it unlikely that Hardcastle had overlooked interviewing the house guests, but he guessed that the DDI had assumed they would endorse Naylor's claim that he had spent the weekend at his country estate.

'You know me, Marriott,' said Hardcastle. 'Sir Royston Naylor ain't out of the woods yet.'

'But his butler was adamant that—'

'His butler is very keen to hang on to his job,' said Hardcastle, 'and he'll say anything his master tells him to. Don't forget that most of the people who worked at Kingsley Hall have been dismissed, or gone to the war. And the butler and his missus might be next. That Naylor is a hard-headed businessman, and he'd sack the Drakes without a second thought.'

Marriott was now thoroughly confused. 'But how will this old soldier help, sir? He won't know what Naylor looks like.'

'Exactly, Marriott. We'll arrange for him to have a glim of Sir Royston. Fetch Wood in here.'

A minute later, DS Wood stepped into the DDI's office. 'Yes, sir?'

'Sergeant Marriott will find out from Inspector Sankey at Rochester Row who this old soldier was who identified the dead from Washbourne Street, Wood. Tomorrow morning, I want you to take him up to the offices of Sir Royston Naylor at Vauxhall Bridge Road so he can get a look at him. Then he can tell us if he's ever seen Naylor hanging around Washbourne Street, particularly on the night that Annie Kelly was topped.'

Aware that Albert Jackson would no longer be living at Washbourne Street, Wood went straight to the Salvation Army refuge at Vandon Street off Buckingham Gate.

'Yes, Sergeant, Mr Jackson is here,' said a young lady attired in the Army's uniform, complete with its distinctive poked bonnet. 'I'll get him for you.'

'I'm Detective Sergeant Wood of Cannon Row police station, Mr Jackson,' said Wood, when the old soldier appeared.

'Oh, aye.' Jackson took his pipe out of his mouth and nodded. 'What's the problem, then?'

'I want you to meet me tomorrow morning in Vauxhall Bridge Road.'

'Why?'

'I'd like you to have a glim at a man who you might have seen hanging around Washbourne Street, Mr Jackson. It's possible that he's someone we're particularly interested in.'

'Right, guv'nor. What time?'

'About quarter to ten.'

On the Friday morning, Detective Sergeant Wood and ex-Sergeant Albert Jackson, formerly of the Oxfordshire and Buckinghamshire Light Infantry, waited on the same side of the road as Naylor's offices, but a yard or two down from the entrance.

At exactly ten o'clock the entrepreneur's Rolls Royce Silver Ghost drew into the kerb.

'Have a stroll up there, Bert,' said Wood, who by now had not only got to know Albert Jackson, but had heard his entire life story twice, 'and get a good look at the toff who's getting out of the Rolls.'

'Right, guv'nor.' Doing as Wood had instructed, Jackson hurried along the pavement and almost collided with Naylor as he alighted from his Rolls Royce. 'Begging your pardon, sir,' he said, touching his cap. 'The old eyesight's not what it was, not after I got me Blighty one.'

'Ah, one of our heroes,' said Naylor, and glanced at Jackson's empty sleeve. 'I hope you know how much we appreciate your sacrifice.' He seized Jackson's left hand and shook it vigorously. Relinquishing his grasp, he took out his wallet and opened it. 'There you are my man,' he added magnanimously, and handed the old soldier one of the new type of pound notes that had been issued to replace sovereigns at the outbreak of the war. 'A little something to help you on your way. And good luck to you, my man.'

'Thank you, sir,' said Jackson, touching his cap again. 'Very kind of you, I'm sure, sir.'

Naylor strode into his office building, and Albert Jackson walked down the road to rejoin DS Wood.

'Well, Bert,' said Wood, 'I've got to hand it to you. You don't only get a good look at the man, but you take a quid off him into the bargain.'

Jackson grinned. 'The army don't only teach you how to kill people, guv'nor.' he said. 'You picks up a few other skills an' all.'

'But had you seen him before, Bert?'

'No, guv'nor, never set eyes on him afore today.'

'Well?' Hardcastle broke off his conversation with Marriott, and looked up expectantly as Wood entered his office.

'It was a washout, sir. Jackson swears he's never seen Naylor before.'

'Dammit!' exclaimed Hardcastle. 'Someone must've seen the bloody man hanging around there. All right, Wood, you can go.'

'It is possible that Naylor's not Annie Kelly's murderer, sir,' said Marriott hesitantly. He knew that once Hardcastle had made up his mind about a suspect it was very difficult to persuade him that he might be wrong. What was more, as Marriott knew only too well, the DDI was often proved to have been right in his suspicions.

'Maybe,' said Hardcastle reluctantly, 'but I've still got a feeling about him. It don't make sense, a man of his standing consorting with prostitutes. If he was so keen to have it up why didn't he find some society girl? There's plenty of ragtime girls about who are willing to jump into bed with a million-aire without him taking the risks of being seen picking up Victoria trollops in broad daylight.'

'He did have a fling with Lady Sarah Millard, sir.'

'Yes, but he picked her up on a street corner, Marriott. No, there's more to Sir Royston than meets the eye. He's a man who fancies a common tart, and he'll likely do it again. You mark my words, Marriott.'

'According to Dr Spilsbury, sir, Annie Kelly was two months pregnant, and that might have had something to do with her murder.' Marriott was having difficulty in following Hardcastle's latest line of thinking. Just because one prostitute had been killed did not necessarily mean that there would be others. 'Of course, we might have another Jack the Ripper on our hands, sir. One of his victims was called Kelly: Mary Kelly.'

'Very helpful, Marriott,' said Hardcastle, a sour expression on his face. 'I think we'll have Naylor followed. Put a couple of men on it next Wednesday. That seems to be his favourite day for having a bit of jig-a-jig.'

Marriott was becoming increasingly concerned at Hardcastle's unwavering obsession with Naylor as the murderer, but could not think of any way in which he could divert the DDI from his belief that the entrepreneur was Annie's killer. 'Anyone in particular, sir?' he asked.

'I'll leave it to you, Marriott, but make sure they know they're not to be spotted by Naylor. If he finds out that I'm having him tailed, he'll likely kick up a fuss with someone who's got a bit of clout. I don't care too much about that, but it'd make our job much more difficult.'

'Very good, sir.' Marriott left the office before Hardcastle had time to add his usual caveat that Catto was not to be used. In Marriott's view, Catto was the very man for the job.

NINE

Continually frustrated by an enquiry that was making little progress, Hardcastle spent the weekend at home. But he was unable to relax; his mind kept returning to the problems surrounding Annie Kelly's murder, and his recurring suspicion that Sir Royston Naylor was somehow involved.

All three of the Hardcastles' children were working for most of Saturday and Sunday. Kitty was early turn on the buses each day, and Maud's hospital had received an above average number of wounded officers from that charnel house of the British Army, the Somme. For that same reason the Post Office had more telegrams than usual to deliver, and deemed it necessary for Walter to work a twelve-hour shift on Sunday as well as on Saturday.

As was his custom on a Sunday, Hardcastle wound the

clock on the mantelpiece, and after lunch settled down to read the newspaper.

To add to his exasperation, Alice chose that particular afternoon to renew her plea that it was time for the family to acquire a motor car.

Hardcastle tossed aside the newspaper. 'Do you know what a car would cost, Alice?' he asked irritably.

'Yes, I do, as a matter of fact. There was a nice little Ford advertised in the *Daily Mail* the other day for only £135.'

'*Only* £135?' Hardcastle was appalled. 'D'you know what I earn a year, my girl? No? Well, I'll tell you: it's about £200. How on earth d'you imagine we can afford to buy a car on that sort of wage?'

Unabashed by her husband's outburst, Alice persisted. 'That station-sergeant who lives round the corner in Cosser Street has got a car, Ernie.'

'Yes, and he's stationed at Marlborough Street nick on C Division. With all those clubs and other dives on his toby you can bet your life he's copping backhanders for turning the occasional blind eye. I'll tell you this much, if I was there instead of Bill Sullivan there'd be some sorting out.' Sullivan, the DDI on C Division was heartily disliked by Hardcastle. He was renowned for his sharp suits, curly-brimmed bowler hat, and rattan cane. His mode of dress coupled with his monocle had earned him the sobriquet of 'Posh Bill with the Piccadilly window' among both policemen and villains. It was rumoured that he had a small mirror glued inside his hat so that he could check the tidiness of his hair whenever he entered a building. Hardcastle dismissed him as a poseur.

'Oh, you're impossible, Ernest.' Alice's use of her husband's full name indicated the extent of her irritation with his intransigence. She threw down her knitting and retired to the kitchen to make a cup of tea.

Hardcastle, now in a worse mood than before, returned to the *News of the World*, and continued to read the account of the previous day's sinking of five ships by a German U-boat off Nantucket Island.

'If that don't bring the Americans into the war,' he muttered to himself, 'nothing will.'

* * *

Hardcastle was in no better a mood when he arrived at Cannon Row police station on the Monday morning.

As usual, the station officer had laid out the station books for the DDI's inspection.

'There's been nothing since you initialled them on Friday evening, sir.'

'Nothing?' exclaimed Hardcastle in disgust. 'Surely to God, someone must've committed a crime somewhere. I can see I'll have to have a word with my detectives. They're not putting themselves about on the manor. Neither, it seems, are the uniformed men,' he muttered as a parting shot.

The station officer deemed it impolitic to reply, and replaced the books on the shelf at the back of the office.

'Marriott,' shouted Hardcastle as he reached the top of the stairs.

'Yes, sir?' The sergeant followed the DDI into his office.

'There's been nothing in the crime book since Friday evening. What are those detectives of mine doing, eh? Surely the winter patrols would have nicked somebody over the weekend.' The winter patrols were Uniform Branch officers who aspired to be full-blown detectives, and whose task was to patrol the streets in plain clothes stopping and searching likely suspects.

'I'll have a word with them, sir.' Hardcastle's comment was a slight not only on the officers concerned, but upon Marriott also whose job it was to supervise them.

'Any developments with the Annie Kelly enquiry?' asked Hardcastle.

'No, sir.' It seemed to Marriott that the DDI was intent on being disagreeable this morning. 'Wood's taking up the observation on Sir Royston Naylor on Wednesday, sir,' he reminded Hardcastle, in an attempt at placation.

'Who have you put with him?' demanded Hardcastle.

'Catto, sir.' Marriott spoke hesitantly, knowing what reaction to expect.

'Catto? Why him, Marriott? He's no bloody good for a job like that.'

'There's no one else, sir. Lipton's at the Old Bailey all this week with the Army and Navy Stores robbery, and Carter's at Bow Street with—'

'Yes, all right, Marriott. I don't want chapter and verse. I just hope that Catto don't make a Mons of it.' The implication was that Marriott would be to blame if anything went wrong, and in particular, if Naylor realized he was being followed. 'On second thoughts, put them on Naylor today.'

'Today, sir? But Wednesday's the day he usually goes to—' 'I know what he usually does, Marriott,' snapped Hardcastle, 'but after that fiasco with Lady Sarah Millard last week, he might decide to change his routine.'

'Very good, sir,' said Marriott, and left the office to make the arrangements, relieved that, at last, he was able to escape the DDI's unreasonable wrath.

It so happened that Hardcastle's decision proved, yet again, that he had an instinct for predicting human behaviour. But doubtless the DDI would claim that it was a talent that resulted from his years of experience in what he called 'the art of thief-taking', but which encompassed the entire gamut of malefactors. However, even he could not have foreseen the outcome of the observation he had ordered.

Detective Sergeant Herbert Wood was no less skilled at his particular forte, that of conducting discreet surveillance on a suspect, than Hardcastle was at thief-taking. Instead of waiting near Victoria railway station, he decided that he and Catto would begin their observation at the head office of Naylor's clothing manufactory in Vauxhall Bridge Road at the time when Naylor usually left.

At ten minutes to six the two detectives took up their posts.

'Grab hold of a cab, Henry, and tell the driver to park a few yards down the road facing Victoria. Tell him it's police business, and that he's to wait for further instructions.'

'Why are we doing that, Skip?' asked Catto.

'Because if Sir Royston takes off in his Rolls and we haven't got the means to follow him, we'll be in trouble with the DDI before we've even started, Henry, that's why. Now, stop wasting time, and do it.' Wood did not like having his orders questioned any more than did Hardcastle. 'And don't forget to take the cab's plate number, otherwise the DDI won't allow the expenses.'

Convinced that everybody today was in a bad mood, Catto crossed the road and flagged down the next taxi he saw. Producing his warrant card, he told the driver to wait for further instructions.

Ten minutes later, at exactly six o'clock, Naylor came out of his office, crossed the pavement to where his driver was waiting with the Silver Ghost, and dismissed him.

'I knew it,' said Wood. 'He's changed the day he goes hunting for a tart.'

As his Rolls Royce disappeared towards Victoria, Naylor hailed a cab and climbed in.

Wood and Catto raced down the road to where their taxi was parked and leaped aboard.

'Follow that cab,' shouted Wood, employing a phrase beloved of crime-fiction writers, but rarely used in real life.

Naylor's taxi drove past the prostitutes gathered at the corner of Wilton Street without its passenger affording them a second glance. The cab continued through Grosvenor Gardens and Belgrave Place, and finally stopped outside a house in Cadogan Place.

'Well, I'll be damned!' exclaimed Wood. 'That's where Lady Sarah Millard lives.'

'What do we do now, Skip?' asked Catto, as Wood paid off the cab.

'We hang about, Henry, maintain a discreet observation, as we say in the trade, and see what happens next.'

Sir Royston Naylor alighted from his cab and strode up to the front door. Moments later he was admitted by a trim, smiling housemaid.

'That's not the first time he's called there, Henry,' said Wood. 'The maid obviously recognized him.'

'That Lady Sarah doesn't give a damn, does she, Skip?' said Catto. 'I reckon she's turned the place into a high-class knocking shop. Might be good for doing her for running a brothel.'

'It's only a brothel if there are two or more toms working there, Henry,' said Wood tersely. 'I should've thought you'd've known that.'

Following that latest reproof, Catto lapsed into silence.

The two detectives loitered near the Millard house, trying to look inconspicuous.

Ten minutes later, another cab pulled up outside the house and an army officer got out. He too was admitted without question by the maid.

'Bloody hell!' said Catto. 'If that's another client there's going to be a few fireworks.'

'Yes, it might well be another trick, Henry,' said Wood with a laugh. 'If it is, Her Ladyship needs to sort out her diary. Either that or they should form an orderly queue in the hall.'

But the two A Division officers did not have long to wait for the riddle to be solved.

Minutes later, the barefooted figure of Sir Royston Naylor came running out of the house, his face clearly etched with fear. His hair was disarranged, his shirt was unbuttoned and he was holding up his trousers, the braces still hanging down. In his free hand he held a pair of shoes and his jacket, the skirt of which was dragging on the ground.

Almost immediately the army officer appeared on the doorstep, a revolver in his hand. The next moment he discharged the weapon, the round passing harmlessly over Naylor's head.

'If I ever catch you with my wife again, I'll make sure the next one hits you, you white-feather bastard,' yelled the officer.

'Ye Gods!' exclaimed Wood. 'It's Sarah's husband. Go and feel Naylor's collar, Henry,' he shouted, and without a thought for his personal safety, raced across to the man with the gun. 'I'm a police officer,' he said as he drew closer. 'Hand over that weapon at once.'

'Don't be damned silly, man. I'm Lieutenant Colonel Millard of the Royal Field Artillery, and I'm entitled to possess this weapon.'

'But you're not entitled to fire it at people in the streets of London,' said Wood, 'and I'm arresting you for discharging a firearm with intent to endanger life. Now, hand it over.'

By now Millard's temper had cooled, and he realized that he was in serious trouble. Having no desire to exacerbate the situation, he meekly surrendered his revolver.

The maid appeared in the doorway. 'Will you be in for dinner, sir?' she asked.

'No, he won't,' said Wood, as he seized Millard's arm and pushed him across to the opposite side of the road to where Catto had Sir Royston Naylor in a firm hold.

'Where are we taking them, Skip?' asked Catto.

'We're on Chelsea Division's ground, Henry. I suppose we'd better take them into Gerald Road nick, and I'll telephone Cannon Row from there.' Having made that decision Wood hailed a cab, and he and Catto bundled the two prisoners into it. He made sure that Naylor sat on one of the jump seats, while Millard was placed in the opposite corner. Wood sat beside Millard; Catto beside Naylor. Each held their respective prisoner in a firm grasp. The last thing the detectives wanted was to have the two men engaging in a fist-fight within the confines of a London cab.

Marriott entered Hardcastle's office with a broad grin on his face.

'What is it, Marriott?'

'Wood and Catto have just arrested Colonel Millard and Sir Royston Naylor outside Lady Sarah Millard's house, sir,' said Marriott, and outlined the circumstances of the two men's detention. 'It seems that Millard caught Naylor having a tumble with Lady Sarah.'

Hardcastle leaned back in his chair and roared with laughter. 'By God, Marriott, you've just made my day. Where are they?'

'At Gerald Road nick, sir.'

Much to Marriott's surprise, Hardcastle snatched at his telephone and asked the operator to put him through to DDI Richard Garwood at Chelsea police station. It was an indication of the pleasure he was deriving from the situation that he had not asked someone else to make the connection for him. Usually he would have nothing to do with what he called 'that damned newfangled instrument'.

'Dick, it's Ernie Hardcastle on A.' And he went on to tell the Chelsea DDI what Marriott had reported.

'Yes, I've just heard,' said Garwood. 'Good knock-off by your lads. Can't have bloody soldiers playing cowboys on the Chelsea Division. The locals wouldn't like it at all. I'll bet half of them are on the telephone to the Commissioner right now.'

'Would you mind if I dealt with it, Dick?' asked Hardcastle, and told Garwood about the murder of Annie Kelly and his suspicion that Naylor was somehow involved. 'We know that Naylor had been screwing Lady Sarah on several occasions previously.'

'Only too glad for you to take it off my hands, Ernie,' said Garwood. 'D'you want me to get my lads to escort these two idiots over to you?'

'There's no need, Dick,' said Hardcastle. 'My two lads are still there. Perhaps you'd be so good as to tell them to bring the prisoners over here.'

*   *   *

It had gone eight o'clock by the time that Sir Royston Naylor and Lieutenant Colonel Millard were brought to Cannon Row police station. Hardcastle had wisely directed that they be kept in separate cells for fear that a fight might break out between them. He decided to interview Millard first, and instructed Marriott to bring him to the interview room.

'Now look here—' Millard began arrogantly, but got no further.

'Sit down and shut up,' snapped Hardcastle.

'I'm not accustomed—'

'I said sit down and shut up,' Hardcastle said again. Once Millard was seated, the DDI sat down opposite him, took out his pipe and began slowly to fill it. He looked up, carefully appraising the army officer. 'I am Divisional Detective Inspector Hardcastle, head of the CID for the Whitehall Division.'

'Well, Inspector . . .' Millard tried to get a word in, but the DDI was having none of it.

'Do you have any idea how much crime I have to deal with on this division, Colonel, apart from all the additional regulations that police have to enforce as a result of the war? What's more, I have Buckingham Palace, the Palace of Westminster, St James's Palace, and all the government offices in Whitehall within my bailiwick including, I may say, the War Office and the Admiralty. And, as if that's not enough, I also have Holyrood House in Edinburgh, and Windsor Castle. But what am I doing this evening? Dealing with two grown men who were behaving like a pair of street hooligans.'

'That man was in bed with my wife, Inspector,' protested Millard. 'I arrived home on leave from the Front and that's what I found. A damned white-feather johnny taking advantage of my absence while I'm fighting for King and Country.'

'That doesn't justify firing a revolver in the street to the common danger, Colonel,' said Hardcastle mildly. 'It certainly doesn't sound like the responsible behaviour of an army officer. However, I'm more interested in Sir Royston Naylor.'

'Who?' Millard looked genuinely puzzled.

'Naylor was the man you chased out of your house, Colonel. He's the head of a firm that makes uniforms for the army.'

'Is he, by Gad? I might've guessed he'd be some sort of profiteer. Well, Inspector, I've never heard of him, and I'd never met him until this evening. He wants to think himself damned lucky he's still alive. I'm an exceedingly good shot and he should be grateful I intended to frighten him rather than kill him.'

'So, there's nothing you can tell me about Naylor.'

'Not a thing, Inspector, other than that he was having an affair with my wife. Who will soon be my ex-wife. I shan't hesitate to cite him in divorce proceedings.'

'Very well, Colonel, I don't think you can help me any further.' Hardcastle had no intention of telling Millard that his wife had been in the habit of picking up men at Victoria railway station and bedding them. That would involve his officers giving evidence in the divorce court, and the Commissioner much preferred that his officers did not become involved in matrimonial proceedings. In any event, it seemed that Colonel Millard had adequate grounds for divorcing his wife without any testimony from the police.

'D'you mean I can go, Inspector?'

Hardcastle laughed. 'No, it doesn't, Colonel. You'll appear before the Bow Street magistrate tomorrow morning, charged with discharging a firearm on the public highway with intent to endanger life.'

'For God's sake man, I didn't hit anyone. I deliberately fired high. This will ruin my career.'

'I can only suggest that you should have thought of that before you decided to take a pot-shot at Sir Royston Naylor, Colonel. Incidentally, you'll probably finish up at the Old Bailey on account of it being a felony.'

'But there's a war on. I'm needed at the Front.'

'That is not a matter for me, Colonel Millard. Incidentally, this whole sorry business will be reported to the Provost Marshal of the Army. What happens to you after that is a matter for the military.'

Millard rose unsteadily to his feet, his shoulders slumping as he realized that his reckless act would almost certainly result in his being cashiered.

'Fetch Naylor in here, Marriott,' said Hardcastle, 'once you've taken Colonel Millard back to his cell.'

Sir Royston Naylor appeared more contrite than on the previous occasion he had been interviewed by Hardcastle.

'What is it with you?' demanded the DDI. 'I'd've thought that the fracas you were involved in last time would have taught you a lesson, but no, you had to keep seeing Lady Sarah despite my warning.'

'It was all a misunderstanding, Inspector,' said Naylor.

'A misunderstanding?' Hardcastle laughed. 'I can see that, Sir Royston. An extremely serious misunderstanding. On your part, of course.'

'I had no idea that Colonel Millard would be coming home on leave.'

'Neither, it would seem, had Lady Sarah,' observed Hardcastle mildly. He was quite enjoying Naylor's discomfort.

'What will happen now, Inspector? Will there be a court case?'

'I regret to say that you do not appear to have committed any offence, so you will not be charged.'

'Thank you,' said Naylor. 'I promise you I'll keep out of your way in future. I have to say it's a relief that I'll not have to go to court.'

'Oh, but you will, Sir Royston. Colonel Millard told me that he intends to divorce his wife, and he'll most certainly cite you as a co-respondent. That means that you can look forward to an appearance at the Royal Courts of Justice in the Strand at some future date. The newspapers will love it; they always make a big thing of a society scandal.'

'Oh my God, that publicity will ruin me,' complained Naylor.

'Very likely,' said Hardcastle. 'That'll be you and Colonel Millard ruined together. And all for the sake of a bit of jig-a-jig with Millard's ragtime girl of a wife.'

TEN

'Good morning, Inspector.' The assistant provost marshal's chief clerk looked up from the pile of reports on his desk. 'You'll be wanting to see the colonel, no doubt.'

'Is he here, Sergeant Glover?'

'Yes, he is, Inspector. The colonel's always in bright and early.' Glover conducted the two detectives into Lieutenant Colonel Frobisher's office, and immediately sent his assistant for tea.

'Ah, Mr Hardcastle,' said Frobisher, standing up to shake hands with the DDI and Marriott. 'How can I help you this morning?' he asked. 'Another deserter perhaps? Please take a seat, gentlemen.'

'A rather more serious matter, Colonel,' said Hardcastle, secretly relishing the disquiet that his announcement was about to cause. 'Yesterday evening two of my officers arrested Lieutenant Colonel Hugo Millard of the Royal Field Artillery.'

'Good God!' exclaimed Frobisher, a shocked expression on his face. 'Whatever for? Not desertion, surely? Colonels don't usually absent themselves.'

'Discharging a firearm on the public highway to the common danger.' Hardcastle made the statement bluntly, and went on to tell the APM the circumstances of the arrest. 'In short, Colonel Millard arrived home on leave from Flanders to discover that his missus was being screwed in the marital bed by a man named Sir Royston Naylor, and Millard didn't much care for it.'

'I should think not,' said Frobisher, somewhat taken aback by Hardcastle's earthy language, to which, even after knowing him for some years, he had yet to become accustomed. 'I imagine he will appear at court, then, Inspector.'

'Most definitely, Colonel. Ten o'clock this morning at Bow Street.'

'What's the likely outcome?' asked the APM.

'Difficult to say. It is a felony, of course, and he could be sent for trial at the Old Bailey.'

'But, surely, as an army officer—' began Frobisher.

'Apart from the magistrate probably saying that as an army officer Millard should have known better,' said Hardcastle, seeing no reason to excuse the colonel's behaviour, 'he will most likely say that it is definitely a matter for the civil jurisdiction. However, subject to a ruling from higher authority, he might prefer that the army deals with it, as there's a war on. But in the end, it'll probably mean that there'll be a powwow between the army and the Director of Public Prosecutions.'

'It would certainly be preferable from the army's point of view if we were to deal with it,' said Frobisher. 'Not that I can see us avoiding the publicity that the whole business is likely to attract. Incidentally, was it his service revolver that he fired, Inspector?'

'Yes, it was,' said Hardcastle, although he could not quite understand what difference it would have made if Millard had fired some other weapon. 'It's in the police property store at the moment and will be produced at court.'

Frobisher glanced at his watch. 'His unit won't have been informed, I suppose.'

'As I said, he was on leave, Colonel, and I gather he's serving on the Western Front somewhere, so there was no question of sending for one of his unit's officers to give evidence of character. Not that it would be needed at this stage. In any event, I suppose it would have to have been a full colonel, or even a general.'

'God, what a mess, and all because of an unfaithful wife,' said Frobisher, shaking his head. 'It's happening a lot these days, Inspector, and it's this damned war that has to answer for it. Decent moral behaviour seems to have gone all to pot.' He sighed, and glanced at the clock. 'In that case, I suppose I'd better go to court myself. There ought to be someone there from the army. Will you be going, Mr Hardcastle.'

'I wouldn't miss it for anything, Colonel,' said Hardcastle, with a laugh.

'I'm most grateful to you, Inspector,' said the APM, mistakenly assuming that Hardcastle was doing him a favour. 'I'm not sure what happens in these circumstances.'

Hardcastle, Marriott and Frobisher arrived at Bow Street just as Lieutenant Colonel Hugo Millard was about to be arraigned.

There was a hubbub of conversation in the public gallery at the appearance in the dock of so senior an army officer in full uniform, and the reporters in the press box began to scribble furiously.

'Before I take a plea is there an officer here from Colonel Millard's regiment?' enquired the Chief Metropolitan Magistrate, his gaze raking the court. His question was a necessary formality; he could not assume that Lieutenant Colonel Frobisher, resplendent though he was in service dress, Sam Browne and a brassard bearing the letters APM, was such an officer. Apart from which, other army officers had been drawn to this unusual spectacle, and were gathered in the public gallery.

'Lieutenant Colonel Frobisher, sir,' said the APM as he stood up. 'I am the assistant provost marshal for the London District.'

'Come into the witness box, Colonel.' The magistrate indicated impatiently with a flourish of his hand, and waited while

Frobisher skirted the back of the court and mounted the two steps into the box. 'Is this a matter that the army would be prepared to deal with, Colonel?' he asked, fingering his Old Etonian tie. 'Subject to any ruling by the Director of Public Prosecutions, of course. Or even the Attorney-General.'

'I'm not in a position to answer that question at this stage, sir. I would need to consult the army's lawyers.'

'Very well,' said the magistrate. 'Perhaps you'd be so good as to do so. In the meantime, I shall remand Colonel Millard into military custody for eight days. I dare say you can take care of that, Colonel Frobisher. After that, I expect to see him here again to answer the charge, or to be told that the DPP is content to allow the military authorities to deal with it.' He scribbled a few words in his register before glancing up. 'Next.'

A roughly dressed man stepped into the dock, clutching a cloth cap. 'Morning, guv'nor,' he said in a gravelly voice. 'Nice day.'

'Frank Duckett, Your Worship,' said the PC gaoler. 'Charged with being drunk and disorderly in Wellington Street.' Duckett was well known to the magistrate for his frequent appearances. 'I'm guilty, sir.' Duckett entered a plea before the clerk was able to put the charge to him. 'And I'm very sorry.'

'I think the best thing is for me to take Colonel Millard to Wellington Barracks in a taxi, Inspector,' said Frobisher, as he and the two detectives walked down the passageway that led to the gaoler's office. 'The commanding officer there will have the unenviable task of providing twenty-four-hour escorts while Millard's confined there. God knows where he'll get a roster of half-colonels from.'

'Perhaps you'd keep me informed, Colonel. My officers will have to give evidence whether it's at the Old Bailey or before a court martial. I presume that Millard will be court-martialled in any event.'

'I imagine that's inevitable, Mr Hardcastle. Conduct unbecoming an officer and a gentleman would be one charge, even if he appears before a civilian court and they impose another penalty. Nevertheless, I can foresee a few days of frantic indecision at the War House until a solution is arrived at. I doubt they've ever been confronted with a case like this before.' Frobisher appeared to derive some sadistic pleasure from that prospect. 'By the way, I have some information regarding your

Seamus Riley. If you'd care to call on me later today, I'll tell you what little I've learned.'

It was late that same afternoon when Hardcastle returned to the APM's office in Horse Guards.

'Did you get Colonel Millard settled, Colonel?'

Frobisher made a sour face. 'The commanding officer at Wellington Barracks was not best pleased, Inspector. In fact, he seemed to resent having a Gunner officer mixing with his precious Brigade of Guards. However, about Seamus Riley . . .'

'You said you'd learned something, Colonel.'

'All rather negative, Inspector. The records office of the Royal Irish Fusiliers has no record of the Seamus Riley you're interested in. As I'd anticipated, there are quite a few Seamus Rileys on their roll, but none who joined at about the time you mentioned.'

'I wonder where he went, then,' mused Hardcastle aloud.

'If I might make a suggestion, sir . . .' said Marriott.

'Yes,' said Hardcastle.

'The date that Mr Underwood, the dairyman, said that Riley left his employment was just before Easter.'

'What's that got to do with it, Marriott?'

'It's possible that he returned to Ireland to take part in the Easter uprising, sir.'

Hardcastle was on the point of dismissing Marriott's suggestion as preposterous when the APM spoke.

'I was about to make the same observation as Sergeant Marriott, Inspector.'

'I suppose I'll have to get a message to the Dublin Metropolitan Police, then,' said Hardcastle gloomily. The prospect did not please him. 'Thank you for your assistance, Colonel.'

The following day, Hardcastle embarked upon the wearisome task of tracking down the mysterious Seamus Riley.

'I suppose I'll have to talk to Superintendent Quinn, Marriott.'

'Why, sir?' Marriott was somewhat puzzled by the DDI's announcement. 'What does Special Branch have to do with Riley?' Patrick Quinn was the head of the Yard's branch that dealt with political extremism, among other matters, and in Marriott's view, was unlikely to be interested in the murder of a prostitute.

'If Riley *was* involved in the Easter uprising, Marriott, as Colonel Frobisher suggested, Mr Quinn's people might know where I can find him. If they don't, they'll be able to talk to the SB in Dublin. With a bit of luck they might know something.' Hardcastle seized his bowler hat and umbrella, but decided that the short walk across to Scotland Yard did not warrant his overcoat. 'Not that I hold out much hope. In my experience, even if SB knew something, they'd most likely keep it to themselves.'

Superintendent Patrick Quinn was standing behind a huge oak desk set across the corner of his office. He was a tall, austere-looking man with a grey goatee beard, an aquiline nose and black, bushy eyebrows. He looked up from the dossier he was reading, his piercing blue eyes studying the inspector who now stood in front of his desk.

'Well, Mr Hardcastle, what is it you want to see me about?' Quinn spoke with a soft Mayo accent.

'It's a matter of a murder I'm dealing with, sir.'

'Explain yourself, man. I don't have all day.'

'No, sir.' Hardcastle went on quickly to outline his interest in Seamus Riley, and the possibility that he had returned to Ireland to take part in the Easter uprising.

'What makes you think that?'

'It was a suggestion put forward by the assistant provost marshal, sir.'

'Really? Well, I can tell you that I don't regard the army as knowing too much about Irish republicanism, Mr Hardcastle. All their officers were at Fairyhouse races in County Meath, fifty miles from Dublin, when the uprising started. However, I'll speak to my Special Branch colleagues in Dublin. If I discover anything, I'll let you know. In the meantime, find out as much as you can about this man. If he's an Irish rebel and he's back here, I need to know. Good day to you, Mr Hardcastle.'

'Any luck, sir?' asked Marriott, when the DDI returned.

'Luck don't enter into it, Marriott,' snapped Hardcastle. He was not at all happy about his interview with the head of Special Branch, coming away, as he had, without any information. 'Mr Quinn wants us to find out as much as we can about Riley.' It seemed to the DDI that he was going to finish up doing SB's work for them, and that they would contribute nothing to the discovery of Annie Kelly's murderer.

'Another trip to Greenwich, then, sir?'

'Exactly,' said Hardcastle, glancing at his watch. 'And there's no time like the present.'

'Right, sir.' Marriott was unconvinced that Seamus Riley was a likely suspect for the murder of Annie Kelly, but at least, Hardcastle had momentarily lost interest in Sir Royston Naylor.

'Ah, the gentlemen from the police.' Cyril Underwood looked up as the two detectives entered his dairy. 'And how can I help you today, Inspector?'

'Seamus Riley,' said Hardcastle. 'Are you sure you've no idea where he was living prior to his departure?'

'As I said before, all I can tell you is that he left here to join the Royal Irish Fusiliers.'

'Well, he didn't,' said Hardcastle. 'I've had a check made with the military and he definitely did not join the RIF.' With some misgiving, he thought that Riley might have joined some other regiment. But it would be impossible to search the records of the entire British Army, standing now at almost two million men under arms.

'Oh, well, that's what he said he was going to do.'

'And you've no idea where he was living when he was working for you, Mr Underwood?'

'The only thing I can tell you is that he sometimes mentioned his landlady, a Mrs Eales.'

'D'you know of this woman, Mr Underwood?' asked Marriott. 'Or where she might live?'

'No, I'm afraid not, sir. She's certainly not a customer of mine.'

'How did Riley get to work? Did he come by tram, or walk, or ride a bicycle?'

Underwood thought about that for a while. 'Now you come to mention it, Inspector, he walked. I remember he came in here one morning looking like a drowned rat. He said that he'd been walking in the rain for about ten minutes. Does that help?'

'It might,' said Hardcastle, angry that Underwood had not seen fit to tell him this on his last visit.

'That's something, I suppose, sir,' said Marriott as he and the DDI left the dairy.

'All we have to do now, Marriott,' muttered Hardcastle, 'is

to find a Mrs Eales who lives within ten minutes' walk of
Underwood's dairy. Well, I'm not traipsing round the streets of
Greenwich trying to find her. That's a job for one of the DCs.'

On his return to Cannon Row, Hardcastle promptly instructed Detective Constable Herbert Wilmot to find Mrs Eales
without delay.

At ten o'clock on the Thursday morning, Wilmot reported
that a Mrs Agnes Eales lived at an address in Plumstead Road,
Woolwich, and that she let out rooms.

'Come, Marriott,' said Hardcastle, 'we'll see if we can lay
this wretched enquiry to rest once and for all.'

'Mrs Agnes Eales?' Hardcastle raised his hat to the middle-
aged woman who opened the door of the house in Woolwich.

'Yes, I'm Mrs Eales.' The woman gazed at the two men,
wondering what they were doing on her doorstep, and what
they wanted.

'We're police officers, madam.' Hardcastle produced his
warrant card, and introduced himself and Marriott.

Mrs Eales looked alarmed. 'It's not my boy Fred, is it?'

'Fred?'

'He's in the army in France, the last I heard. Has he been
wounded?'

'Not to my knowledge, madam,' said Hardcastle. 'We want
to talk to you about a dairy roundsman by the name of Seamus
Riley.'

'Oh, that's a relief. You'd better come in.' Mrs Eales led the two
policemen into her parlour, and immediately offered them tea.

'Very kind, Mrs Eales,' murmured Hardcastle.

While Agnes Eales was in the kitchen making a pot of tea,
Hardcastle gazed around the room. Scrupulously clean, it was,
nonetheless gloomily furnished. Net curtains covered the
windows, and a quantity of bric-a-brac seemed to cover every
available surface.

'What regiment is that fellow in, Marriott?' asked Hardcastle,
pointing at a framed photograph of a soldier, prominently
displayed on the mantelshelf.

Marriott stepped across to the fireplace and studied the print
of a young man, little more than a boy, in army uniform
standing in a stiff pose beside a torchère. 'The Irish Guards,
sir. That's the Star of St Patrick on his cap.'

'I thought I recognized it,' said Hardcastle. 'So, what d'you gather from that, eh, Marriott?'

'That Seamus Riley might be in the Irish Guards and not the Riffs, sir?'

'Exactly. If Riley was keen to join up, he might have taken Mrs Eales's son as an example. And Riley might be a sympathizer to the Republican cause.'

'With respect, I doubt it, sir,' said Marriott, appalled at yet another of Hardcastle's bizarre assumptions. 'The Irish Guards were raised in 1900 as a compliment to the way Irish regiments acquitted themselves in the Boer War. I think you'll find that they're true to King and Country.'

Further discussion on the matter was stemmed by the arrival of Mrs Eales with a tray of tea. 'D'you take milk and sugar, gentlemen?' she enquired.

'Both, thank you,' said Hardcastle, 'and so does Sergeant Marriott the last time I asked him. Now, about Seamus Riley,' he added, accepting a cup of tea.

'Such a nice young man,' said Mrs Eales, as she sat in an armchair facing the two detectives. 'He left here just before Easter.'

'Did he say where he was going?'

'Only that he was going to enlist. Some Irish fusilier regiment, so he said.'

'Did he ever say anything about home rule for Ireland, Mrs Eales?' asked Marriott.

Agnes Eales laughed. 'He'd occasionally spout off about it, but I never took him seriously. The Irish are always going on about that, particularly them from the south. He was from Dublin, so he told me.'

'Did your son Fred have any particular reason for joining the Irish Guards?' asked Hardcastle.

'Not really, but apparently the recruiting sergeant was in the Irish Guards, and he convinced Fred that it was the best regiment in the army. Fred didn't really care which regiment he joined, so he was quite happy to sign up with them.'

'Did Mr Riley leave anything behind when he went?' asked Marriott, trying to steer Mrs Eales back to the enquiry.

'Yes, he did leave a suitcase with a few things in it. He said he'd come back and collect it, but he never did. I hope he's all right.'

'Did he ever mention a young lady called Annie Kelly, Mrs Eales?' asked Hardcastle.

Agnes Eales did not answer immediately, but spent the next few moments pouring more tea.

'I think he was sweet on a young girl at one time,' she said eventually. 'I think she was called Annie, and he told me that she lived in Nelson Street. That's not far from here.'

Hardcastle knew that that was where Annie had lived with her parents. 'And was he seeing her up until he joined the army?' he asked.

'I don't really know, Inspector.'

'I wonder if we might have a look at this suitcase that Mr Riley left behind.'

Mrs Eales hesitated. 'Well, it is rather private. Is there something wrong?'

Hardcastle decided that he had to tell Riley's former landlady why the police were interested in him. 'Annie Kelly has been murdered, Mrs Eales.'

'Oh, good heavens. When was this?'

'The end of last month,' said Marriott.

'But you surely can't think that young Seamus had anything to do with it. I mean he was in the army by then.'

'Did he come back after he joined up?' asked Hardcastle. 'Did you ever see him in uniform?'

'Well, no, now you come to mention it, but I thought . . .'

'The suitcase, Mrs Eales,' prompted Hardcastle.

'It's in the cupboard under the stairs,' said Agnes Eales, clearly distressed that she might have harboured a murderer.

Marriott dragged the suitcase into the hall and opened it. There were a few items of worn clothing, a half-used writing pad and a diary. But the diary had no entries in it.

'There's this, sir.' Marriott held up a small dog-eared piece of pasteboard. 'It's a membership card that says Seamus Riley is a member of Sinn Fein, sir.'

'What's Sinn Fein, Marriott?'

'It's Gaelic for "We ourselves", sir. It's a political party in Ireland that seeks independence.'

'I thought as much. We'll take it with us.' Hardcastle turned to the landlady. 'Thank you very much, Mrs Eales,' he said, 'but we'll not bother you any further.'

ELEVEN

On Friday morning, Hardcastle arrived at work at his usual time of eight o'clock. At the top of the stairs leading to his office, DC Catto was waiting.

'What are you hovering there for, Catto?' demanded Hardcastle without pausing. He took off his hat and coat, sat down behind his desk, and began to fill his pipe. 'Well, come in, man.'

Catto approached. 'There's a message from Special Branch, sir.'

'Spit it out, Catto.'

'Superintendent Quinn wishes to see you at half past nine promptly, sir.'

'Very well.' Irritated at this peremptory command, Hardcastle dismissed Catto, lit his pipe, and began dealing with the reports and expenses claims that his clerk had placed in a pile on the corner of his desk.

At twenty-five past nine, Hardcastle donned his hat, seized his umbrella, and made his way downstairs and across the roadway that separated Cannon Row police station from New Scotland Yard's central building.

To add to his frustration, he was kept waiting until Quinn deigned to see him.

'Do you have any information for me, Mr Hardcastle?' asked Quinn, when eventually the DDI was admitted to the superintendent's office at a quarter to ten.

Hardcastle recounted the conversation that he and Marriott had conducted with Mrs Eales, and finally produced the Sinn Fein membership card. 'And we found this among Riley's belongings, sir,' he said, handing Quinn the small piece of pasteboard that had been in the Irishman's abandoned suitcase.

Quinn placed the card in the centre of his desk and spent a few moments studying it. 'Interesting, but all rather academic now, Mr Hardcastle,' he said. 'Late on Wednesday evening, I received information from the Special Branch in Dublin that your Seamus Riley was among those killed when the General Post Office in O'Connell Street was shelled by the British.

That, of course, is absolute proof that Riley was a republican activist. I would have let you know sooner, but I was rather busy all day yesterday.'

'I see, sir. Thank you,' said Hardcastle stiffly. He was furious that his trip to Woolwich to interview Agnes Eales had been unnecessary, and had wasted time that could usefully have been employed searching for Annie Kelly's real killer. 'Do you wish to keep that, sir?' He waved a hand at the membership card.

'Yes indeed, Mr Hardcastle. I'll have it filed away. We never know when such snippets of information might come in useful. Good day to you, Mr Hardcastle.'

Hardcastle nodded briefly and left the office. He concluded, not for the first time, that Special Branch filed everything, whether it was useful or not.

'Marriott,' shouted Hardcastle, as he reached the top of the stairs.

'Yes, sir?' responded Marriott, as he followed Hardcastle into his office.

'A complete waste of time,' muttered Hardcastle. He was still fuming that Quinn had not seen fit to inform him of Riley's death as soon as he received it. It would have been a matter of simplicity to send one of his officers across to Hardcastle to tell him what had been learned. But he had long ago discovered that such was the secrecy that surrounded the activities of Special Branch that Quinn would not share information with anyone who did not need to know it. And that included his own detectives.

'What did Mr Quinn have to say, then, sir?'

'Seamus Riley's dead, Marriott. Far from joining the Royal Irish Fusiliers, he was killed when the British Army shelled the GPO in O'Connell Street. Unfortunately, Mr Quinn was unable to tell us this before we went to Woolwich to see Mrs Eales.' Infuriated though he was at Superintendent Quinn's delay in passing on this information, Hardcastle would never, under any circumstances, criticize a senior officer to a subordinate one. 'So, now we'll have to start afresh, but I'm still of the opinion that Sir Royston Naylor's our man.'

'Yes, sir,' said Marriott. It seemed that there was no way to steer the DDI away from his determination that Naylor was Annie Kelly's killer.

*   *   *

The DPP had happily ceded the case of Lieutenant Colonel Millard to the army, having no desire to prosecute a case involving a senior serving officer. For its part, the army preferred to avoid the publicity that would surround an Old Bailey trial, but, as it happened, the trial of Millard did attract unwelcome and widespread newspaper interest. As a result of those dual decisions the army acted with an uncharacteristic swiftness and a general court martial was convened within the week.

On Monday the sixteenth of October, Hardcastle, DS Wood, DC Catto and Frobisher arrived at the Duke of York's Headquarters in Kings Road, Chelsea, at ten o'clock.

An impressive court had been assembled in one of the lecture rooms of the headquarters. The president, a brigadier-general, was flanked by a judge-advocate in wig and gown, a colonel of the General Staff, and two lieutenant colonels, one from the South Wales Borderers, the other from the Machine Gun Corps. These officers, wearing medals and swords, were seated behind an ordinary table, their highly polished field boots visible beneath it. On the blanket-covered table were carafes of water and glasses, and two red leather-covered books: *King's Regulations* and the *Manual of Military Law*.

Deprived of his Sam Browne and sword, Millard entered the courtroom accompanied by his defending officer, Lieutenant Colonel Rollo Prentice, a brother artilleryman. Both faced the court and saluted in unison. Already present at a table on the other side of the room were Lieutenant Colonel Rupert Cavendish the prosecuting officer, and his assistant, a young major.

The members of the court were sworn in, and the judge-advocate read the charge.

'How say you, Colonel? Guilty or not guilty?'

'Guilty, sir,' replied Millard in a strong voice. He had been advised that it would be in his best interests not to waste the court's time by contesting the charge.

'May we have the facts, Colonel Cavendish?' said the president.

The members of the court listened carefully as the prosecuting officer gave the details of Millard's regrettable behaviour.

'How many rounds did the accused fire, Colonel?' asked the president.

'One, sir,' said Cavendish.

'And no one was hit?'

'No, sir.'

The president turned to the defending officer. 'Do you wish to make a plea in mitigation, Colonel?'

Prentice stood up, hitched up his sword, and ran a thumb down the inside of his Sam Browne cross belt. 'Sir, may it please the court, Colonel Millard has been in command of a field artillery brigade that formed a part of the 46th Division engaged in the Somme offensive. I do not have to emphasize the strain such a battle places upon commanders. On Sunday the eighth of October, Colonel Millard left France for a well-deserved seven-day furlough and arrived at his home in Cadogan Place at about seven o'clock on the following day. There he found that his wife was in bed with a man. Not unnaturally, discovering his wife in such a compromising situation inflamed Colonel Millard's temper. He chased the man out of the house, and fired a round over his head. Colonel Millard assures me that he had no intention of wounding the man, but merely to frighten him. He now bitterly regrets his impetuous action and realizes that it was a foolish thing to do.'

'*Flagrante delicto*, as one might say,' commented the president, an amused smile playing around his lips.

'Exactly so, sir.'

'Thank you, Colonel Prentice.' The brigadier-general toyed briefly with a sheet of paper. 'Has the man that Colonel Millard chased from the house been identified?' He knew that it was not uncommon for a man like Millard to return home from active service to discover that his wife had been unfaithful. Although it was not necessary for the court to have this information, the president saw no reason to shield the man who had cuckolded the accused. He knew that the name, if given in open court, would be entered in the record of the proceedings, and doubtless would find its way into the pages of the more scurrilous national press.

'Yes, sir,' said Prentice. 'I am informed that he is Sir Royston Naylor, the owner of a company that manufactures military uniforms.'

'Sir Royston Naylor, you say?' The president wrote down the name and repeated it loudly, not wanting there to be any risk of it being unheard by members of the press.

'That is correct, sir,' said Prentice.

'Very well,' said the president. 'The court will now withdraw to consider sentence.'

Frobisher stood up and turned to the still seated Hardcastle.
'That means that *we* withdraw, Inspector,' he whispered. 'It's
different from the civilian practice. In courts martial it happens
the other way round. The members stay where they are, and
we are the ones who go out.'

'Damned funny business,' muttered Hardcastle, yet again
bemused by the practices of the military, and struggled to his
feet.

Once in the draughty corridor, along with everyone else
who had been in court, Hardcastle lit his pipe.

'How come that a lieutenant colonel is in command of a
brigade, Colonel? Shouldn't that be a brigadier-general?'

'Not in the artillery, Inspector. An artillery brigade is what
other regiments call a battalion.'

'I see. What happens now, Colonel?' asked Hardcastle, sorry
that he had raised the question. He had decided, some time
ago, that he would never understand the military.

'The court will decide what to do with Millard, Inspector,
and then it's all over subject to confirmation by the general
officer commanding,' said Frobisher. 'In the meantime, the
members will be enjoying a cup of coffee while we're left
out here to freeze.'

Sure enough a mess steward appeared bearing a huge tray
of coffee, and was conducted into the courtroom by the court
orderly, an elderly sergeant whose medals jangled irritatingly
every time he moved.

A full forty minutes elapsed before the court reconvened,
and the unfortunates in the cold corridor were allowed back.
Millard and his escort were marched in by the court orderly.

'Colonel Millard, the court has considered your conduct
with the utmost care, and has taken note of the defending
officer's plea in mitigation,' began the president. 'However,
whereas your anguish at discovering your wife with another
man can be fully understood, it is still no excuse for reck-
lessly discharging a firearm. As an officer, and a senior one
at that, such conduct must be marked with condign punish-
ment. You will, therefore, be reduced in rank to major with
seniority effective from the date of your original promotion
to major, subject to confirmation. March out.'

'Bit harsh, I thought,' said Frobisher, as he, Hardcastle, Wood and Catto made their way out to Kings Road. 'Won't do his career any good.'

'Harsh?' echoed Hardcastle. 'An Old Bailey judge would probably have sent him to prison,' he said. 'And then his career would have been finished.'

'Maybe so,' admitted Frobisher. 'However, considering the losses we're sustaining, Millard will soon be back up to half-colonel, but he can forget about any promotion beyond that.'

'Will he go back to Flanders?' asked Hardcastle.

'I shouldn't think so, Inspector. He'll be sent to the RFA depot at Woolwich pending a posting to another unit. He'll probably finish the war as an instructor somewhere in this country.'

'Done himself a favour then,' murmured Hardcastle.

Hardcastle arrived early on the Tuesday morning and immediately sent for Marriott.

'Yes, sir?'

'Are all the detectives in, Marriott?'

'Yes, sir.'

'Good. Send them down to that newsvendor by Westminster Underground station to buy these papers.' Hardcastle handed Marriott a list.

'Very good, sir.' Marriott took the list. 'Will you be paying for them, sir?' he asked.

'Certainly not, Marriott. They can have them back once I've done with them.'

Fifteen minutes later, Marriott returned with an armful of Tuesday's national dailies.

As the president of the court martial had anticipated, they carried a full account of the previous day's proceedings at the Duke of York's headquarters. And more.

Many of them had acquired a photograph of Sir Royston Naylor, one of which showed him entering his Rolls Royce outside his offices in Vauxhall Bridge Road. With typical Fleet Street doggedness, some reporters had tracked down Lady Sarah Millard and included details of the Millards' house in Cadogan Place together with a photograph. One organ of the yellow press had erroneously linked Earl Rankin's family lineage with that of the Royal Family.

Another paper had published a photograph of Kingsley Hall

in Buckinghamshire. The caption boldly stated that 'poor' Lady Naylor lived there alone 'while her adulterous husband was in bed with a hero's wife'.

'That lot should please Sir Royston, Marriott,' chuckled Hardcastle, pushing the pile of newspapers aside. 'Just think what they'll have to say when the Millards' divorce case comes up.'

A constable appeared in the doorway of the DDI's office.

'There's a Sir Royston Naylor downstairs, sir. He wishes to see you.'

'Well, he needn't think he can come bowling in here to see me whenever he feels like it, millionaire or not,' said Hardcastle. 'I wonder what he wants.'

'I don't know, sir,' said the PC, 'but he seemed fair upset about something.'

Hardcastle laughed. 'I'll bet he is.' He was tempted to instruct the station officer to deal with Naylor, but decided that it would be amusing to see what he had to say. 'Show him up, lad.'

When Naylor entered the office, almost apoplectic with rage, he was clutching a copy of the *Daily Herald*.

'I want to know the meaning of this, Inspector,' he blustered, brandishing the newspaper. 'This is libellous. How could you possibly allow them to print this sort of stuff about me?'

'Are you suggesting that the release of information about your philandering is a contravention of the Defence of the Realm Act, Sir Royston?' asked Hardcastle mildly. 'I don't see that it damages the war effort. If it had, the censor would have barred it. Apart from anything else, I have no control over what the newspapers publish. I'm only a simple policeman.' He waved a hand at the paper Naylor was holding. 'What you have there is a report of a court martial, Sir Royston, and legitimate speculation resulting from it. It's nothing to do with me, so I suggest you speak to the army.'

'I'm going to sue this Millard,' spluttered Naylor. 'He doesn't know who he's dealing with.'

'I thought his intention was to cite you, Sir Royston,' suggested Marriott, taking his lead from Hardcastle, 'when he starts proceedings to divorce his wife.'

'But the woman was willing,' protested Naylor, as though her readiness to embark upon an affair exonerated him from any liability in the matter.

'Makes no difference,' said Hardcastle, by now tiring of the industrialist's posturing. 'And if you'd be so good as to stop wasting my time, I've a murder to solve. Good day to you.'

'You've not heard the last of this,' shouted Naylor, and collided with a chair in his hurry to get out of Hardcastle's office.

'By the time I get to hear of all the things I've not heard the last of, Marriott, it'll take about a year to listen to them all,' said Hardcastle, as Naylor could be heard stomping down the stairs.

TWELVE

'I think we'll pay Lady Sarah Millard a visit, Marriott,' said Hardcastle, once Naylor had left his office.

The DDI was becoming more and more impatient at his lack of progress in finding the killer of Annie Kelly, and was still annoyed at having unnecessarily wasted a morning interviewing Agnes Eales at Woolwich. As for the incident of Naylor cuckolding Hugo Millard, that had been an amusing diversion, but added nothing to the pitiful ragbag of evidence that had been accumulated. Now Hardcastle was looking for a different avenue of enquiry.

'Lady Sarah? Is that wise, sir?'

'Don't see why not, Marriott.'

'But what d'you hope to learn from her that we don't know already, sir?'

'Despite being a flighty, spoilt society girl, Marriott, I think that young Lady Sarah is more intelligent than your average tom,' said Hardcastle. 'Having frequented Victoria for some time, she might be able to shed some light on any men who were Annie Kelly's regular tricks. I'm thinking that one of them put Annie up the spout and topped her, because her pregnancy would've made trouble for him. And I don't think that that would've been a swaddy who'd only got across her the once and then disappeared into the night, so to speak. No, Marriott, we're looking for a regular. And someone who's expecting a peerage might just be such a candidate,' he added, loath to give up on Sir Royston Naylor.

'But Lady Sarah's not likely to speak freely if Colonel Millard's there, sir.'

'*Major* Millard,' corrected Hardcastle, a stickler for such minutiae. 'He got demoted. Anyway, he had seven days leave, and that expired last Sunday. He'll be at Woolwich now, not that I think he'd have stayed with his slut of a wife any longer than he had to, not now he's decided to get shot of her.'

'When d'you want to pay her a visit, then, sir?' Marriott was not sure that the DDI's proposal would be of any assistance in finding Annie Kelly's killer. He had taken the view that Lady Sarah Millard was a cosseted and vacuous society girl who thought that playing at prostitutes was just a bit of fun. And he doubted that she had the wit to have taken note of anything of importance, or to recognize any of the men who had consorted with the murdered woman.

Hardcastle pulled out his hunter and glanced at it. 'No time like the present, Marriott.' He thrust his watch back into his waistcoat pocket, donned his coat and hat, and seized his umbrella.

'Good morning, sir.' The housemaid at the Millards' Cadogan Place house bobbed at the sight of the two men on the doorstep.

'We're police officers, miss, and we'd like to speak to Lady Sarah Millard if she's at home,' said Hardcastle.

'I'm afraid she's moved, sir. The colonel's put the house up for sale.'

'I see,' said Hardcastle, deeming it unnecessary to correct the housemaid's error about her master's rank. 'D'you happen to know where Lady Sarah's gone?'

'She wrote the address down somewhere, sir. If you'd care to step into the hall, I'll see if I can find it for you.'

The two detectives followed the young woman into the house, and waited while she went in search of the details of Lady Sarah's present whereabouts.

'I've found it, sir.' The housemaid returned waving a slip of paper. 'She's at Artillery Mansions in Victoria, at least for the time being. She said as how it's not permanent.'

'Thank you, miss,' said Hardcastle, once Marriott had written the address in his pocketbook.

'At least it's on our ground, sir,' said Marriott, when he and the DDI were back in the street.

'Artillery Mansions,' said Hardcastle. 'A very suitable

place for a Gunner's soon-to-be ex-wife. That damned place
haunts me.'

'Are you thinking of Rose Drummond, sir?'

'Yes, I am, Marriott.' Only two months ago, Hardcastle had
been saddled with investigating the murder of a German spy,
Rose Drummond, whose body had been found in Hoxton
Square, Shoreditch. She had been a resident at Artillery
Mansions where she had held soirées for senior army officers
and members of parliament from who she had hoped to extract
information. It was an enquiry that had taken Hardcastle and
Detective Sergeant Aubrey Drew of Special Branch to the
little town of Poperinge in Belgium at a time when the Germans
on the Messines Ridge were shelling it.

Lady Sarah Millard's apartment was on the first floor of
Artillery Mansions, and the woman herself answered the door.
That surprised Hardcastle; he had imagined that she would
have had a butler, or at least a maid. Perhaps, he thought flip-
pantly, even a 'madam'.

'Oh, it's you, Inspector.'

Hardcastle raised his hat. 'Indeed, Lady Sarah, and I'd like
a word with you.'

'You'd better come in.' Although the girl did not seem too
happy at the arrival of the police, she showed the two detectives into a sparsely furnished sitting room, containing only
a sofa, a couple of armchairs, and a small escritoire under the
window.

Lady Sarah noticed Hardcastle's sweeping gaze. 'I've not
had time to furnish it fully, yet,' she said, and then, dismissing
that problem as a matter of no importance, she changed the
subject. 'I suppose you've come about that dreadful business
with Hugo and Royston.'

'That's no longer of interest to me,' said Hardcastle bluntly.
'But I understand that Major Millard intends to divorce you,
and cite Sir Royston Naylor as co-respondent. I dare say that
makes you extremely unpopular with both of them, having
been responsible for your husband's demotion, and attracting
unwanted publicity for Sir Royston into the bargain. I don't
suppose your father, Lord Rankin, is too pleased either.'

'I've ruined everything.' Sarah was near to tears. 'I never
meant it to happen; it was all a terrible mix up.'

'A mix-up?' scoffed Hardcastle. 'I'd've called it stupidity, but it's something you'll have to live with, I suppose.' He had no intention of wasting sympathy on the Millard woman. To him, she appeared to be an empty-headed flibbertigibbet who went through life doing exactly as she pleased, without regard to anyone else's views or opinions or feelings. 'However, I'm more concerned with the fate of Annie Kelly, and finding her killer.'

'I don't see how I can help you, Inspector.'

'How long were you playing at being a harlot, Lady Sarah?'

Sarah Millard obviously did not like that word, and attempted to look offended. 'About a month, I suppose,' she admitted.

'Did you know Annie Kelly?'

'I spoke to her a few times.'

'This was when you were soliciting in the Victoria area, I presume. I ask that because I've also been told that you tried your luck in Soho for a while, but got warned off.'

'What makes you think I was ever in Soho?'

'I'm a policeman, Lady Sarah, and it's a policeman's job to know about things like that. Where were you soliciting, Shepherd Market? That's the usual stamping ground for whores.' Ruby Hoskins had told Hardcastle this, but, as usual, he was intent upon checking. Not that where Sarah Millard had been plying her immoral trade had much bearing on the matter in hand.

'Yes, I was there for a while.' The girl answered in a whisper and glanced at the floor.

'But it was only in Victoria that you came across Annie Kelly, was it?'

'Yes.'

'Do you know any of the men she went with?'

'Not by name. Sometimes I would send someone to her.'

'What d'you mean by that, Lady Sarah?' asked Marriott.

'I wouldn't entertain soldiers.' Lady Sarah raised her chin slightly as if the very idea appalled her. 'If one approached me, I'd send him to one of the other girls.'

'So, you only dealt with officers and the titled gentry, did you?' enquired Hardcastle sarcastically.

'Only because they tended to have more money.' To Lady Sarah it seemed a perfectly logical reason for declining to share ten minutes in some sleazy room with one of the common soldiery.

'Did you send many men to Annie Kelly?' asked Marriott.

'I can't remember.'

'Did Sir Royston ever go with her?' Hardcastle was beginning to lose patience with the earl's daughter, and believed that she was being deliberately obstructive.

'I don't know.' Sarah tossed her head, regarding the DDI's questions little short of impertinent. 'Maybe.'

'Very well,' said Hardcastle, as he and Marriott stood up. 'I'll not trouble you further.'

Sarah Millard remained seated and silent.

'We'll see ourselves out,' said Hardcastle pointedly.

Having deliberately slammed Sarah's front door, Hardcastle descended to the ground floor with Marriott hurrying after him.

'D'you think she was telling the truth when she said she didn't know if Naylor had been with Annie Kelly, sir?' asked Marriott as the pair emerged into Victoria Street.

'Truth!' responded Hardcastle fiercely. 'That young whore wouldn't know the truth if it came up and bit her on the arse. But I'm still sure that Sir Royston had something to do with Annie's death, and I reckon that the noble Lady Sarah is covering for him. For all we know, he might be paying her to keep her mouth shut. Particularly as she'll not be getting much money from the galloping major. And I dare say that Lord Rankin's cut her off without a penny, because he can't have failed to read the report of the court martial in *The Times*. But we shall see, Marriott, we shall see.'

'I wonder if Annie Kelly ever worked Shepherd Market, Marriott,' said Hardcastle, when the two of them were back at Cannon Row police station.

'I suppose it's a possibility, sir.' Marriott was unsure where the DDI's latest thought was leading.

'Sarah Millard admitted that she knew Annie, and she might've persuaded her that the pickings in Mayfair were more profitable than in Victoria. And if that's the case, one of the whores up there might know of someone she was seeing. And that someone might just be our killer.'

'D'you want me to send a couple of the DCs up there, sir?' suggested Marriott hopefully, relieved that the DDI seemed to be veering away from Sir Royston Naylor as his principal suspect.

Hardcastle stared at his sergeant. 'Certainly not, Marriott.

It's far too important an enquiry to trust to the likes of Catto and company. We'll go ourselves.'

'When, sir?' Marriott had known instinctively what the DDI's answer would be, and foresaw another evening that he would not be spending with his family.

Hardcastle took out his watch and studied it. 'I should think that nine o'clock this evening will catch most of them, Marriott,' he said, and dropped his watch back into his waistcoat pocket.

'D'you want Mr Sullivan informed, sir?' Marriott was aware that, as a matter of courtesy, the DDI of the St James's Division should be told that Hardcastle was venturing on to that division's area.

'It's got nothing to do with Mr Sullivan, Marriott,' responded Hardcastle curtly, 'unless he wants to solve our murder for us.'

The DDI's dislike of Sullivan was clear, and Marriott deemed it politic to remain silent. It was the nearest that Hardcastle had ever come to criticizing another senior officer in his hearing.

The taxi set down the two detectives at the southern end of Queen Street, and they crossed Curzon Street to Shepherd Market.

'This area is called Mayfair because they used to hold the May Fair here in the eighteenth century,' said Hardcastle, giving Marriott the benefit of another of his potted history lessons. 'But it became too riotous, and was abolished.'

'Very interesting, sir,' said Marriott.

It was fortunate for Hardcastle that at that moment, a uniformed policeman entered the market from Shepherd Street. As a result, the assembled prostitutes, congregated outside The Grapes public house began moving towards Hardcastle and Marriott.

'Stay where you are,' exclaimed Hardcastle, extending both arms sideways.

The women were now trapped, but the policeman seemed perplexed by Hardcastle's action.

'I'm a police officer,' Hardcastle shouted.

'Is that a fact?' said the policeman. 'Who are you, then?'

'DDI Hardcastle of A.'

'Want any help, sir?'

The prostitutes, now apparently resigned to the fact that this was a police raid stood in a group, talking to each other.

'I'm not here to arrest you,' said Hardcastle, as he and

Marriott walked up to the disconsolate group. 'I want to know if any of you knew Annie Kelly. She was murdered at the end of last month in Victoria, and I want to catch whoever did it.'

There was a renewed hubbub of conversation, and eventually one young woman stepped forward.

'I knew her, guv'nor.'

'Who are you?' asked Marriott.

'Eliza Crabtree,' said the girl, an attractive wench, no more than seventeen years of age.

'When was this?' asked Hardcastle.

'Around August, I s'pose. She was up here a few times, but then she sheered off back to Victoria.'

'Did you ever see Annie Kelly with this man?' asked Marriott, producing a copy of the newspaper that contained a photograph of Sir Royston Naylor taken after Major Millard's court martial.

'Yeah, I did,' said Eliza, without hesitation. 'He come up here looking for her quite often. But if she weren't here, he'd have another of us. I had him a couple of times.'

'Was there anyone else that Annie saw regularly?' asked Hardcastle.

'No, not what I know of, mister.'

'All right, Eliza, thanks,' said Hardcastle.

'I was about to nick her, sir,' said the C Division policeman, who by now was standing next to the DDI.

'Well, don't,' said Hardcastle firmly. 'She's just been very helpful in a murder I'm investigating.'

'Very good, sir.' The PC saluted, and walked away.

'Well, Marriott,' said Hardcastle, as they made their way back to Curzon Street, 'all that's done is to put Naylor at the top of my list.'

'I thought he was there already, sir,' said Marriott, risking a jocular comment, but received only a glassy stare from Hardcastle in return.

For the next two days, Hardcastle sat in his office and fretted. He checked reports and signed expenses claims, but it was clear to anyone who knew him well that the Kelly enquiry was festering away in his fertile brain.

On Friday he sent for Marriott.

'I'm not happy that we've got all we can from the Millard girl, Marriott. I think we'll go round and see her again.'

'But she's already said she doesn't know if Sir Royston ever went with Annie Kelly, sir.'

'She was lying, Marriott. I'll tell her that if I charge her with obstructing police, I'll make sure all her whoring will come out in open court. She won't like that, and her father, the Earl Rankin, will like it even less. Especially now that the publicity about Major Millard's court martial has died down.'

'It'll come out in the divorce court anyway, sir.' Marriott thought that Hardcastle was wasting his time, or worse, and was looking for something to do just to relieve his boredom. But, as was so often the case, Marriott was proved wrong.

Hardcastle hammered on the door of Lady Sarah Millard's apartment three times, but received no answer.

'She's not there, sir,' volunteered Marriott.

'I'd rather worked that out for myself, Marriott,' said Hardcastle sarcastically, and returning to the ground floor, he knocked on the caretaker's door.

'Yes, sir? Can I help you?' The caretaker was a man of some fifty years, dressed in black trousers, a white shirt and waistcoat, and a green baize apron.

'I'm Divisional Detective Inspector Hardcastle, and I'm anxious to have a few words with Lady Sarah Millard.'

'Not seen her this morning, sir,' replied the caretaker. 'Mind you, she might've slipped out when I was busy, but she don't usually go out of a morning. But I can't keep track of everyone,' he muttered defensively. 'There's a lot of people living here.'

'D'you have a key to her apartment?' Hardcastle asked. It had occurred to him that some benefit might be gained from looking around Lady Sarah's apartment in her absence.

'I do, sir,' said the caretaker hesitantly, 'but aren't you supposed to have a search warrant? I mean is it legal?'

'This says it is.' Hardcastle withdrew a search warrant that he had executed some days previously in connection with an entirely different matter, and briefly flourished it under the caretaker's nose.

'That's all right, then,' said the relieved caretaker. 'I don't want to get into no trouble with the management, you see, sir. I do have my position to consider.'

'Very wise,' commented Hardcastle. 'By the way, what's your name?'

'Harris, sir. Ted Harris.'

'When you're ready, then, Mr Harris.'

The caretaker fetched a bunch of keys, and led the two detectives back upstairs to the first floor.

'All right, Mr Harris,' said Hardcastle, once the caretaker had opened the door to Lady Sarah's apartment. 'You can leave this to us. If you give me the key, I'll return it to you when we're done.'

'I s'pose that'll be all right, sir.' Somewhat reluctantly Harris handed over the key, and returned to his office.

'Right, then, Marriott, we'll have a gander round and see if we can find anything interesting.'

'Yes, sir.' Marriott was greatly concerned about Hardcastle's illegal search. He was, however, secure in the knowledge that if it was queried none of the opprobrium would fall on him. But apart from that he had no idea what the DDI hoped to find.

After a cursory glance around the sitting room, Hardcastle pushed open the door to the only bedroom. 'Stone the bloody crows!' he exclaimed. 'That's all we need.'

Lying on the bed was the fully clothed body of Lady Sarah Millard, her eyes staring sightlessly at the ceiling.

Marriott moved swiftly across the room, seized the girl's wrist and felt for a pulse. 'Nothing, sir,' he said, glancing at Hardcastle. 'There are red marks on her neck; it looks like manual strangulation.'

'I think we'll let Dr Spilsbury be the judge of that, Marriott,' said Hardcastle. 'Best get on to him straight away. And summon up a couple of men from the nick. I dare say Harris has got a telephone in his office.'

'There's one in the sitting room, sir,' said Marriott, and returned there to do the DDI's bidding.

Ten minutes later, having run all the way from Cannon Row police station, Detective Constables Catto and Carter arrived. They knew that when the DDI summoned them to the scene of a murder, he would accept no excuses for delay.

'You and Carter stand guard on this apartment, Catto, and don't touch anything. I'm going down to have a word with the caretaker.'

'Has she been murdered, sir?' asked Catto innocently.

Hardcastle stared at the unfortunate detective. 'Well, Catto, she's not bloody well taking a mid-morning nap, that's for sure.' And with that crushing comment the DDI descended to the ground floor.

'Everything all right, sir?' asked the caretaker.

'No, Mr Harris, everything's not all right. Lady Sarah Millard's been murdered.'

'Ye Gods!' exclaimed Harris. 'Whatever happened?'

'I was hoping you might be able to tell me,' said Hardcastle. 'Have you noticed any strangers coming in here during, say, the last twenty-four hours?'

Harris ran a hand round his chin, and shook his head. 'Can't say as how I have, sir.'

'Well, then, d'you know of any of Lady Sarah's regular visitors? A man most likely.'

Once again Harris shook his head. 'Lady Sarah was a nice young lady, sir. Well, being a lady in her own right, like, she would be, wouldn't she?'

'Yes,' said Hardcastle pensively. He had no intention of sharing details of Lady Sarah's murky past with a caretaker.

'She always kept herself to herself, as you might say,' added Harris, 'and she never give no trouble.'

'Very interesting,' said Hardcastle impatiently, 'but did she have any male visitors?' he asked again.

'Not that I know of, sir.'

It was an hour or more before Dr Bernard Spilsbury arrived. With his customary efficiency, he first glanced around Lady Sarah's bedroom, his eyes taking in any detail that might help him in his determination of the cause of the young woman's death. Moving across to the bed, he made a visual examination of the corpse before beginning the routine of taking temperatures and all the necessary tests that followed.

'You seem to be making a habit of finding murder victims in Artillery Mansions, Hardcastle,' said Spilsbury, when he had finished conducting his tests. 'This August just gone, wasn't it, the last one? Edith Sturgess if I remember correctly.'

'Yes, it was. That was after the murder of Rose Drummond in Hoxton. You've a good memory, sir.'

'One needs a good memory in my profession, Hardcastle. Now, about this woman . . .' Spilsbury waved a thermometer at the body of Lady Sarah. 'My initial opinion is that she died as a result of manual strangulation. I'll be able to confirm that once I open her up. As to time of death, you'll have to wait until then as well.' He began to put away his instruments. 'Have the cadaver removed to St Mary's at Paddington, Hardcastle, there's a good fellow.'

'Of course, Dr Spilsbury.'

Hardcastle had instructed Marriott to send for Detective Inspector Charles Stockley Collins, head of the Yard's finger-print bureau, and he arrived as Dr Spilsbury was leaving.

'How d'you do, Collins?' Spilsbury nodded briefly in the fingerprint expert's direction.

'Very well, sir, thank you,' said Collins. He turned to Hardcastle. 'I'll see what I can find for you, Ernie, but from what Marriott told me, I doubt I'll find any that have earned a place in my index.'

'I think you're right, Charlie,' said Hardcastle, 'but we've got to try. Might come in useful when I nick the bloke who did it.'

'You think you will?'

'You can put money on it, Charlie.'

'I'll keep my money in my pocket, thanks all the same, Ernie.' Collins knew of Hardcastle's reputation for solving murders.

Hardcastle and Marriott arrived at St Mary's hospital at ten o'clock on the Saturday morning.

As usual, Dr Spilsbury had started early, and had finished by the time the detectives appeared in his examination room.

'As I predicted, Hardcastle, she died as a result of manual strangulation. It's interesting that her murder was similar to that of Annie Kelly.'

'In what way?' asked Hardcastle, his interest immediately aroused.

'The thyroid cartilage had been broken. As in the Kelly case, I would say that considerable force was applied by a right hand, or even both hands.'

'Same killer, then,' suggested Hardcastle.

'It's possible, Hardcastle,' said Spilsbury. 'Or it might be a coincidence.'

'Some coincidence,' muttered Hardcastle.

'D'you have a suspect in mind?' asked Spilsbury.

'Yes, I do, sir. How long had Lady Sarah been dead?'

Spilsbury looked thoughtful. 'I would say not more than

twenty hours, and not less than ten. That's the best I can do for you.'

'It's enough, sir, and thank you, once again.'

'I hope you catch him.'

'I shall, sir, I shall,' said Hardcastle.

Marriott nodded in agreement. He, too, knew of Hardcastle's reputation, but had no idea how the resourceful DDI was to realize his promise.

'I suppose we'd better go and see the Earl Rankin, Marriott,' said Hardcastle, as they left St Mary's hospital, 'and tell him his daughter's been murdered. You'd better find out where he lives.'

'Pont Street, Chelsea, sir,' said Marriott, with a measure of self-satisfaction. He was aware that, at some stage, the DDI would want to know. 'And a country estate in Queen's Magna, Hampshire.'

'And I suppose the Rankins will be down there, seeing as how it's Saturday,' said Hardcastle gloomily, 'but we'll give Pont Street a try first on the off chance.' And without further ado, he hailed a cab.

THIRTEEN

The detectives' taxi stopped outside a large, gabled red-brick mansion in Pont Street.

'Don't forget to note the plate number, Marriott,' said Hardcastle, as he marched up to the front door.

'Yes, sir.' Marriott did not have to be reminded to record that important detail; it was required in order to substantiate a claim for expenses from the Receiver to the Metropolitan Police. But Hardcastle always said it.

'Are you reporters?' The butler who opened the door surveyed the two policemen disdainfully.

'No, we're not,' snapped Hardcastle. 'I'm Divisional Detective Inspector Hardcastle of the Whitehall Division, and I wish to see Lord Rankin on an important matter.'

'I do beg your pardon, gentlemen. You'd better come in,' said the butler, suddenly adopting a far more conciliatory attitude.

Hardcastle and Marriott entered the large hall, in the centre of which was a round table on which were a number of coats and hats, and an army officer's cap bearing the badge of the Coldstream Guards.

'I'm afraid you've come at a somewhat inopportune moment, Inspector. We have just heard that his lordship was killed yesterday on the Somme.'

'I didn't realize he was serving,' said Hardcastle, now at a loss to know how to break this further distressing news.

'Oh yes, sir. He was a career soldier in the Coldstream Guards, and he was commanding a brigade of the Guards when he was killed.'

'This is going to be difficult, Mr . . .?'

'Bristow is my name, sir. Might I enquire in what respect it is difficult?'

'I came here to inform the family that Lady Sarah Millard has been murdered.'

'Oh my God!' exclaimed Bristow, his customary deferential reserve vanishing. He paused in thought for a moment. 'The Rankins' eldest son is here together with the countess, sir. It might be better if you were to talk to him, and he could perhaps break the news to Her Ladyship at a more propitious moment. Not that I can imagine when that would be.'

'That might be for the best,' said Hardcastle, thankful that he did not have to present the grieving Lady Rankin with word of her daughter's shocking death.

'Perhaps if you would care to step into the library, sir. Her Ladyship is in the drawing room, together with Master Geoffrey.' Bristow paused and hurriedly corrected himself. 'Earl Rankin as he now is, of course.' He showed Hardcastle and Marriott into a book-lined room that led off from the back of the hall, and disappeared to find the Rankins' eldest son.

The door opened to admit a young man in the uniform of a captain, the distinctive two-button grouping indicating that, like his late father, he was a Coldstream Guards officer.

'Bristow tells me that you wish to see me, Inspector.'

'I'm afraid so, Lord Rankin,' said Hardcastle.

'No, it's my father who's Lord Rankin and . . . oh, you're quite right, Inspector. It'll take time for me to grow accustomed to the title. I'm afraid I have other things on my mind at the moment. Obviously, Bristow told you of the death of my father.'

'Indeed, sir,' said Hardcastle. 'But I'm sorry to have to say that I bring you further distressing news.'

'Oh God! It's not my brother Archie, surely?'

'No, sir. It's about your sister, Lady Sarah Millard.'

'Oh, I see.' Geoffrey Rankin's face assumed a stony expression. 'We don't talk about Sarah, Inspector. Not after the disgrace she brought upon the family. I suppose you know about this awful business of her being unfaithful to Hugo, and the court martial, and all that.'

'Yes, sir, I was present at that hearing. No, I'm sorry to have to tell you that Lady Sarah is dead.'

'Ye Gods! How much more can this family take? My apologies, gentlemen. Do please sit down.' Geoffrey Rankin sank into a chair and waited while the detectives seated themselves. 'What happened?'

'She was murdered, Lord Rankin,' said Hardcastle bluntly, appreciating that there was no way to avoid stating the bald fact.

'Murdered?' Rankin passed a hand over his forehead. 'Was it one of the men she was seeing?'

'I don't know at this stage, sir,' said Hardcastle stiffly. 'Enquiries are in hand, but I have to say that it seems likely.'

'I don't know how I'm to break this to my mother. The shock of my father being killed has completely unnerved her. What this latest tragedy will do, God only knows.' It was obvious that the new Lord Rankin was at a loss.

'Have you just returned from the Front, Lord Rankin?' asked Marriott.

'Not recently, no. I came back from Wipers about a month ago. I'm at the Royal Military College at Sandhurst, training young officers. It's just as well that I'm at home in the circumstances.'

'It might help us if you knew of any men that Lady Sarah was seeing, Lord Rankin,' continued Marriott. That Geoffrey Rankin had been back in the country for only a month made it unlikely, but it was a question that had to be asked.

'I'm afraid not. I'm sorry, you are?'

'Detective Sergeant Marriott, sir. It's just that we are anxious to trace anyone who might have known your sister.'

'Someone she might've slept with, I suppose you mean,' said Rankin in a tone of voice that revealed his disgust at his sister's behaviour. 'No, Sergeant, I can't help you, much as I would like to.'

Hardcastle stood up. 'Thank you, Lord Rankin. I'm sorry to have been the bearer of bad news, but I was duty bound to inform you.'

'Of course. Thank you, Inspector.' Young Rankin crossed the library floor and tugged at a bell pull. 'I'll have Bristow show you out. Has Sarah's body been released for burial yet?'

'Not yet, sir,' said Hardcastle. 'That'll be a matter for the coroner, of course. But I'll let you know as soon as possible.'

'Yes, I quite understand.' Geoffrey Rankin turned as the butler appeared in the doorway. 'Perhaps you'd show these officers out, Bristow.'

'Very good, My Lord,' murmured Bristow. He had quickly adapted to Geoffrey Rankin's new status.

The two CID officers followed Bristow into the hall. 'A sad day for the family, sir,' he said as he handed them their hats and coats.

Back at Cannon Row police station, Marriott followed Hardcastle into his office.

'What's next, sir?' he asked.

'We'll have Sir Royston Naylor in, and give him a talking-to, Marriott, that's what's next,' said Hardcastle. 'In the meantime, we'll adjourn to the Red Lion where you'll have the privilege of buying me a pint.'

'Very good, sir.' Marriott grinned, secure in the knowledge that neither he nor Hardcastle ever paid for their beer in the pub outside Scotland Yard.

'D'you intend to *arrest* Sir Royston Naylor, sir?' asked Marriott, when he and Hardcastle were back in the DDI's office.

'Not yet,' said Hardcastle. 'According to Dr Spilsbury, Lady Sarah was topped between ten and twenty hours before we found her. That means that she was murdered on Thursday sometime between two o'clock and midnight. Personally, I'd hazard a guess at sometime later on Thursday evening. I think we'll have a run down to Wendover and have a word with the butler. What was his name?'

'Edward Drake, sir, and his wife Gladys is the cook-general.'

'Ah yes, of course it is.' Hardcastle was playing his usual game of pretending to forget names. 'If we have a word with him before Sir Royston Naylor has time to rig up an alibi, we might catch him on the hop.'

'D'you really think Naylor's our man, sir?'

'I'm convinced of it, Marriott. Convinced of it.'

'When d'you propose going, sir?' Marriott was afraid that Hardcastle intended to go this afternoon, or even worse, tomorrow morning. The DDI had never been averse to working right through a weekend.

'We could go this afternoon, I suppose,' said Hardcastle impishly, 'or maybe tomorrow. Sunday would be a nice day for a run out to Buckinghamshire.'

'Yes, sir,' said Marriott flatly.

Hardcastle laughed. 'It's all right, Marriott, don't get yourself in a lather, we'll go Monday morning. That'll give Naylor time to lull himself into a false sense of security. Go home and see your children. And give my best to Mrs Marriott.'

'Thank you, sir,' said a relieved Marriott. As a CID officer he saw all too little of his wife and children. 'And my regards to Mrs H.'

Only Alice Hardcastle was at home that Saturday evening. Kitty and Maud were both on duty, and Wally had gone to the Bioscope picture house in Vauxhall Bridge Road with a workmate of his to see *The Vagabond*, Charlie Chaplin's latest comedy.

After dinner, Hardcastle spent the evening reading a book before he and Alice turned in for an early night.

On Sunday morning, following his usual practice, Hardcastle walked down to the newsagent on the corner of Kennington Road to buy a copy of the *News of the World*, and an ounce of St Bruno tobacco.

'Keeping you busy, Mr Hardcastle, are they?' Horace Boxall had owned the newsagent and tobacconist shop for as long as Hardcastle could remember.

'Busy enough, Horace. I'll have a box of Swan Vestas too.'

Boxall put the newspaper, tobacco and matches on the counter, took Hardcastle's shilling and handed him the change.

'I see some big noise in Austria was assassinated yesterday, Mr Hardcastle.'

'Really,' said Hardcastle, feigning some interest in the matter. 'It's on page three, I think.'

Hardcastle opened the *News of the World*, and found the item to which Boxall had referred. The prime minister of Austria, Count Karl von Stürgkh had been shot dead in a Vienna restaurant by a journalist, Friedrich Adler.

'Never heard of him, but I don't suppose he'll be much of a loss,' commented Hardcastle, and pocketed his tobacco and matches. 'One more Hun we won't have to worry about.'

From Boxall's, Hardcastle made his way to the nearby licensed grocer's shop run by the know-all Mr Squires.

'Good morning, sir,' said Squires. 'I see the war's not going too well. The battle of the Somme's still dragging on, and we seem to be getting nowhere.'

'Bit of an expert on warfare, are you, Squires?' said Hardcastle. He was always irritated by the grocer whose opinions of the way in which the war should be conducted were expressed with total disregard to the facts.

'I reckon they should get rid of that General Haig. I don't think he knows what he's doing.'

'Perhaps you should volunteer for the army, Squires, and get out there to give him the benefit of your advice.'

'Nothing I'd like more, Mr Hardcastle,' said Squires earnestly, 'but I'm a martyr to the arthritis. Not fit, you see.'

'Well, I hope it don't stop you from reaching for a bottle of that Johnnie Walker's Red Label.'

Squires placed the bottle of whisky on the counter. 'I'll just put it in a bag for you, Mr Hardcastle. I'm not supposed to sell spirits on a Sunday, but seeing you're a policeman, I suppose it'll be all right. That'll be four and sevenpence, sir.'

'That's gone up,' complained Hardcastle as he handed over two half crowns.

'It's the war, sir,' said Squires mournfully, and gave Hardcastle fivepence change. 'You mark my words, it'll be six shillings before this war's out.'

'Six bob for a bottle of Scotch, Squires?' scoffed Hardcastle. 'That'll be the day.' He was still laughing as he left the shop.

It was with his usual feeling of relief that Monday morning came, and Hardcastle set off for the police station.

'Ready for a trip to Wendover, then, Marriott?' asked

Hardcastle, rubbing his hands together in anticipation of finally bringing Sir Royston Naylor to book. But there was a surprise in store for the detectives.

The young woman who answered the door of Kingsley Hall was attired in riding breeches, knee boots and a grey woollen jumper-blouse, and her long blonde hair was dressed into a single plait. For some moments she studied the two bowler-hatted men without comment.

'Good morning, madam,' said Hardcastle. 'I'm—'

'My lady,' corrected the woman haughtily. 'I'm addressed as my lady. And I'm not looking for a butler or a footman, thank you very much. We got rid of Drake and his wife and we've found replacements who'll be starting next week. Anyway, how did you know there was a vacancy?'

'I'm Divisional Detective Inspector Hardcastle of the Metropolitan Police, and this here's Detective Sergeant Marriott. I presume you're Lady Naylor.' She certainly appeared to be about the 25 years of age that Drake had said she was. But the butler had also described her as a nervous type who was ter-rified of Zeppelins. The woman standing in front of Hardcastle now did not seem to fit that description. In fact, she seemed very confident of herself, and was a well-built attractive woman, albeit somewhat coarse of feature.

'I am Lady Henrietta, yes, and what do the police want with me, might I ask?'

'It's not you I wanted to talk to, Lady Naylor, but with Sir Royston.' Hardcastle did not subscribe to the erroneous form of address that Naylor used to his wife.

'Well, Inspector, Sir Royston ain't here, but I suppose you'd better come in.' Lady Naylor spoke with an affected accent, and had used the word 'ain't' in much the way that she im-agined the upper classes, to which she aspired, would employ it.

The two detectives followed Kingsley Hall's chatelaine into a richly furnished drawing room, the tall windows of which gave a magnificent view of the sweeping grounds to the rear of the house.

With an imperious wave of her hand, Lady Naylor invited Hardcastle and Marriott to sit down before taking a seat on a chesterfield opposite them. She took a cigarette from a silver box, and lit it with a table lighter. Emitting a plume of smoke, she crossed her legs and leaned back.

'Well, what is it you policemen want?'

'I'm anxious to discover where Sir Royston was last Thursday, Lady Naylor.'

'Why?'

'According to information received—'

Lady Naylor threw back her head and laughed. 'That's a nice policeman's phrase,' she said. 'What's it really mean?'

'I have been told that Sir Royston might have witnessed a serious crime on Thursday, and I'd like to talk to him about it.' Hardcastle was struggling with this interview. He had not expected to meet Lady Naylor, but had hoped to speak to Edward Drake, the butler. That Drake had now apparently been dismissed, along with his wife, had put the DDI in a difficult position.

'I can tell you straight off that he couldn't have seen anything. He came down here on Thursday morning and stayed until yesterday afternoon. He had to go back to London on account of his having important war work to deal with. Sir Royston is responsible for making army uniforms for our gallant lads at the Front.'

'I see.' Hardcastle harboured doubts about the alibi that Lady Naylor had provided for her husband.

'Does Sir Royston have an apartment in London, Lady Naylor?' Marriott was playing Hardcastle's game; he knew that the Naylors had a house in Grosvenor Gardens, but was interested to see what Lady Naylor had to say.

'If he has, it's nothing to do with you.' Lady Naylor appeared affronted at being addressed by a mere sergeant. 'He always stays at his club when he's in Town. It's the Carlton, you know. It's *the* club for all the bigwigs in the Conservative Party.' The implication was that Naylor enjoyed the status of a Tory grandee.

'Why did you sack your butler?' asked Hardcastle.

'Unreliable,' said Lady Naylor.

'Oh? In what way?'

'He kept disappearing, and I can't abide unreliable staff.'

'Most unfortunate,' murmured Hardcastle. 'Did he do it often?'

'Often enough. There was the weekend of the twenty-third to the twenty-fifth of last month. He just vanished with no explanation. Sir Royston had a shooting party down here, too. It was most inconvenient, and we had to get a girl in from the village to help out.'

'And you've no idea where Drake went, Lady Naylor?'

'None,' replied the woman. 'When he turned up again on the Tuesday, I gave him his cards, and his wife. She wasn't much of a cook despite always quoting that Mrs Beeton woman.'

'I don't wonder you got shot of them, then,' said Hardcastle. It had not escaped his notice that, according to his late employer, Edward Drake had been absent from Kingsley Hall over the very period that Annie Kelly had been murdered. And yet, Drake had vouched for Sir Royston Naylor's presence that weekend, and had described the shooting party. It was beginning to look very much as though Drake was implicated in the murder of the Kelly girl, but why?

'Now, if you've finished talking about my former butler, and you've nothing more to talk about, I'm about to go riding.' Lady Naylor stubbed out her half-smoked cigarette and stood up.

Hardcastle maintained an air of sullen taciturnity for the entire journey back to London. Marriott had guessed that this might happen, and had had the foresight to buy a copy of the *Daily Mirror* at Wendover station to read on the train.

The DDI still persisted with his moody silence in the cab back to the police station, refraining for once from offering Marriott his usual advice about the confusion in cab drivers' minds between Cannon Row in Westminster and Cannon Street in the City of London.

Acknowledging with a grunt the station officer's report that all was correct, Hardcastle mounted the stairs to his office.

'Come in, Marriott.' The DDI sat down and reached for his pipe.

'Not a very successful trip, sir,' ventured Marriott, somewhat apprehensively.

'That bloody woman knows something, Marriott. She knew why we were asking about Naylor, but she trumped us. What the hell made him go down to Wendover on a Thursday morning, eh?'

'I don't think he did, sir,' said Marriott.

'Of course he didn't,' muttered Hardcastle. 'Why would he do that? She's giving him an alibi, that's what that's all about.'

'We could let Wood have a word with Naylor's chauffeur, sir,' suggested Marriott.

'No, he'd only tell his guv'nor, and I don't want Naylor alerted. Mind you, Her Ladyship's probably done that already.'

'What about this story of Lady Naylor's that Drake disappeared at the very time that Annie Kelly was topped, sir?'

'Flimflam, Marriott. On the other hand,' continued Hardcastle thoughtfully, 'it's just possible that Drake did the deed. If Sir Royston paid him enough to make his troubles go away. If it was Naylor who put Annie Kelly in the family way, that is.'

'And if Lady Naylor's right about Drake being adrift during the weekend that Annie was topped, we don't know where he was when Lady Sarah Millard was done in.'

'No, we don't, Marriott, but I'm not having it. That bastard Naylor's in this business up to his neck.' The DDI spent a few moments filling his pipe and lighting it. 'Fetch Wood and Carter in here; that Carter seems to have his head screwed on the right way.'

'You wanted us, sir?' enquired DS Herbert Wood, as he and DC Gordon Carter appeared in the DDI's office.

'Yes, Wood. Hilda, Lady Naylor, what calls herself Lady Henrietta, is married to Sir Royston Naylor who you arrested in what you might call interesting circumstances.' Hardcastle afforded Wood a wry smile. 'I want you and Carter to find out everything you can about her. Don't leave any stone unturned, so to speak. And be discreet about it. That Lady Naylor is one cunning woman.'

'Very good, sir,' said Wood. 'How soon d'you want to know?'

'Yesterday,' exclaimed Hardcastle, and waved a hand of dismissal.

On Tuesday morning, Hardcastle made another surprise announcement. 'I think we'll go down to Woolwich and have a word with Major Millard, Marriott.'

'D'you think he might've had something to do with the death of his wife, sir?' Once again, Marriott was taken aback at this latest twist in the DDI's thinking. 'I mean, he was at the Front when Annie Kelly was topped.'

'I'm not suggesting he had anything to do with Annie Kelly, Marriott. Only that he might've done for his missus.'

'But what possible motive could he have had?'

'She got him demoted, Marriott, indirectly of course, and

a juicy divorce would do his career even more harm than it's been done already.'

'I suppose we'd better go down to Woolwich and find out, then, sir,' said Marriott, resigned to what he thought would be another wasted excursion. He did not think that there was anything to be gained by interviewing Millard, but as the DDI would be the first to point out, it would be a neglect of duty not to do so.

It was almost noon when Hardcastle and Marriott arrived at the guardroom of the Royal Artillery Barracks in Repository Road, Woolwich.

A bombardier stood up as the two bowler-hatted detectives entered. 'Can I help you, sir?' he asked, adding the 'sir' because he was unsure who the newcomers were, and it was better to be safe than incur the wrath of two commissioned officers.

'I'm Divisional Detective Inspector Hardcastle of the Whitehall Division, Bombardier.' Hardcastle had learned from Marriott that a Gunner NCO with a two-bar chevron was not addressed as 'corporal'.

'Who was you wishing to see, Inspector?'

'Major Millard,' said Hardcastle.

'I'll try the officers' mess first, on account of he's likely in for lunch. One moment.' The bombardier made a telephone call, and after a brief conversation replaced the receiver. 'He's there, Inspector.' He crossed to an open door that led to the cell passage. 'Knocker, come out here.'

A soldier appeared. 'Yes, Bomb?'

'Take these two policemen across to the officers' mess, Knocker. They want to have a word with Major Millard.' The bombardier turned to Hardcastle. 'Gunner White will escort you, Inspector.'

After following Gunner White through the complex design of the barracks, the two detectives eventually arrived at the mess.

'May I help you, gentlemen?' asked a young subaltern, seeing two strangers in the entrance hall.

'I'd like a word with Major Millard,' said Hardcastle. 'I was told at the guardroom that I'd find him here.'

'He's in the anteroom. I'll show you the way.'

'Do all right for themselves here, don't they, Marriott?' whispered Hardcastle, gazing around in awe at the sumptuous furnishings, and at some of the mess silver that was displayed in cabinets, as he and Marriott followed the young officer into the anteroom.

'Two visitors for you, Hugo,' said the subaltern.

Millard put down a copy of *The Times* and stood up. 'Ah, I do believe it's Inspector Hardcastle,' he said, 'and what brings you all the way to Woolwich?'

'You do, Major.'

'I thought so. You want to talk about the death of my wife, I suppose.'

'Among other things, Major.'

'Take a seat. May I get you a drink?'

'No thank you,' said Hardcastle. 'Where were you on Thursday the nineteenth and Friday the twentieth of this month, Major Millard?'

'My word, you cut to the chase very quickly, Inspector. Are you thinking that I had something to do with her murder?'

'Perhaps you'd just answer the question, Major.'

'Easily,' said Hugo Millard. 'I was duty field officer all last week. Confined to barracks, as you might say.'

'Is there anyone who can confirm that, sir?' asked Marriott.

'Indeed there is.' Millard crossed to a nearby table, and spoke briefly to a lieutenant-colonel who was sipping a whisky and reading a copy of *The Field*. Moments later the two officers joined Hardcastle and Marriott.

'This is Colonel Orton, my commanding officer, Inspector,' said Millard as the two CID officers stood up. He turned to Orton. 'Perhaps you'd be so good as to tell Inspector Hardcastle what I was doing last week, Colonel.'

'Hugo was field officer of the week, Inspector. He was in barracks for the entire seven days.' Orton wore a puzzled look. 'Might I enquire why you want to know?'

But it was Millard who replied. 'I think the inspector is labouring under the misapprehension that I'd murdered my wife, Colonel.'

'Oh I see.' Orton laughed and returned to his table. He clearly thought that Millard was joking.

'Now we've got that out of the way, Inspector, are you any nearer finding who murdered Sarah?'

'I have one or two irons in the fire, Major Millard,' said Hardcastle stiffly. He had no intention of telling the artillery officer that suspicion had now turned to Drake, mainly because he was far from convinced that the Naylors' former butler was involved.

'I'm pleased to hear it, Inspector. I have to tell you, though, that marrying Sarah Rankin was all a terrible mistake: a heady romance arising out of summer balls and punting on the river, and a marriage entered into in haste at the outbreak of war.' Millard shook his head at the pointlessness of it all. 'And now it's over. All it really achieved was losing me a Bath star.' He pointed casually at the cuff of his tunic, now bearing but a solitary crown.

FOURTEEN

That afternoon, Detective Inspector Charles Stockley Collins called on Hardcastle.

'I found a few fingerprints in the Millard girl's apartment, Ernie, but nothing that compares with anything in our records.'

'Didn't expect that you would, Charlie,' said Hardcastle.

'One set I found belonged to the caretaker, but that's to be expected. And another set were Lady Sarah's. There were a few prints on the locker beside the bed where the body was found. I don't know whose they were, but it looked as though someone had placed his hand flat on the locker to steady himself.'

'Could be the murderer, I suppose,' said Hardcastle gloomily, 'but I shan't know until I've nicked him. But I still favour them being Sir Royston's.'

It was a frenetic forty-eight hours for Wood and Carter, during which time they slept very little.

Their priority was to find the public house closest to Naylor's Edmonton clothing factory, and that evening they found one called The Angel, appropriately in Angel Road. As Wood had anticipated there were several girls there who worked for Sir Royston. Fortunately, they proved to be very forward young women.

'Not often we see two well set-up gents like you in here,' said one young girl, brazenly starting a conversation.

'Thought we'd come in for a drink seeing as how there were so many pretty girls in here,' said Wood.

'Well, you've come to the right place, love. My name's Maisie by the way. What's yours?'

'Bert,' said Wood, 'and this is my mate Gordon,' he added, indicating Carter.

'And what do you two do to earn a crust, love?'

'Civil service,' said Wood tersely, not wishing to disclose that he and Carter were police officers. 'Just finished work, have you?'

'Yeah, thank Gawd.'

'What d'you do for a living, then, Maisie?'

'Make uniforms for the army, don't we, and me fingers is raw from pushing the stuff into the machines. I dunno how soldiers manage to wear it. Likely take all the skin off of 'em, I wouldn't wonder, poor buggers.'

'Still, the pay's all right, I suppose,' said Wood. 'Being war work.'

'All right?' scoffed Maisie. 'No it bloody ain't, not working for that skinflint Naylor. And you have to watch yerself, an' all. Very free with his hands is Naylor.'

'Is he the boss, then, this Naylor?'

'Yes, Sir Royston bloody Naylor. And he fancies hisself, an' all.'

'D'you mean he likes the ladies?' queried Carter, joining in the conversation.

'Not arf. If you feels a hand on yer arse, it's sure to be the guv'nor's. 'Ere, Ethel, come over 'ere,' she said to a nearby comely wench who was holding a glass of port and lemon.

The girl called Ethel joined them, and cast a lingering glance at the two detectives. 'Found yourself a man, then, Maze? 'Bout time an' all. You want to watch her, mister,' she said to Wood. 'On the lookout for a beau is our Maze. Any man'll do,' she added with a coarse cackle.

'Never mind all that daft talk, Ethel. Tell 'em about Naylor's hands.'

'I've had 'em all over me,' said the girl in matter-of-fact tones. 'One minute you're working away at the machine and the next thing you know is him having a feel of yer tits. Him a married man an' all.'

'I'll bet his wife doesn't know about that,' said Gordon Carter.

'Know about it!' exclaimed Ethel. 'How d'you think she landed him? Hilda Mullen was one of us, but she never objected to him having a feel. In fact, if anything, she played up to him. Next thing we know she's transferred up the office, and in no time at all she's on her way to a church wedding. By way of his bedroom, I wouldn't wonder.'

The following day, Wood renewed his acquaintanceship with Naylor's chauffeur, and garnered a little more information.

'Still shuffling backwards and forwards to the Carlton Club, mate?' he asked, crossing the road from the tram stop.

'Gets bloody boring, guv'nor, I can tell you,' said the chauffeur, confiding that his name was Sam.

'I see there was a bit in the paper about him the other day. Got mixed up with some army officer's wife.'

Sam laughed. 'That's the guv'nor all right. Always has an eye for the girls, does Sir Royston.'

'So it seems,' said Wood. 'No wonder he keeps his wife tucked away in the country.'

'If you knew her, you wouldn't blame him,' said Sam. 'A right cow, that one. She used to work in his factory, you know. Came from Brighton, so I hear.'

That piece of information caused the two detectives to take a trip to the coast where they were able to add a little more to their rapidly increasing knowledge of Lady Naylor.

What they learned at the Sussex seaside resort meant that most of Wednesday was spent at the General Register Office at Somerset House in the Strand where births, marriages and deaths were recorded. The DDI had implied, somewhat forcefully, that the enquiries about Lady Naylor were to be made as quickly as possible, but it was not until half past five on the Wednesday that DS Wood reported back. But the delay was grudgingly acceptable to Hardcastle; he knew that Wood was a good enquiry officer. Not that he would ever tell him.

'Well, Wood, what've you found out?'

'I've prepared a report, sir,' said Wood, offering a sheaf of paper.

'I should hope you have, Wood, but sit down and give me the bare bones.'

'Lady Naylor was born Hilda Mullen in Brighton on the twenty-sixth of January 1891, sir. She went to a school in the area, and did a lot of sea swimming. According to one or two of the local people we spoke to, she was very keen on it, and very good at it.'

'Yes, she looked a fit young woman,' commented Hardcastle. 'She was just off horse riding when Sergeant Marriott and me saw her on Monday.'

'When she was thirteen, she got a job as a scullery maid at a big house in Preston Park, travelling there every day on a bicycle from where she lived in the centre of Brighton,' continued Wood, after referring to his notes. 'But she got the sack for thieving.' Anticipating the DDI's next question, Wood added, 'But she wasn't prosecuted, sir, so there's nothing in records. When she was fifteen, that was in 1906, she went to London, to Edmonton, and got a job in the clothing factory there.'

'So, that's where she met Naylor, I suppose,' said Hardcastle.

'Yes, sir, but not until five years later when he bought the factory.' Wood went on to tell the DDI what he and Carter had learned from Maisie and Ethel, the two factory girls they had met in the Angel Arms at Edmonton. 'Sir Royston was a widower; his first wife died in 1912, apparently from consumption.'

'A carney little trollop, this Hilda Mullen, then, Wood.'

'So it would seem, sir. I've found out a bit more about Sir Royston, too. He bought the factory in 1911 when it was going downhill. But the war saved the business from going under when he got a contract from the War Office in 1914 for the manufacture of army uniforms. Not only did he make a lot of money, some of which went into the right pockets, if you take my drift, sir, but he got his knighthood last year.'

'You mean he greased a few palms as a way to getting a title.'

'That seems to be the general view from various people I've spoken to, sir, yes.'

'And I've no doubt that Lady Naylor will do anything she can to hold on to Royston Naylor no matter what he gets up to. She certainly seemed to enjoy being lady of the manor. What's more, I'm bloody sure she's giving her husband an alibi, and from what you say, he likes to have a tumble with any woman who's willing. I suppose she puts up with it, so she can carry on being called Her Ladyship.'

'That's the impression I got from the girls who worked with Lady Naylor, sir, when she was Hilda Mullen.'

'And now she calls herself Lady Henrietta, be damned,' scoffed Hardcastle. 'The cheek of the woman. Anyway, well done, Wood,' he said, once again breaking his rule of complimenting a junior officer.

'Thank you, sir,' said Wood, somewhat taken aback by this rare word of praise.

'I've had an idea, Marriott,' said Hardcastle, the moment he arrived at the police station on Thursday morning.

'You have, sir?' Marriott was always wary of the DDI's announcements that he had 'had an idea'.

'I want Edward Drake found. If Lady Naylor's to be believed, though I'm not sure I do believe her, he might have had something to do with our two murders. If he'd topped them as a favour to Sir Royston, he might've been paid enough to vanish once the deed was done, so to speak. On the other hand, and assuming for a moment he's innocent, I'm sure he could tell us a thing or two now he's free of the shackles of Kingsley Hall.'

'I'll have a word with the local village bobby, sir. They usually know everything that's happening on their manor.'

'I suppose there's an outside chance that he might be able to tell you something,' said Hardcastle sceptically. He had no great opinion of other police forces, but his severest condemnation was reserved for the City of London Police, the force that dominated the square mile in the centre of the Metropolitan Police District. In the DDI's view, its existence was nothing short of impertinence, and an interference in the policing of London. 'Be a good idea if you went down there, Marriott. You're more likely to get him to open up than if you talk to him on that telephone thing.'

'The police house in Kingsley, please,' said Marriott, as he boarded the waiting taxi at Wendover railway station.

'Ah, you're that policeman from London, sir. I thought I recognized you, the minute you come through the ticket barrier,' said the cab driver. 'I took you and that other policeman to Kingsley Hall a couple of times, didn't I?'

'Yes,' said Marriott, and unwilling to offer any explanation for his return, lapsed into silence. Cab drivers were notorious for spreading gossip, and it was bad enough that news of renewed police interest in the occupants of 'the Hall', as it was known locally, would be circulating within the hour.

The police house, a double-fronted cottage, was on the fringe of the village of Kingsley. Only a blue lamp and the word POLICE on the roof of the porch, distinguished it from its neighbours.

Marriott removed his bowler hat as he stepped through the open door. Seated behind a desk was a woman in her forties. She had a pencil pushed into her hair, and there was a pile of papers in front of her.

'Good morning, sir,' said the woman, glancing up.

'Good morning, ma'am. I'm Detective Sergeant Marriott of the Whitehall Division of the Metropolitan Police. Is the constable at home?'

'Not at the moment, Mr Marriott, but he's bound to be in shortly for his dinner. I'm Mavis Cordell, his wife. I expect you could use a cup of tea seeing as how you've come all the way up from London. Whitehall, you say?' She made it sound as though Marriott had just arrived from the moon.

'That's very kind, Mrs Cordell, thank you,' said Marriott. 'A cup of tea would be most welcome.'

'I've just been filing some of my Jack's reports, and doing the weekly return for the inspector at divisional headquarters in Wendover,' said Mavis Cordell, 'but I'm about finished. Come into the parlour and make yourself comfortable while I make the tea,' she added, removing the pencil from her hair and leading the way into a comfortable sitting room.

It was well known, and indeed expected, that the wives of village policemen in the county constabularies acted as unpaid deputies. As such they frequently dealt with members of the public, often solving their domestic problems without resort to their husbands, and recording details of petty crime.

No sooner had Mrs Cordell served Marriott with tea and biscuits than Jack Cordell arrived. He was a large red-faced man with a flowing moustache who appeared old enough to be approaching the end of his service.

'Mavis tells me you're from London, Sergeant.' Cordell extended a hand and seized Marriott's in a vice-like grip before sitting down, unbuttoning his tunic and removing the bicycle clips from his trousers. 'You'll find we do things a bit different down here and no mistake.'

'I'm sure you do, Mr Cordell, and I'm hoping that your local knowledge might help me out,' said Marriott. 'I trust I can speak to you in confidence,' he added, not wishing to waste too much time.

'Of course you can, Sergeant, and the name's Jack, by the way. Anything you have to tell me stays between these four walls.' Cordell removed a pipe from the inner recesses of his tunic, and began to fill it with tobacco.

'It's more a case of what you can tell me, Jack,' said Marriott.

'Fire away, then, Sergeant, and I'll do what I can to help you.' Cordell spoke between puffs as he lit his pipe.

'My guv'nor, DDI Hardcastle of the Whitehall Division, is interested in Sir Royston Naylor and his wife. I won't go into details, but it's important that we find out what we can about them.'

'Ah, the folks up at the Hall,' said Cordell, tugging briefly at his moustache. 'I make a routine visit there from time to time, but they never seem glad to see me.' He stood up. 'If it's all the same to you, Sergeant, I'll get Mavis to come in. She knows quite a lot about the Naylors, and she can be trusted, being of the cloth as you might say.'

'By all means, Jack.' Marriott knew from previous contact with village policemen that the wife knew as much, and sometimes more, about the goings-on in the bailiwick for which her husband was responsible.

Cordell opened the door of the parlour and shouted for his wife. 'Sergeant Marriott's interested in the Naylors up at the Hall, Mavis,' he said, once his wife had joined them.

'Made a lot of money out of the war, has that Royston Naylor,' said Mavis Cordell as she sat down and arranged her skirt. 'And as for his wife, well, she's got ideas above her station, and that's a fact.'

'So I believe,' said Marriott, intrigued by the openness of the PC's wife.

'Lady Muck they calls her in the village, Mr Marriott, and her only a factory girl afore she got wed to Sir Royston, and she's half his age. She's a proper madam, and full of hoity-toity airs and graces, but in truth she's no better than she ought to be. And another thing: she always comes down to the shop on her horse. Showing off, I call it. What's more she dresses in men's riding breeches and sits her nag astride. I've never seen the like of it. Well, that's not what you expect of a lady. All the real ladies round here ride side-saddle. Them as still has horses, of course. The army has taken most of them for the war effort.'

'I understand that Sir Royston recently sacked his butler.' Marriott was amused by Mrs Cordell's assessment of what constituted a lady, but wished to get on with his enquiry with as little delay as possible.

'That wasn't Sir Royston's doing,' said Cordell, laying down his pipe and taking a sip of his tea. 'It was Her Ladyship who gave poor old Ted Drake and his wife the push. From what I hear, Lady Naylor couldn't stand having him around. Reckoned he had superior ways, whatever that meant. Funny that, considering how she carries on.'

'Have you any idea when the Drakes were dismissed, Jack?'

Cordell picked up his pipe and scratched his moustache with the stem. 'Towards the end of September, I seem to recall,' he said thoughtfully. 'As a matter of fact, Ted dropped in here to say goodbye. Blooming shame, really. He was there before the Naylors arrived, you know. I reckon he'd been in service up at the Hall for nigh-on twenty years. Started off as second footman, and finished up as butler, but that was when the old viscount was there. Now he was a real gentleman, was his lordship.'

'Have you any idea where they went after they were dismissed, Jack?' Marriott asked.

'They went up to London.' Cordell stood up and crossed to a small bureau. 'I've got the address here somewhere, Sergeant.' After a brief search he produced a piece of paper. 'Yes, here we are. Him and Gladys took rooms in some place called Ufford Street in Lambeth. I s'pose you'd know where that is, being a London copper.'

Marriott smiled. 'Not necessarily, Jack. London's a big place.'

'Aye, I s'pose so. Never been there myself, but perhaps Mavis and me will have a trip up there once I retire, and when the war's over. Any road, to get back to Ted, he reckoned he'd saved a bit to tide him over, and said that him and his missus stood a better chance of getting a position in the Smoke. Personally I'd've stayed well clear of London what with the bombs and that, but if you're out of work I suppose you've got to go where it is.'

'I'll take a note of that address,' said Marriott, taking out his pocketbook.

'I don't know what else I can tell you, really, Sergeant,' said Cordell.

'I've heard that Sir Royston hosted shooting parties from time to time, Jack.'

'Ay, that he does. In the season, of course. Last one was the end of September, just before Ted Drake got the sack.'

'Was Ted Drake there that weekend?' asked Marriott.

'Bound to have been,' said Cordell. 'They'd never have given him time off when something like that was going on. Any road, him and his missus lived-in at the Hall, and I've never known them go anywhere on their days off.' The PC seemed mystified by Marriott's question. 'Naylor fancies himself as quite the country squire, having a butler at his beck and call, but between you and me, Sergeant, he's not the gent he'd have you believe. Even so, there's talk round the village of him getting made a lord. Mind you, what with Sir Royston being a Tory, and Asquith being a Whig, I don't give much for his chances. But he certainly has some highfalutin guests down here, wining and dining them. Charlie Webster, who does a bit of beating for Naylor, reckons there's quite a few turn up at the Hall what've got handles to their names. Certainly gives Her Ladyship the chance of lording it.'

'What did you find out?' asked Hardcastle when Marriott returned to the police station at about three o'clock that afternoon.

'Quite a lot of the information came from Mrs Cordell, who seems to act as a sort of part-time constable, sir. Doing the paperwork, filing reports and dealing with callers.'

'Does she indeed?' Hardcastle scoffed. 'If I asked Mrs H to give me a hand out solving a murder, I'd get a very dusty answer, Marriott.'

'I don't think I'd get much help from my missus either, sir,' said Marriott, before going on to tell Hardcastle what he had gleaned from PC Cordell and his wife. 'He also told me that Drake and his wife have taken rooms in Ufford Street, Lambeth, while they look for work.'

'That's not far from where I live,' said Hardcastle. 'I think we'll go and see Drake at this here Lambeth drum of his, and see what he's got to tell us.'

'D'you intend to go now, sir?' asked Marriott, who was feeling somewhat tired after his excursion to Buckinghamshire.

'Nothing like striking while the iron's hot, Marriott,' said Hardcastle, donning his hat and coat, and picking up his umbrella.

Ufford Street, a turning off Blackfriars Road in Lambeth, consisted of terraced dwellings occupied for the most part by those in lower managerial positions, or who were bookkeepers or clerks.

Hardcastle knocked at the door of the house where PC Cordell had told Marriott that Drake was living.

A man in shirtsleeves and an unbuttoned waistcoat answered the door.

'Yes?' He glanced suspiciously at the two men on his doorstep. 'We don't buy goods at the door.'

'We're police officers,' said Hardcastle. 'We're looking for a Mr Edward Drake.'

'He's not here,' said the man.

'D'you mean he's gone out?' asked Marriott.

'No, he's moved.'

'How long was he here, then?'

The man scratched his head. 'About a week, then he upped and left. Him and his missus took a room here while they were looking for somewhere permanent, so he said. We put a card in the newsagent's shop on the corner saying we'd got a room to let. Now that our boy Len's in the Royal Flying Corps it was going spare.'

'Have you any idea where he went?' asked Hardcastle.

'No, sorry, he never said.'

'Did he say if he was looking for work, Mr er—?'

'Green's my name, Harry Green. No, he never mentioned what he was doing. I don't even know what his trade was. But him and Mrs Drake seemed very nice people. Perhaps he was down on his luck, but he settled the rent without a quibble. He was quite the gentleman, if you know what I mean.'

'Yes, I do, Mr Green,' said Hardcastle. 'Thank you. If he should return for any reason, perhaps you'd ask him to contact me at Cannon Row police station in Whitehall. I'm Divisional Detective Inspector Hardcastle.'

'Yes, I will.' Harry Green paused. 'He's not in any trouble, is he?'

'No, not at all,' said Hardcastle. 'I just want to follow up on something he told me the last time I spoke to him.'

'I wonder where he's gone, sir,' said Marriott, once he and Hardcastle were walking back to Blackfriars Road in search of a cab.

'He's done a bunk,' exclaimed Hardcastle. 'That'll be guilty knowledge, Marriott, you mark my words. There's more to Mr Drake than I first thought.' It was a rare admission on the DDI's part that he might have underestimated the Naylors' former butler.

'So, what do we do now, sir?'

'We find him, that's what we do,' said Hardcastle, as though the answer to Marriott's question was obvious.

But Marriott knew how difficult it would be to find a man in London. Particularly, as he and Hardcastle were beginning to suspect, he did not wish to be found.

'Fetch Wood and Carter in here, Marriott,' said Hardcastle when he arrived at work on Friday morning.

When the two officers appeared, Hardcastle reminded them of his conversation with Lady Naylor the previous Monday.

'She sort of hinted that Drake the butler might've had something to do with these two murders, Wood.'

'Is that likely, sir?' asked Wood.

'I have to say I've got grave doubts about it, Wood,' said Hardcastle, 'but it don't mean we don't have to find out. There's only one problem: Drake's run. Leastways, after he got the push by Lady Naylor, he gave the local police in Kingsley an address in Lambeth. But when Sergeant Marriott and me went there the bird had flown, so to speak. And that makes me suspicious. So, Wood, I want you and Carter to find him.'

'Have we any idea where he might be, sir?' asked Wood.

'No, but I suppose he's somewhere in London. Might be a good idea to try the domestic agencies for a start, them as places displaced butlers, as you might say.'

'Very good, sir.' Wood responded calmly, but he was secretly horrified at the near impossible task that the DDI had just set him.

'Perhaps I've been putting all my eggs in one basket, Marriott,' said Hardcastle once Wood and Carter had left to set about their unenviable task.

'How's that, sir?'

'It's possible that we're looking in the wrong direction, and that Sir Royston Naylor ain't the murderer.'

'Drake, then, sir,' suggested Marriott, pleased that Hardcastle now seemed partially to have abandoned his fixation with Naylor.

'Shan't know until we find him, but in the meantime I think we'll have a word with Naylor.'

'Do we know where to find him, sir?'

'Of course we do, Marriott. He arrives at Vauxhall Bridge Road at ten o'clock every morning. We'll have a chat with him in his office, and if he ain't in a talkative mood we'll invite him round to the nick for a cup of tea.'

FIFTEEN

D S Wood and DC Carter started work on finding Drake as soon as they had left the DDI's office.

'I suppose we'd better take Mr Hardcastle's advice, Gordon, and start looking for the Drakes at one of the agencies that places domestic staff.'

'But where do we start, Skip?' Carter was quite depressed at the enormity of their task.

'I know of one in Chelsea,' said Wood, 'and if they haven't got the Drakes on their books, they'll know of other agencies. Then we keep on trying until we find him.'

'But we could be walking for a month at that rate,' complained Carter.

'Look on the bright side, Gordon,' said Wood. 'It might only take a fortnight. Anyway, you get a boot allowance.'

As he had anticipated, the Chelsea agency had no butler named Edward Drake on its list, but referred Wood to another agency. After he and Carter had unsuccessfully approached a further four agencies, they eventually found that the unemployed butler's name was on the books of a bureau in Elizabeth Street, Pimlico.

'Yes,' said the grey-haired principal, taking a small card from a drawer, 'we do have a Mr and Mrs Drake on our register. Seeking vacancies together as butler and cook.'

'Do you have an address for them, ma'am?' asked Wood.

'Our clients' details are confidential,' said the woman, returning the card to the drawer, and firmly shutting it.

'This is a murder enquiry, ma'am,' said Wood. 'Mr Drake is possibly a vital witness, and we need to interview him without delay.'

'Oh!' The woman dithered momentarily. 'In that case, I suppose I could let you have the details, but in the strictest confidence you understand.' She took out the card again.

'Of course,' murmured Wood, who had no intention of treating the Drakes' address with any degree of confidentiality.

'Mr and Mrs Drake are currently employed as shop assistants at the Army and Navy Stores in Victoria Street. I am informed that they are living in the company's hostel accommodation behind the store in Howick Place.'

'Thank you,' said Wood.

Wood and Carter made their way immediately to the Army and Navy Stores where they eventually located the company's security officer, a retired policeman named Parry.

'They're at work at the moment, Skipper,' said the security officer, a former Uniform Branch inspector whose last station had been at Walham Green in Fulham. 'How seriously are they wanted?'

Wood gave Parry brief details of police interest in the Drakes. 'To be honest with you, Mr Parry, I don't think they're strong suspects,' he said finally, hoping that he was right.

'Supposing I were to ask them to call at the nick to see your Mr Hardcastle when they've finished work? That'll be at six o'clock this evening.'

Wood considered Parry's suggestion for a moment or two. If the Drakes were alerted to police interest and absconded, he would be in serious trouble with the DDI. On the other hand to detain them while they were on the shop floor might create a greater problem than it solved. He took a chance.

'I think that would be the best idea, Mr Parry,' said Wood, secretly crossing his fingers.

*   *   *

'I hope for your sake Edward Drake turns up,' said Hardcastle, when Wood reported the arrangements he had made with the Army and Navy Stores security officer.

Wood hoped so too. 'I don't think there's any doubt, sir,' he said hopefully. 'They were easy enough to find. It's not as if they were covering their tracks.'

Much to Wood's relief, a constable appeared in Hardcastle's office at half past six to report that Mr and Mrs Drake had arrived at the police station, and were in the interview room.

'I understand that you wish to see us, Inspector.' Edward Drake stood up as Hardcastle and Marriott entered the room.

'Indeed, Mr Drake.' Hardcastle nodded in Gladys Drake's direction. 'Mrs Drake,' he murmured.

'How can we help you, then, Inspector?' asked Drake, resuming his seat.

'I'm told you were dismissed from the Naylors' employment, Mr Drake,' Hardcastle began.

'On Tuesday the twenty-sixth of September, Mr Hardcastle,' said Drake. 'It's not a date I'm likely to forget,' he added bitterly.

'Were you given any reason for your dismissal?'

'None. Her Ladyship appeared in the servants' hall and told us she had no further need of our services, just like that. Any proper lady would have sent for me and given me my notice in the drawing room. I've never seen the like of it in all my forty-four years in service, but to come below stairs and give me the bird, just like that, well, it beggars belief.'

'And you left immediately?'

'We did. Those were Her Ladyship's instructions. She didn't even offer us transport to the railway station, even though Jesse Paxton, the handyman, could have taken us in the shooting brake. I had to fork out for a taxi for Gladys and me. Downright disgraceful, I call it. However, those of us in service have a loose sort of society. Well, it's not a society as such, but butlers know each other, and the word's gone out, if you know what I mean. I very much doubt that Lady Naylor will succeed in getting a replacement for me and Gladys. At least, nobody of quality.'

It was evident to Hardcastle that Drake bore a grudge against the Naylors, and from what he had been saying it was justified.

'After your dismissal, Mr Drake, I went to Kingsley Hall and spoke to Lady Naylor. She told me that she had sacked you because you were absent from duty from the twenty-third to the twenty-fifth of September. That was the weekend of Sir Royston's shooting party. She further said that it was when you returned on Tuesday the twenty-sixth, she dismissed you for that unauthorized absence.'

'That's preposterous, Mr Hardcastle,' spluttered Drake.

'It's nonsense,' agreed Gladys Drake. 'We were there the whole weekend working our fingers to the bone. Ted was on the go from morning till night. And, I'll tell you this much, Inspector, some of them stuck-up so-called gentry Sir Royston had down there didn't know how to behave themselves, no more did their wives. From what I heard there were some strange goings-on during that Saturday night. People flitting from one bedroom to another, if you take my meaning.'

'But Sir Royston was there the whole time, was he, Mr Drake?' asked Marriott.

'Yes, he was,' said Drake, 'but I told you that when you came down to the Hall.'

Mrs Drake laughed. 'And he was running about after his influential friends like a sheepdog, Mr Marriott.'

'What about Lady Naylor, Mrs Drake?'

'She was there too, but she was took ill on the Sunday with the gripe in her belly, so we heard on the Monday morning. Never put in an appearance all day. What's more she sent for me on the Monday afternoon and had the cheek to blame it on something I'd cooked. That damned woman – pardon my French – wouldn't know a decent meal if it was put in front of her. I dare say she'd complain about the cooking even if she went to Buckingham Palace.'

'When I came to see you both at Kingsley Hall, Mr Drake,' said Hardcastle, 'you told me that Lady Naylor was one of the best. An absolute peach and a lady in her own right, I think you said.'

Drake afforded the DDI a bleak smile. 'It's called loyalty to one's employers, Mr Hardcastle,' he said, 'but between you, me and the gatepost, Lady Naylor was an absolute bitch. She had no idea how to behave, and she led poor Sir Royston a dog's life. I think he rued the day he ever married her.'

'One other thing, Mr Drake. When I spoke to you before, you told me that Sir Royston arrived at the Hall for that weekend on the Friday evening. That was the twenty-second of September.' Hardcastle remembered that Ruby Hoskins claimed to have seen Naylor at nine o'clock that evening in Victoria, talking to Annie Kelly.

'He arrived on the Saturday morning, Inspector,' said Drake. 'I'm sorry I misled you, but those were Her Ladyship's instructions, that I should say he came down on the Friday.'

Hardcastle decided it was time to be more open with the Drakes. 'Does the name Lady Sarah Millard mean anything to you, Mr Drake?'

'I think I read something in the paper about her and Sir Royston. Didn't Lady Sarah's husband chase him out of their house and threaten to shoot him?' Drake chuckled maliciously.

'Indeed he did,' said Hardcastle with a wry smile, 'What's more, it resulted in Lady Sarah's husband being demoted to major, but Lady Sarah has since been murdered.'

'Good God! What a dreadful business,' exclaimed Drake. 'I didn't see that, but as I didn't know the lady, I might not have noticed it in the paper.'

'My task now is to find her killer, Mr Drake, but I don't suppose you'll be able to help me with that.'

'I'm afraid not, Mr Hardcastle.'

'Well, thank you for coming in, Mr Drake, and you too, Mrs Drake. I doubt that I'll want to see you again, but perhaps you'd let me know if you secure a post, so that I can find you if I need to.'

Just before ten o'clock on Monday morning, Hardcastle and Marriott were waiting outside Sir Royston Naylor's office in Vauxhall Bridge Road for his arrival.

'Good morning, Sir Royston,' said Hardcastle, as the Rolls Royce Silver Ghost drew into the kerb and Naylor alighted.

The clothing entrepreneur glanced apprehensively at the two detectives. 'What the devil d'you want this time, Inspector?' he demanded.

'A few words with you, Sir Royston.'

'Really? Well, it might interest you to know, Inspector, that I'm a very busy man working for the war effort.'

'So am I,' rejoined the DDI, 'so I'll not waste any more of my time than I have to. Now then, we can either have this little chat out here on the street, or we can go into your nice warm office.'

'What exactly d'you want with me?' demanded Naylor, showing no sign of complying with Hardcastle's suggestion. 'Haven't you badgered me enough? I'll have you know I'm seriously considering making a complaint to the Commissioner about you harassing me.'

'Isn't that fellow a reporter from the *Daily Chronicle*, Marriott?' asked Hardcastle casually. He ignored Naylor's little outburst and pointed at a man, to the DDI a complete stranger, who was leaning nonchalantly against the tram stop on the opposite pavement reading a newspaper.

'I do believe you're right, sir.' Marriott had not seen the man before either.

'You'd better come up to my office, Inspector,' said Naylor hurriedly, and led the way into the building.

'Good morning, Sir Royston.' An elderly uniformed commissionaire saluted as Naylor passed through the entrance hall.

'Morning, Darby.' Naylor mounted the stairs, and swept into his office, ignoring his secretary's greeting.

The office was carpeted and oak-panelled. Naylor settled himself behind a large desk that, Hardcastle thought, had been acquired to emphasize the man's perceived importance of his own standing.

'Well, what is it?' Naylor opened a gold case and took out a cigarette without offering one to either of the policemen.

'Lady Sarah Millard's been murdered, Sir Royston.'

'I saw that in the newspaper, but what has it to do with me?'

'Where were you on Thursday the nineteenth and Friday the twentieth of this month?'

'At Kingsley Hall, and as you've been there pestering Lady Henrietta I'd've thought you'd've known that.'

'And was Lady Naylor there too?'

'Of course she was. How else would she have known that I was there?'

'Tell me about Drake, Sir Royston.'

'What about him?'

'I understand that he was dismissed.'

'Yes, that's correct. But why are you so interested in former members of my domestic staff?'

'Lady Naylor told me that he absented himself for the weekend of your shooting party at the end of September.'

'If that's what she said, then that's the case, but it was Lady Henrietta who dismissed Drake, not me. I'm far too busy to concern myself with the butler and his wretched wife.' Naylor stared out of the window as he replied; it did not escape the DDI's notice.

'Have you any idea where he went when he left your service, sir?' Marriott knew the answer, of course, but was curious to learn if Naylor knew, or would confess to knowing.

'No, none at all, but why all these questions?'

'Because the weekend that Lady Naylor said Drake was absent was the weekend during which Annie Kelly was murdered.'

Naylor laughed. 'Are you suggesting that my butler had something to do with that, Inspector? Really, I think you're wasting my time, and as I said earlier, I do have a business to run.'

'Surely you must have noticed whether or not your butler was at Kingsley Hall that weekend, Sir Royston,' said Marriott.

'He might've been, there again, he might not,' said Naylor airily. 'I think I made the point that matters of staff don't concern me. Apart from anything else, I was far too busy taking care of my guests. There were some very influential people at the Hall that weekend. A peer of the realm among them.'

It was, Hardcastle deduced, an implied threat, but it would take more than that to dissuade him from his duty. He stood up. 'Thank you, Sir Royston, that'll be all for now. I have further enquiries to make, and then I shall need to see you again.'

It was an empty promise; the DDI had no idea in which direction he should turn next in terms of his investigation. But, judging from the expression on Naylor's face, the clothing manufacturer did not know that, and Hardcastle's statement had clearly worried him.

'All very interesting, Marriott,' said Hardcastle, when the two detectives were back at Cannon Row police station.

'D'you think Naylor's lying, sir?'

'I always think Naylor's lying, Marriott; it's in the nature of the beast. What's more I think that his jumped-up cow of a wife is a lying bitch, too. I've little doubt that Drake and his wife were being truthful, but I'm wondering what the real reason was for them being sacked.'

'It could be that Sir Royston found out that we had spoken to Drake the first time we went to Kingsley Hall, sir, and was afraid of what he might've said. Or might say in the future. And I'll bet he's hoping that we haven't traced the Drakes.'

'But it was Naylor who suggested we should check his alibi,' said Hardcastle.

'Yes, sir, but I'd put money on him not guessing that we'd speak to the butler. He probably thought that we'd talk to Her Ladyship.'

'In that case he don't know much about detective work, Marriott,' muttered Hardcastle, 'but he's about to find out.'

'Is he still your favourite for these two toppings, then, sir?' Marriott thought that Hardcastle had unreasonably fixated on Sir Royston Naylor as the only suspect.

'No doubt about it,' exclaimed Hardcastle firmly. 'It's just a case of proving it,' he added, as though that were a minor problem. 'Tell Wood to see me when he's got a moment.'

'Very good, sir,' said Marriott, and crossed to the detectives' office.

'Sir?' DS Wood appeared promptly. When the DDI sent for someone when he had 'got a moment', it meant that he was to attend immediately.

'You've had dealings with Sir Royston's chauffeur, ain't you, Wood?'

'Yes, sir.'

'He must know where Naylor lives in London. He surely don't take him down to Kingsley every night. Well, I know he don't.'

'No, he doesn't, sir. Naylor's got a house in Grosvenor Gardens.'

'So he has, so he has,' said Hardcastle. 'I remember you telling me.' But he had known all along. 'I've got a job for you.'

'Yes, sir?'

'See if you can find out how often Lady Naylor comes up to Town. I know that Drake the butler told me that she never does on account of being scared of the Zeppelins, but having seen her I don't buy it. Anyway, Drake told me his true opinion of her once she'd given him the boot. Hilda Naylor's a devious woman, and I want to know what she gets up to.'

'Right, sir.' Having been given another near impossible task, Wood went on his way wondering how he was to go about

it. But it did not take him long to fathom a way. Detective
Sergeant Wood was a resourceful officer

Herbert Wood descended the area steps of the Naylors' house
in Grosvenor Gardens, and knocked at the door.

A young girl answered, and gazed suspiciously at the man
standing on the step.

'Yes?'

'I'm a police officer, miss,' said Wood, and produced his
warrant card.

'Oh,' said the girl, 'is there some trouble, then?'

'I hope not,' said Wood, 'but I'm calling on all the houses
in this area to warn them about a suspicious character who's
been seen hereabouts.'

'What's he look like?' The girl paused. 'You'd better come
in,' she said. 'It's fair perishing out here.' As if to emphasize the
chill weather, she folded her arms and shivered. 'You could probably do with a cup of tea, too. Cook's just put the kettle on.'

'Thanks, a cup of Rosie wouldn't go amiss,' said Wood.
'I've been on the go since first thing this morning,' he said,
lying glibly.

'This gent's a policeman, Mrs Hampton,' said the girl, as
she ushered Wood into the large, warm kitchen.

'And I suppose he'll be wanting a cup of tea,' said Mrs
Hampton with a smile. 'Well, don't stand there, Kitty girl, get
the cups out. And you'd better sit yourself down, Mr—?'

'Wood, ma'am, Detective Sergeant Wood.'

'What brings you here, then, Mr Wood?' asked the cook,
as she poured hot water into a large brown teapot.

'This man,' said Wood, and produced one of the many photo-
graphs that were similar to those kept in CID offices all over
the capital. They were largely of forgotten men who had been
convicted of some crime or another in the distant past, but
were useful when the police were carrying out what they called
a 'duff' call.

'Ooh, I don't like the look of him,' said Kitty. 'What's he
been up to?'

'He usually pretends he's from the gas company, and asks
if he can check the pipes around the house for leaks,' said
Wood, making up his story as he went along. 'And once inside
and left on his own, he steals whatever's to hand.'

'Well, he'll get short shrift in this house,' exclaimed Mrs Hampton, placing her hands on her ample hips. 'I've got a large rolling pin here. He'd get more than he bargained for, and that's a fact.' And with that statement of intent, she poured the tea.

'I suppose you're kept busy in a house of this size,' suggested Wood casually, as he accepted the offer of a slice of home-made fruitcake.

'Not really,' volunteered Mrs Hampton. 'Most times there's only Sir Royston here, and more often than not he eats at his club, the Carlton in St James's, apart from breakfast. He does like a good breakfast, does Sir Royston.'

'Widower is he, then?' enquired Wood offhandedly.

'Bless you, no, Mr Wood.' Mrs Hampton lowered her voice. 'Between the three of us, he's got a right tartar of a missus. Lady Henrietta she calls herself. When she's up here there's the very devil to pay. Nothing's right for her, and her as common as muck an' all. And when the two of 'em is here together there's always a row. I think he made a mistake when he married her.'

'Come often, does she?'

'All too often, and that's a fact. I've had more run-ins with her than I've had hot dinners. She'll do it once too often, and then I'll give in my notice. A good cook can always get a placing.'

'How does the butler get on with her?'

'Huh! He doesn't, not no more. Give in his notice a month or more back, and Her Ladyship ain't been able to get a replacement. Word gets out you know, Mr Wood.'

'So I believe,' said Wood, finishing off his cake. This was exactly what Drake had told Hardcastle.

'It was her turning up here on a Sunday of all days, last month, it was. She weren't expected, particularly as Sir R was down at Kingsley Hall. But in flounces Her Ladyship on the Sunday afternoon, bold as brass, and demanding dinner.'

'Which Sunday was that?' asked Wood, his disinterested air concealing his excitement at this revelation.

Mrs Hampton crossed to a calendar. 'The twenty-fourth of September, Mr Wood. Come as a surprise to all of us. Being Sunday we was hoping for a quiet day.' She turned to the maid. 'Ain't that so, Kitty?'

'Yes,' agreed Kitty. 'What with the master being down at Kingsley Hall for his shooting party we thought that Her Ladyship would be there an' all.'

'Well, she starts lording it about the place, as usual, and had poor Mr Pearce – he was the butler – running backwards and forwards, fetching and carrying, and generally making a nuisance of herself. And as for her language, well, that would've been more suited to the gutter. But that was it as far as Tom Pearce was concerned. He told her straight that he'd been in proper houses and he wasn't going to stand for her tantrums no more. And with that, he ups and leaves.'

'I suppose he got another place, did he?' asked Wood.

'Walked straight into a position round at Belgrave Square. Very nice gent by all accounts. A barrister so Mr Pearce said.'

'I didn't know there were any barristers living in Belgrave Square,' said Wood, who knew of several.

'Oh yes,' said Mrs Hampton. 'A Mr Cedric Kitchen, according to Mr Pearce. Tom said he's a King's Counsel.'

Wood stood up. 'Well, thank you for the tea, and the cake, Mrs Hampton, and don't forget what I said about this man who reckons he's from the gas company.'

'Don't you vex yourself about him, Mr Wood. Once I've laid him out, I'll call a constable.'

SIXTEEN

'Lady Naylor was in London on Sunday the twenty-fourth of September, sir.' It was with some degree of excitement that DS Wood presented himself in Hardcastle's office at two o'clock. He had realized the importance of Lady Naylor's unexpected return to London the moment Mrs Hampton had mentioned it to him earlier that day. 'According to the cook, Her Ladyship turned up at about three o'clock that afternoon.'

'Did she really?' Hardcastle reached for his pipe and briefly toyed with it. 'So she couldn't have known whether Drake was adrift from Kingsley Hall that weekend,' he mused aloud. 'And Mrs Drake, the butler's wife, told me that Lady Naylor had spent the whole of that day in bed on account of having eaten something that upset her.'

'But the night that Lady Naylor was in London was the night that Annie Kelly was murdered, sir,' said Wood, fearing that the DDI might have missed the point.

'The significance of the date hadn't escaped me, Wood,' said Hardcastle mildly. He walked to the door of his office. 'Marriott, come in here, quickly,' he shouted.

'Yes, sir?' Marriott was still struggling into his jacket when he appeared in the DDI's doorway.

'Wood, tell Sergeant Marriott what you've just told me.'

Wood repeated the information he had obtained from the cook at the Naylors' Grosvenor Gardens dwelling.

'Interesting, sir,' commented Marriott.

'It's more than interesting, Marriott,' said Hardcastle, and turned his attention to Wood once again. 'Did this Mrs Hampton say why Lady Naylor had come up to London? I mean, did Her Ladyship tell Mrs Hampton why she'd come?'

'No, sir. At least, she didn't say. But she did have a row with the butler, name of Thomas Pearce, and he put in his notice there and then, and walked out.'

'Did this informant of yours say where this Pearce fellow went, Wood?'

'It seems he got a post almost immediately with a Mr Cedric Kitchen, a King's Counsel, sir.'

'That rings a bell. Where does he live?'

'Belgrave Square, sir. I've got the exact address.' Wood knew that that would be Hardcastle's next question, and had made the necessary enquiries.

For a few moments, Hardcastle sat in contemplative silence. 'What was the name of that chap that Inspector Sankey took to identify the victims of the bomb at Washbourne Street, Wood?'

'Albert Jackson, sir,' replied Wood promptly. 'An ex-sergeant. Lost an arm at Festubert last year.'

'That's the fellow. Didn't you take him to cop a gander at Sir Royston?' The DDI knew perfectly well that he had.

'Yes, sir,' said Wood, 'but he claimed never to have seen Sir Royston before. What's more Sir Royston gave him a quid on account of his being a wounded soldier. "One of our heroes", I think he called him.'

'Yes, well never mind all that,' continued Hardcastle, still giving some thought to the matter of Lady Naylor's surprise visit to London. 'Get hold of Jackson and fix somehow for him to have a look at Lady Naylor. See if he's ever clapped eyes on her before.'

'But she seems to spend most of her time at Kingsley Hall, sir,' protested Wood.

'Well, I know that, Wood.' Hardcastle let out a sigh of exasperation. 'So you'll have to take him down there, won't you? Sergeant Marriott will tell you the name of the local copper, and where to find him. He'll probably be able to give you a hand out to set up an observation. From what Mrs Drake told me, Lady Naylor makes a habit of riding her horse down to the village to do some shopping.' Having decided against smoking, the DDI replaced his pipe in the ashtray. 'On second thoughts, Marriott, it might be as well if you went down there too, seeing as how you know the PC.'

'How soon d'you want this done, sir?' asked Marriott.

'As soon as Wood can find this here Albert Jackson.'

'Very good, sir. Are we allowed to charge for a meal for Mr Jackson?'

'Yes, but make sure you get a receipt, otherwise I can't allow the claim. In the meantime, Marriott, you and I will go round to Belgrave Square and see what this ex-butler of the Naylors has to say.'

It was six o'clock when Hardcastle and Marriott arrived at the Belgrave Square house occupied by Cedric Kitchen, KC.

'We're police officers,' said Hardcastle to the butler who opened the door. 'You're Thomas Pearce, I presume.'

The butler looked somewhat surprised to be addressed by name. 'Indeed, sir, but you have the advantage of me.' He opened the door wide, and the two detectives stepped into the hall.

'We'd like to have a word with you, Mr Pearce.'

'Well, sir, I—'

At that moment, however, the drawing room door opened and a man appeared. He was well built and at least six foot tall, with a shock of auburn hair and bushy sideburns.

'Who is it, Pearce?' But before the butler was able to answer, the man took off his spectacles and crossed the hall in a couple of strides. 'Good heavens, it's Hardcastle, surely?' He shook hands with the DDI and then stood back. 'We crossed swords at the Bailey about eighteen months back. A rather nasty robbery with violence if memory serves me aright.'

'Indeed, sir,' said Hardcastle. 'I thought I recognized the name when it was first mentioned to me. This is Detective Sergeant Marriott,' he added, indicating Marriott with a wave of the hand.

'Well, what can I do for you?'

'It's rather a case of what your butler can help me with, sir.'

'Is it, by Jove?' Kitchen roared with laughter. 'I don't believe you're going to tell me the butler did it, whatever it is. Think you'll be in need of a lawyer, Pearce?' he asked, glancing at his manservant. 'I know one or two, but it'll cost you a pretty penny. You know what these legal fellows are like: charge a fortune for getting you convicted.' He turned back to the DDI. 'What's it all about, Hardcastle? Pearce ain't in any sort of trouble, is he?'

'No, sir, not at all. It's to do with a double murder I'm investigating.' Hardcastle went on to explain about the murders of Annie Kelly and Lady Sarah Millard, and that Pearce's knowledge of his previous employers might be able to assist in the police investigation.

'Ah, yes, I read something about the Millard girl's death. Nasty business, especially coming on top of that court martial involving her husband. Reading between the lines, I gather she was doing some amateur whoring.'

'Yes, sir,' said Hardcastle. 'That is so.'

'I don't suppose that pleased Lord Rankin. He was her father, you know.'

'Yes, I knew that,' said Hardcastle.

Kitchen nodded. 'Yes, of course you would.'

'Lord Rankin's dead, sir. Killed at the Somme commanding a brigade, the Friday before last.'

'Was he, by God? Terrible business, this war, Hardcastle.' Kitchen shook his head. 'So where does old Pearce here fit into your jigsaw?'

'As he was formerly butler to Sir Royston and Lady Naylor, sir,' said Hardcastle, 'he might be able to help in my enquiry. Between you and me, I've got suspicions about the Naylors' involvement in this matter.'

'Oh, don't beat about the bush, Hardcastle.' Kitchen laughed again. 'You think Royston Naylor's up for these murders.'

'It's a possibility I'm considering, sir.'

'Well, I don't know why we're all standing in the hall. Come into the drawing room.' Cedric Kitchen led the way, and invited the two policemen to take a seat. 'You'd better dash away and get us some whisky, Pearce, and bring a glass for yourself. Then you can submit to Mr Hardcastle's interrogation. But be careful what you say, because he'll take it all down in writing, and he'll have you up before the beak before you know where you are.'

'Very good, sir,' said Pearce gravely, and left the room to return moments later with a silver salver bearing a decanter of whisky and glasses. 'Shall I pour, sir?'

'Yes, I'm sure these two officers won't be averse to a drop of Scotch. That is the case, ain't it, Hardcastle?'

'Most kind, sir,' murmured Hardcastle.

'Pour yourself one, Pearce.' Kitchen turned to the DDI. 'I think it'd be better if I were out of the way, Hardcastle? You never know, I might finish up appearing in this case.'

'As you wish, sir.' Hardcastle was unconcerned about Kitchen's presence, or any later involvement, but knew from previous experience that butlers often spoke more freely in the absence of their employer. Not that he had any concerns in this case; Kitchen and Pearce seemed to share a unique relationship.

'Let me know when Mr Hardcastle is leaving, Pearce, just so I can make sure he's not making off with any of the family silver.' And with that parting shot, and another guffaw of laughter, Kitchen retired to his study, clutching his tumbler of whisky.

'How can I help you, then, sir?' asked Pearce.

'Sit down, man. I understand that you left the employment of Sir Royston Naylor on Sunday the twenty-fourth of September.'

'I can see you're well informed, sir.' Pearce parted the tails of his morning coat and took a seat opposite the two CID officers.

'One of my sergeants had a talk with Mrs Hampton.'

'Is she still there?' asked Pearce. 'I'm surprised after the way Lady Naylor treated the staff. Mrs H is a very good cook, and she could get a place anywhere.'

'Yes, she's still there,' said Hardcastle, 'but she told me that you had a bit of a set-to with Lady Naylor on the day you left.'

'One of many, sir, but the last one was why I left. You can put up with so much, but there comes a time when enough's enough. She turned up quite unexpected on that day and started throwing her weight about, as usual, demanding this, that and the other. Well, you expect to have to run about after the people you work for. That's why you're there, but you don't expect to be sworn at, and quite vile language she was using, too, and in front of Mrs H. However, sir, I suppose it's only to be expected of a factory girl.'

'I understand that you left immediately, Mr Pearce,' said Marriott.

'In a manner of speaking, sir, yes. I told Her Ladyship that I'd had enough of her language, and was leaving her employment forthwith, and I went up to my quarters and began packing.'

'What was her reaction to that?'

'She said something like good riddance, larded with a few more obscenities, which was no more than I expected from her.'

'Was she still there when you left?' asked Hardcastle.

'No, sir. It took me quite some time to get my things together. I intended to return later to pack my trunk, but I needed a few things because I was going to stay for a day or two with my sister and her husband in Pimlico. Anyway, when I'd finished I went back downstairs, and Lady Naylor had gone. Mrs Hampton said she'd had dinner and left at about half past nine.'

'Any idea where she went, Mr Pearce?' asked Marriott.

'I'm afraid not, sir. Her Ladyship always played her cards close to her chest. The last thing she'd do is to tell the servants what she was up to. And that was half the trouble. In a well-ordered household your employers always tell you their plans. It's only civil, otherwise you can't prepare rooms and meals, and that sort of thing.'

'Well, thank you for that information, Mr Pearce. It's been very helpful. We'll not detain you any longer.'

'I hope I've been of some assistance, sir,' said Pearce, rising to his feet. 'I'll just let Mr Kitchen know you're leaving.'

Cedric Kitchen appeared in the hall as Hardcastle and Marriott were donning their hats and coats.

'Was Pearce able to help, Hardcastle?'

'Indeed, sir. Another piece of the jigsaw, so to speak.'

Kitchen shook hands with each of the detectives. 'Don't doubt I'll see you down at the Bailey one day soon, Hardcastle.'

For most of the taxi journey back to Cannon Row police station, Hardcastle had remained in contemplative silence. But just before he and Marriott arrived, the DDI gave voice to his thoughts.

'You're going down to Kingsley tomorrow, aren't you, Marriott?'

'Yes, sir.' Marriott knew perfectly well that Hardcastle was aware that he was.

'See if you can find out if Lady Naylor arrived at Wendover railway station on the evening of Sunday the twenty-fourth of September. It might be as well if you got that local PC . . . what's his name?'

'Cordell, sir. Jack Cordell.'

'Yes, well, get him to have a word with the local taxi drivers and see if any of them picked up Lady Naylor that evening. Your man Cordell is more likely to persuade these cabbies to speak out than if you asked them.'

At ten o'clock the following morning, Marriott, Wood and Albert Jackson set off from Waterloo railway station. At Wendover, the same cab was waiting on the rank.

'My word, guv'nor,' said the driver, 'you coppers are spending a lot of time down here.'

'As a matter of fact, we've come to make an arrest.' said Marriott.

'Really?' The cab driver turned in his seat, an expression of consuming interest on his face.

'Yes,' continued Marriott, 'we're investigating someone who's been blabbing to people in pubs about police business. That's a very serious matter, of course. Under the Defence of the Realm Act he could finish up spending a couple of years in chokey.' Marriott accompanied his empty threat with a sinister smile; Hardcastle would have been proud of him.

'Oh!' exclaimed the driver, and putting the taxi into gear drove off somewhat jerkily.

When the cab delivered the little party of Londoners at the police house, Marriott told the driver to wait.

In shirtsleeves and uniform trousers, Jack Cordell, the Kingsley village constable, was in his garden staking his dahlias when Marriott, Wood and Jackson approached. He stood up and brushed the soil from his hands and knees as he recognized the Metropolitan Police officer.

'Hello, Sergeant. What brings you back to Kingsley?'

'The Naylors,' said Marriott, and introduced DS Wood and Albert Jackson.

Cordell shook hands with the two sergeants, and was about to do the same with Jackson when he noticed that the man's right arm was missing.

Jackson laughed. 'It's all right, guv'nor,' he said. 'I'm quite used to using the other one now.'

Somewhat awkwardly Cordell shook the old soldier's left hand.

'There is one thing, Jack,' said Marriott. 'My guv'nor's keen to know if any of the local cabbies picked up Lady Naylor from Wendover railway station late on Sunday the twenty-fourth of September. I kept the taxi hanging on in case you wanted to talk to the driver.'

'Leave it to me, Sergeant,' said Cordell, and strode across to the waiting cab.

Sighting the constable, the taxi driver immediately leaped out. 'Good morning, Mr Cordell.'

'It's Jim Charlton, isn't it?' asked Cordell, ignoring the driver's outstretched hand.

'That's me, Mr Cordell.' The cabbie began to look apprehensive.

'Whose taxi was on duty on Sunday the twenty-fourth of September, Charlton?'

'That was me,' said Charlton.

'And did you pick up Lady Naylor and take her to Kingsley Hall?'

'Half a mo,' said Charlton, and reached through the window of his cab to pick up his log. After a moment or two thumbing through it, he looked up. 'Yes, as a matter of fact, I did, Mr Cordell.'

'What time was that?'

'Just before midnight. She must've caught the last train from London.'

Cordell turned to Marriott. 'Anything else you want to know, Sergeant?'

Marriott drew the constable aside, out of Charlton's hearing. 'Ask him if he picked up Her Ladyship on the evening of Thursday the nineteenth of October as well, Jack.'

Cordell turned back to Charlton, and repeated Marriott's question.

Once again, Charlton referred to his log. 'Yes, I did. She must've caught the last train again.'

'Right,' said Cordell, 'and you won't mention this to anyone, particularly anyone up at the Hall. Understood?' The PC glared at Charlton. 'Because if you do, my lad, you'll not only lose your licence for disclosing confidential police information, you might just lose your liberty too.'

'Not a word, on my life,' said the terrified cab driver.

'Thank you, Jack,' said Marriott, when Cordell relayed this latest piece of vital information. 'Just what I wanted to know.' He was having difficulty in suppressing his excitement at what he had just learned. He paid off the cab and sent a worried Charlton about his business.

'Come inside, gentlemen, and I'll get Mavis to make a cup of tea. Then, while you're having that, you can tell me what else I can do for you.'

While Mavis Cordell was dispensing tea and biscuits, Marriott explained why he and Wood had brought Albert Jackson to Kingsley.

'It should be easy enough, Jack,' Marriott continued. 'All we need to do is find Mr Jackson somewhere where he can have a sight of Lady Naylor.'

'Shouldn't be too difficult, Sergeant.' Cordell turned to his wife. 'What day is it that Her Ladyship comes down to the village shop, Mavis?'

'Every day as far as I know,' said the PC's wife. 'She does like showing herself off, does that one.' She glanced at the clock on the mantelshelf. 'You might be lucky if you take a stroll down there as soon as you've finished your tea. She usually shows up about dinner time, and word is that she sometimes goes into the Kingsley Arms for a wet.' Mavis sniffed. 'I ask you, a real lady would never go into a public house on her own, if then, but I suppose because she's married to Sir Royston she thinks the rules don't apply to her.'

Their tea hurriedly consumed, Jack Cordell stood up. 'If it suits you, we'll take a stroll down there now, Sergeant,' he said to Marriott. 'It's only a five-minute walk.'

'If it's all the same to you, Jack, I think I'd better stay here. You see, I've met Lady Naylor before, and if she spots me she might recognize me and wonder what I'm doing here. So I'll leave Sergeant Wood and Mr Jackson to go with you.'

The village of Kingsley was typical of many within a day's journey from London. Opposite the Kingsley Arms was the village green in the centre of which was a lake, home to a few ducks and a proliferation of pond life. There were a few shops on either side of the inn, among them a general store, a post office, a saddler, a chandler, and a gunsmith.

'I dare say you gentlemen could do with a wet while we're waiting.' Cordell took off his striped duty armlet and slipped it into his pocket. 'If we go in the saloon bar, we'll have a good view of the road outside.' He took off his helmet and ducked through the low doorway of the inn.

'Good day, Jack.' The landlord was a huge man in a red waistcoat with brass buttons, his loss of hair compensated by bushy black sideburns. As a preamble to serving his customers, he wiped the top of the bar with a cloth.

'Good day to you, Josh. Three pints of your best, if you please.'

After DS Wood had insisted on paying for the beer, the two policemen and Jackson found a table by the window, and settled themselves with their tankards of ale.

They did not have long to wait. Twenty minutes later, and after another round of beer, they were treated to the sight of Lady Naylor on horseback stopping outside the inn. Attired as usual in men's riding breeches, and a woollen sweater, the hatless Lady Naylor dismounted, tethered her horse to a lamp post, and entered the general store.

'That's Her Ladyship,' said Cordell.

'Well, Bert, have you seen her before?' asked Wood.

'I should say I have,' said Jackson adamantly. 'She was always calling at Washbourne Street. Afore it was bombed, like.'

'What?' Wood was unable to conceal his astonishment. 'What on earth was she doing there?'

'She reckoned as how she was the landlord's agent come to inspect the property and collect the rent.'

'Well, who's the landlord?'

'I haven't the faintest idea,' said Jackson.

'A pound to a pinch of snuff it's Sir Royston Naylor,' muttered Wood.

*   *   *

'Any luck?' asked Marriott, when the trio returned to the police house.

Wood repeated what Jackson had told him, but Marriott gave the impression of being uninterested in this piece of information. He had no wish to attach any importance to Jackson's revelation in the ex-soldier's presence.

'I've no doubt there's a reasonable explanation,' said Marriott, 'but we'll get back to London and have a word with the guv'nor, although I doubt he'll be much interested.' He turned to Cordell. 'Thanks for your help, Jack. I think we'll be getting on our way.'

'If there's anything else I can help you with, you know where I am, Sergeant,' said Cordell.

Marriott, Wood and Jackson left the police house and strolled towards the centre of the village.

'I think we'll have a pint and a sandwich at the pub, and then find ourselves a train back to the Smoke,' said Marriott.

SEVENTEEN

'Well?' barked Hardcastle, when the two sergeants presented themselves in his office.

'What you might call a profitable day, sir,' said Marriott, and went on to relate what they had gleaned from their visit to Kingsley.

'And this here cab driver Charlton was sure that he collected Lady Naylor from Wendover railway station on the nights of the two murders, is he?'

'I'd no doubt that he was telling the truth, sir,' said Marriott. 'I got the impression that Jack Cordell frightened the life out of him.'

'Quite right and proper,' commented Hardcastle. 'Sounds like a good policeman, and him only a country copper, too.'

Marriott said nothing, for fear of setting Hardcastle off on one of his critical comments about provincial police forces.

'So, who owned this Washbourne Street house, Marriott? Before Fritz knocked it down, that is,' continued Hardcastle.

'I've already sent Catto to City Hall in Charing Cross Road

to find out, sir,' said Marriott, having anticipated that that would be Hardcastle's next question.

'Well, where is he?' As ever Hardcastle was impatient to get on with the investigation. 'That sort of enquiry doesn't take all day.'

'I'll see if he's back yet, sir.' Marriott crossed the corridor to the detectives' office, returning moments later with Catto.

'Well, Catto, solved this problem for me, have you?'

'Yes, sir,' said Catto, for once confident that he had the answer that the DDI was expecting. 'The owner of one-forty-three Washbourne Street is Sir Royston Naylor of Grosvenor Gardens.'

'Hah!' Hardcastle smote the top of his desk with the flat of his hand. 'I think we're getting somewhere at last, Marriott.'

'But there's more, sir,' said Catto.

'More? I hope you haven't been overdoing it, Catto. I don't want to see your name appearing in *Police Orders* as discharged worn out.'

Catto risked a grin at Hardcastle's little joke. 'While I was at City Hall I found out that Sir Royston Naylor owns two other properties in Washbourne Street. Numbers one-forty to one-forty-two on the opposite side of the road.'

'Well done, lad,' said Hardcastle, once again breaking his rule about not commending junior officers.

'Thank you, sir.' Catto was astonished at receiving a word of praise from the DDI.

'All right, Catto, don't stand there grinning like a Cheshire cat. I'm sure you've got work to do.'

'What do we do next, sir?' asked Marriott, once the delighted Catto had departed. 'Arrest Lady Naylor?'

'No, Marriott, we arrest 'em both.' Hardcastle rubbed his hands together. 'But we've got to arrange it so that we catch the pair of 'em at the same time.' He lapsed into silence, pondering the problem. 'An observation,' he said finally.

'Where, sir? In London or at Kingsley?'

'In London, Marriott. I'm not wasting time sending Wood down there just to follow the damned woman back here when she decides to come up and collect the rent. And I don't want her nicked on a county constabulary's patch; it makes for complications.' Hardcastle turned to DS Wood. 'Find out from your mate Albert Jackson which day of the week Her Ladyship comes up to collect the rents, Wood.' He shook his head. 'I've never heard the like of it: a titled woman going about collecting rents,' he said. 'I suppose she don't trust a rent collector in case he pockets some of the takings. Frightened of the Zeppelins, be damned. The only thing she's frightened of is that someone might not pay up.'

'Jackson told Wood that Lady Naylor usually comes up to London of a Friday evening, sir,' said Marriott on Wednesday morning. 'He reckons that she likes to get there after the menfolk have been paid, but before they have time to piss their wages up the wall of a local boozer.'

'Seems there's some advantage after all for Sir Royston having got wed to a factory wench, Marriott,' said Hardcastle. 'She knows first-hand how the working classes live, being one of 'em, so to speak.'

'I'll set up an observation for Friday evening, then, sir,' said Marriott. 'But what shall we do about Sir Royston?'

'Get Wood to organize the observation, and he can have the pleasure of arresting Lady Naylor,' said Hardcastle. 'I want you with me because I'm going to collar Naylor the minute he sets foot outside his office on Friday evening. With any luck we'll have him in the nick before the arrival of Her Ladyship. Be a nice surprise for him.' He emitted a self-satisfied chuckle. 'I do believe things are coming together, Marriott.'

By a lucky coincidence both arrests occurred at about the same time.

At half past five on the Friday evening, Hardcastle and Marriott were waiting in a cab in Vauxhall Bridge Road opposite the offices of Naylor Clothing Ltd. Naylor's Rolls Royce arrived at ten minutes to six precisely, and five minutes later Darby, the commissionaire, appeared in the doorway and signalled to Sam, Sir Royston's chauffeur. The chauffeur got out and stood by the passenger door, ready to open it the moment Naylor appeared.

'As usual, he'll be out at six on the dot, Marriott,' commented Hardcastle. 'I do like a man of habit.' Leaping from the cab and instructing the driver to wait, he swiftly crossed the road followed by Marriott.

Naylor looked up in surprise to be confronted by the DDI

and Marriott. 'What the hell d'you want this time, Inspector? I thought I told you—'

'Royston Naylor, I'm arresting you on suspicion of being involved in the murders of Annie Kelly and Lady Sarah Millard,' said Hardcastle, cutting across the manufacturer's protest.

Naylor went red in the face, dropped his walking stick and waved his hands about. 'What on earth are you talking about? Have you taken leave of your senses, man?'

Hardcastle took hold of Naylor's arm as a token of his arrest and led him across the road to the waiting taxi.

Pausing briefly to suggest to Naylor's chauffeur that he was unlikely to be needed this evening, and to hand him the discarded walking stick, Marriott joined Hardcastle and Naylor in the taxi.

'Scotland Yard, cabbie.' Hardcastle turned to Naylor. 'Tell 'em Cannon Row, Sir Royston,' he said jovially, 'and half the time you finish up at Cannon Street in the City.'

'This is a damned outrage,' spluttered Naylor.

DS Wood and DC Catto loitered near 140 Washbourne Street which ran parallel with Vauxhall Bridge Road. At about the time that Naylor was arriving at Cannon Row police station, Lady Naylor alighted from a taxi, and made to enter the house.

'Hilda, Lady Naylor,' said Wood, raising his hat as he stepped into the woman's path, 'we're police officers, and I'm arresting you on suspicion of being involved in the murders of Annie Kelly and Lady Sarah Millard.'

'Have you gone raving mad?' The woman who demanded that she be called Lady Henrietta stared at Wood, apparently unfazed by his awesome statement.

'I shall now take you to Cannon Row police station, madam.'

'My lady,' said Hilda Naylor imperiously. 'I'm addressed as my lady.'

'Please yourself,' said Wood, and hailed a cab.

'Splendid!' exclaimed Hardcastle, when Wood informed him of the arrest of Lady Naylor.

'Her Ladyship's in cell number three, and Sir Royston's in the one next door to it, sir,' said Marriott.

'Ask Mrs Cartwright to see me, Wood.' Hardcastle reached for his pipe and began to fill it.

'You wanted to see me, sir?' asked the station matron as she stepped into the DDI's office a few moments later.

'There's a prisoner in number three cell, Mrs Cartwright, name of Lady Naylor.'

'Yes, sir.'

'I want her thoroughly searched. Sergeant Marriott will wait outside the cell door and take possession of anything you find.'

'Very good, sir,' said Mrs Cartwright.

Bertha Cartwright was far more formidable a woman than appeared to be the case when she was taking the DDI his tea. On those occasions she always seemed to be a mumsy sort of woman, concerned about the welfare of her soldier son and little else.

'On your feet,' she bellowed, as she strode into the cell.

'How dare you shout at me like that,' shrieked Lady Naylor, 'and, I'll have you know, I'm addressed as my lady.'

'I don't care if you're the Queen of Sheba, but all the while you're locked up here, I'll address you anyway I like, dearie. Now then, get that frock off.'

'I'll do no such thing, you fat cow.'

Mrs Cartwright stepped across the cell, and delivered a stinging blow to Lady Naylor's face. 'Do it. Now.'

There was no further argument, and within minutes Lady Naylor was standing naked and shivering in the cell while Bertha Cartwright examined her clothing.

'I shall make a very strong complaint to the highest authority about you,' said Hilda Naylor when the matron had finished, and had told the prisoner to get dressed again. 'You clearly don't know who you're dealing with.'

Without another word, Mrs Cartwright left the cell. 'Nothing, Mr Marriott,' she said. 'Has anyone been through her handbag?'

'I doubt it,' said Marriott. 'I think the station officer put it straight into the prisoners' property store.'

'Better have a look, then, love,' said the matron.

The station officer produced Lady Naylor's handbag, and Mrs Cartwright emptied it on to the desk in the front office.

'There's a bunch of keys, a diary, some sort of account book, a lace-trimmed handkerchief, a pencil in a silver holder, and some visiting cards in a silver case.' Mrs Cartwright identified each item as she moved it from one side of the table to the other. 'Oh, and there's a separate key here, Mr Marriott.'

'I think Mr Hardcastle might be interested in that, Mrs Cartwright,' said Marriott.

'This is only thing that the matron found that might be of interest, sir,' said Marriott.

Hardcastle took the key and examined it closely. 'Was that the only key, Marriott?'

'There was a bunch of keys, too, sir, but I suspect they're for the Washbourne Street properties that Sir Royston owns.'

'Get your coat and hat, Marriott.' Hardcastle stood up. 'We're going to conduct a little test.'

It was half past eight when Hardcastle and Marriott arrived at Artillery Mansions.

Hardcastle knocked loudly on the caretaker's door. 'Mr Harris,' he said, 'has anyone called at Lady Sarah Millard's apartment since I was last here?'

'No, sir, no one,' said Harris.

'Not a Major Millard by any chance?'

'No, sir, no one.'

'Did you perhaps see a woman calling here on, say, Thursday the nineteenth of last month, or even early in the morning the next day?'

'No, Inspector. Like I said when you found that poor lady's body, I never saw anyone go up there.'

'Very well,' said Hardcastle, and he and Marriott made their way up to the first floor.

'D'you think we're in luck, sir?' asked Marriott.

'Any minute now and we'll find out,' said Hardcastle, and producing the key found in Lady Naylor's handbag, he tried it in the lock. 'Aha!' he exclaimed as the door swung open. 'You're an educated chap, Marriott. What was it that Greek fellow said? Wasn't he called Archie someone?'

'Archimedes, sir, and eureka was what he said. It means I've found it.'

'Exactly, Marriott.' Hardcastle walked into the apartment

and glanced around. 'Well, no sense in hanging about here,'
he said. 'We've got what we wanted, and I reckon Lady
Naylor's going to have a bit of a job explaining why she had
that key in her possession.'

When the two detectives had returned to Cannon Row police
station, Marriott produced the necklace found in the basement
of 143 Washbourne Street.

'What about this, sir?' he asked.

'Ah, yes, the necklace. We forgot to show that to Mr and
Mrs Drake.'

'Yes, sir.' Marriott was always mildly amused that the DDI
tended to include him in any failing on his own part. 'But
Mrs Hampton, the cook at Grosvenor Gardens that Wood interviewed, might know if it's Lady Naylor's.'

'Quite right, Marriott,' said the DDI, and shouted for DS
Wood.

'Sir?' Wood appeared almost immediately.

'Take a trip round to Grosvenor Gardens and ask your friend
the cook if she's ever seen this necklace before, Wood. And
don't waste any time.'

'Well, if it isn't Mr Wood.'

'I'm sorry to bother you so late in the evening, Mrs
Hampton, but it is rather important.'

'Come in, Mr Wood. Kitty and me was just having a cup
of cocoa. Perhaps you'd care for one. There's a bit of cold
mutton as well, if you'd like some.'

'Thank you, that would be very nice.' Wood, never one to
pass up the offer of a free meal, followed the Naylors' cook
into the warm kitchen.

'Hello, Mr Wood.' Kitty the parlour maid was seated beside
the fire knitting, and reading a magazine.

'There you are, Mr Wood,' said Mrs Hampton, putting a
cup of cocoa and a plate of meat on the kitchen table. 'Now,
what can I help you with?'

'This,' said Wood, taking the necklace from his pocket.

It needed only a glance for Mrs Hampton to identify it.
'Why, bless you, that's Her Ladyship's,' she said. 'She's not
here at the moment, thank the Lord, but I can return it to her
if it would save you another journey.'

'It's not that simple, Mrs Hampton. You see, it's what we call evidence.'

'Evidence? Whatever do you mean? Are you saying it was stolen? Was it that man you told us about, the one who pretends to be from the gas board?'

'Not exactly.' Wood glanced from Mrs Hampton to Kitty and back again, and concluded that he could take them into his confidence. 'Earlier this evening I arrested Lady Naylor, and my guv'nor arrested Sir Royston.'

'Arrested?' Mrs Hampton put her hand to her mouth. 'Whatever for?'

'In connection with the murder of a prostitute at the end of last month.' Wood decided that he need say no more than that; in fact, he might have said too much.

'Well, I never did. I always knew that woman wasn't to be trusted.' It seemed that Mrs Hampton had already decided that Hilda Naylor was guilty of the crime for which Wood had arrested her.

'But I'd be glad if you kept that to yourselves,' continued Wood, glancing at Kitty as he spoke. He knew that domestic servants had a propensity for gossip, particularly with those below stairs in adjacent houses.

Mrs Hampton emitted a hollow laugh. 'Your secret's safe with us, Mr Wood,' she said, 'much as I'd love to shout it from the rooftops.'

It was close to eleven o'clock by the time that Wood reported back to the DDI.

'Well, Wood, you took your time. What news?'

'Mrs Hampton positively identified the necklace as belonging to Lady Naylor, sir.'

Hardcastle laughed. 'I thought she would.' He took out his hunter, briefly wound it and dropped it back into his waistcoat pocket. 'I think we'll let the Naylors have a night in the cells to think it over, Marriott. And then in the morning, we'll see what they have to say for themselves.' He stood up and put on his coat and hat. 'See you at eight o'clock tomorrow, Marriott.'

On Hardcastle's instructions, Sir Royston Naylor had been placed in the interview room. Languishing in an uncomfortable cell overnight had not, however, in any way reduced his

boorish attitude. If anything, it had increased it, but before
Naylor had a chance to protest at his detention Hardcastle
flung the necklace on the table.

'Seen that before, Sir Royston?'

'I, er—' The entrepreneur clipped on a pair of pince-nez
and peered closely at the item of jewellery. 'No, I can't say
that I recall having seen it before.'

Hardcastle laughed. 'It belongs to your wife, doesn't it?
And I suggest you bought it for her.'

'I suppose it's possible.' Naylor was hesitant in his reply,
and Hardcastle knew instinctively that he was prevaricating.

'Let's stop beating about the bush, Sir Royston. That necklace was found alongside the murdered body of Annie Kelly in
the basement of one of your properties, number one-four-three
Washbourne Street.'

'I'm sorry, but I don't know anything about it.' By now all
the fight had left Naylor.

'I suggest that you murdered Annie Kelly and deliberately
left that necklace there to throw suspicion on your wife.'

'I told you, I know nothing about it,' said Naylor desper-
ately.

'You didn't get on with your wife, did you, Sir Royston.'
Marriott had been fully briefed by DS Wood about the latter's
conversation with Mrs Hampton, the cook at Grosvenor Gardens.
'In fact, I'd suggest that you regret ever having married her.'

'Not at all, I—'

'I have it on good authority that you and she were always
fighting,' Marriott continued, 'especially at your London house,
and probably at Kingsley Hall, too.'

'The truth of the matter is that you were deceived by Hilda
Mullen into believing that she was pregnant: the oldest trick
in the book,' said Hardcastle. 'And that's why you married
her. It wouldn't do for a man who had been knighted by the
king to have an illegitimate child around the place. Particularly
when he had hopes of a peerage.'

'Then you discovered that you had made Annie Kelly pregnant.' Marriott joined in again, pressing Naylor. 'And she
started making demands that you divorce your wife and marry
her, or at least provide her with a substantial sum of money.
But you couldn't be sure that she'd stay quiet, even if you
paid up.'

'I didn't know anything about her being pregnant.'

'Well, the post-mortem examination of that poor girl revealed that she was two months up the spout, and that the sprog was yours,' said Hardcastle brutally. Neither he nor Dr Spilsbury had any way of knowing if that were the case, but the DDI guessed that Naylor would not be sufficiently knowledgeable to know it either.

'I think I ought to send for my lawyer,' said Naylor.

'I haven't finished yet,' said Hardcastle, 'and I'll tell you when you can see a solicitor. Now I turn to the matter of the late Lady Sarah Millard.'

'What about her?' asked Naylor listlessly.

'You'd been having it up regularly with her while her gallant husband was at the Front fighting for King and Country. But it came as a bit of a surprise when he turned up at Cadogan Place waving his pistol and threatening to kill you. And if the publicity that followed that unpleasant incident wasn't enough, Major Millard was going to divorce his wife and cite you as co-respondent. And that, Sir Royston, would certainly have put the kibosh on any hopes you had of settling your arse on the red benches of the House of Lords. So you decided that the only way to deal with that little problem was to murder Lady Sarah.' Hardcastle decided that it would not help him to secure an admission from Naylor if he mentioned the key to Lady Sarah Millard's Artillery Mansions apartment that was found in Lady Naylor's handbag.

'This is preposterous,' exclaimed Naylor, but he was clearly rattled by Hardcastle's allegations.

'Very well. Put him down, Marriott, and we'll see what Her Ladyship has to say about the matter.'

At their first meeting, Hardcastle had formed the opinion that Hilda, Lady Naylor, was a feisty woman. In similar vein to her husband, her confinement overnight had done little to diminish her arrogance.

She began speaking the moment that Hardcastle and Marriott entered the interview room. 'You obviously know who I am,' she said haughtily, 'and I'll warn you that I intend to complain to the highest authority. Sir Royston has some very influential friends in Whitehall, and if you think you can just arrest me on a whim, well, you're much mistaken, Inspector.'

'That was quite a speech for someone who started out life as an uneducated scullery maid in Brighton, who was sacked for thieving and then went on to become a factory girl who married the boss.' Hardcastle took out his pipe and began slowly to fill it. 'And all that swimming you did must've given you some pretty powerful muscles.' It was not a casual observation; he had a very good reason for saying it.

That Hardcastle knew so much of her background momentarily discomfited Hilda Naylor, but she quickly recovered. 'I don't see that bettering myself is anything to be sneered at,' she snapped.

Hardcastle placed the necklace on the table and sat back without comment.

For a few moments Hilda Naylor's gaze was transfixed by the platinum dog collar necklet beset with diamonds. 'What's that?' she asked eventually.

'A necklace, Lady Naylor, and Detective Sergeant Marriott here found it close to where the body of Annie Kelly was found in the ruins of one of the Washbourne Street houses owned by your husband.'

'Really?' Hilda Naylor affected ignorance. 'And what has it to do with me?'

'It's your necklace, Lady Naylor,' said Marriott. 'We've had it valued by a jeweller, and he put a price on it of about three hundred and fifty pounds. Hardly the sort of thing a prostitute could afford.'

Sir Royston's wife sneered. 'And what makes you think that it's mine?'

'It's been identified by members of your staff, and they're in no doubt that they saw you wearing it on several occasions.'

'I suppose you're talking about Drake, my former butler and that wretched little wife of his. Well, they're lying. Just because I sacked them they'd say anything to make me look bad. I dismissed them because they were unreliable, often absent and insubordinate.' Lady Naylor spoke cuttingly, as though any statements of an ex-servant and his wife were beneath consideration.

'Your husband also identified that necklace as yours,' said Hardcastle mildly, taking another of the unsubstantiated gambles to which Marriott had grown accustomed. 'Furthermore, he said that he hadn't seen you wearing it after

Monday the twenty-fifth of September. And that, Lady Naylor, was the date of Annie Kelly's murder.'

'That doesn't mean anything. I didn't see it after that date either.'

'So, you admit the necklace is yours,' said Marriott.

'It might be.' Hilda Naylor, realizing that she had made a mistake, attempted to backtrack on her statement.

'Are you suggesting that Sir Royston murdered this poor girl?' asked Hardcastle.

'I really have no idea, but he and I were both at Kingsley Hall that weekend. So neither of us could've done it.'

Hardcastle had no intention of revealing details of DS Wood's conversation with Mrs Hampton, a conversation that confirmed that Lady Naylor was in London on the Sunday prior to the discovery of Annie Kelly's murder. It would be time enough to adduce that evidence at the trial. And Hardcastle was now, at last, convinced that there would be a trial.

'You must have to have pretty strong hands to manage that horse of yours,' commented Hardcastle in a disinterested way, as though he were merely making conversation.

'I'm a good horsewoman, even though I say it myself,' said Hilda Naylor, mistakenly assuming that Hardcastle was paying her a compliment.

'Strong enough to strangle someone, I should think.'

'What d'you mean by that?'

Hardcastle took another risk. 'You were frightened that if Annie Kelly made a fuss about being pregnant by your husband it would put the kibosh on any chance your husband might have of getting himself a peerage. And I suggest that you decided to do away with Annie, and do away with the problem at the same time.'

'Rubbish!' Hilda Naylor almost spat her denial, but Hardcastle noticed that her cheeks had reddened.

'And then there's this.' The DDI produced the key that Mrs Cartwright had found in Lady Naylor's handbag.

'What's that supposed to do with anything?' The woman cast a disdainful glance at the key.

'It's the key to Lady Sarah Millard's apartment in Artillery Mansions, and it was found in your handbag.'

'Nonsense! You must've put it there in some silly attempt to make me look guilty.'

'Guilty of what, Lady Naylor?' asked Marriott mildly.

'I had nothing to do with that woman's murder, if that's what you're suggesting.'

'Your husband seems to think you did,' said Hardcastle mildly.

'I don't believe it.' But it was fairly obvious that she did believe that her husband had made a statement implicating her in the murder.

'Well, you'll have a chance to argue it out at the trial. Put her back in her cell, Marriott, and then come back here.'

'What's next, sir?' asked Marriott, when he returned from locking up Lady Naylor.

'Get hold of Mr Collins in Fingerprint Bureau, and ask him to come over here as quickly as he can. I want him to take Lady Naylor's dabs and compare them with those he found in Lady Sarah's apartment.'

EIGHTEEN

Hardcastle was in no hurry to re-interview Sir Royston Naylor, and dropped into the matron's room alongside the charge room.

'Any tea on the go, Mrs Cartwright?'

'Always got a cup for you, Mr Hardcastle. It's just made.' Bertha Cartwright took a large brown teapot from the stove and poured a cup of tea for the DDI.

'It looks as though you'll have to give evidence at the Old Bailey, Mrs Cartwright.' Hardcastle sat down at the small table. 'Lady Naylor doesn't believe that you found that key in her handbag,' he said, helping himself to a ginger snap.

'She'd lie through her teeth, that one,' scoffed the matron. 'I'll happily swear on a stack of Bibles that I found it. And Mr Marriott *and* the station officer were there when I did.'

'Your lady wife's put it all down to you, Sir Royston.' Hardcastle spoke in matter-of-fact tones as he concentrated on slowly filling his pipe.

'What d'you mean by that?'

'She reckons that it was you who murdered Lady Sarah.'

'That's preposterous,' exclaimed Naylor. 'Why would I do such a thing?'

'To avoid an unsavoury court case. Major Millard was going to divorce his wife and cite you as a co-respondent. And that would've put paid to any ideas you had about becoming Lord Naylor of Kingsley.'

'That's absurd,' protested Naylor.

Marriott, sitting beside Hardcastle, thought it absurd also, but he was no longer surprised when the DDI made outrageous allegations. It so often achieved the desired result.

Hardcastle nodded sagely. 'Yes, I thought so too, Sir Royston. It seemed to me that Lady Naylor wanted to see you dressed up in ermine more than you did.'

'I had nothing to do with it.' Naylor remained silent for a few moments. 'That bloody woman has been nothing but trouble to me. I don't know why the hell I married her.'

'I suppose it's the old, old story: you mistook lust for love,' said Hardcastle, with a flash of earthy wisdom as he stood up. He turned to Marriott. 'Put him down.'

'Are you keeping me here, Inspector?' asked Naylor, a note of incredulity in his voice.

'Most certainly,' said Hardcastle. 'You might not have done the deed, but I'm far from convinced that you're totally innocent in this affair.'

It was not until three o'clock that same afternoon that Detective Inspector Collins was able to give Hardcastle the result of his fingerprint comparison.

'I've got good news for you, Ernie.'

'It's about time I had some,' muttered Hardcastle.

'I've compared the fingerprint impressions I took from Lady Naylor with those I found in Lady Sarah Millard's flat at Artillery Mansions.'

'Well, don't keep me in suspense, Charlie.'

'They're a match.'

'With the dabs you found on the bedside locker?'

'The very same,' said Collins.

'Good work, Charlie,' said Hardcastle. 'You'd better get the mothballs out of your Old Bailey suit because we're going to trial.'

*   *   *

'When am I going to be released?' demanded Hilda Naylor
haughtily. 'I've been here for nearly twenty-four hours, and
I can assure you that Sir Royston will be taking legal action
regarding this matter. It's an outrage.'

'As I told you earlier,' began Hardcastle, 'a key to Lady
Sarah Millard's apartment at Artillery Mansions was found in
your handbag—'

'And I told you that I—'

'Just be quiet and listen,' snapped Hardcastle. 'The key was
found in your handbag, and I have just received confirmation
that your fingerprints were found on a bedside locker in the
same apartment next to the bed where Lady Sarah's body was
found. But first, I shall deal with the murder of Annie Kelly
. . .' The DDI held out his hand for the file that Marriott was
holding, not that he needed it. 'A platinum and diamond
necklet that has been positively identified as your property
was found close to the body of the Kelly woman. I shall
shortly charge you with both those murders.'

'It's a lie, a bloody filthy lie. You bastards are stitching me
up. I never had nothing to do with those murders. I never had
no key, and I've never seen that bloody necklace before.' Lady
Naylor's hitherto cultivated control over her speech finally
vanished, and her factory-girl persona came to the surface. 'It
was Royston, he done for 'em.'

Hardcastle turned to his sergeant. 'I suppose you'd better
write that down, Marriott,' he said mildly.

'You can't prove any of this,' protested Hilda Naylor.

'That remains to be seen,' said Hardcastle mildly. 'However,
I shall produce witnesses at your trial who'll testify to your
possession of the key, and your ownership of the necklace.'
But then Hardcastle adopted an avuncular tone that Marriott
did not hear too often. 'I've a feeling there's something you
want to tell me, Lady Naylor.'

'Does either of you have a cigarette?'

Marriott produced his packet of Gold Flake and offered it.

'Thank you.' Hilda Naylor smiled as Marriott struck a match
and leaned forward to light her cigarette. She had suddenly
become much less hostile than previously.

'I'm surprised you smoke,' said Hardcastle, maintaining his
kindly tone of voice, 'seeing as how you're a strong swimmer,
and a very good horsewoman.'

'I used to swim a lot as a girl, in the sea at Brighton, but not any more,' said Hilda Naylor. 'I had high hopes of swimming the Channel one day, but then I married Sir Royston and he bought me a fine stallion. He's been very good to me, and I'd do anything for him.'

This was an entirely different woman from the haughty chatelaine of Kingsley Hall who the two detectives had first encountered. But Hardcastle was cynical enough to conclude that it was a charade.

'I heard a rumour that he's being considered for a peerage,' continued Hardcastle, as though he were carrying on a polite conversation rather than questioning a murder suspect. But the DDI was a skilled interrogator.

'Oh yes,' agreed Naylor's wife. 'No more than he deserves, of course. He's worked very hard for the war effort. That's what got him his knighthood in the first place, you know. He had to go to Buckingham Palace to be invested by the King.'

'I suppose you knew about him meeting Annie Kelly, Lady Naylor,' suggested Marriott. 'And that he'd got her pregnant.'

'Of course I did.' Lady Naylor threw back her head and laughed. 'He's like all men,' she said. 'A pretty girl appears and he's putty in her hands. Of course I knew.'

Which is how you *trapped him*, thought Hardcastle. 'And you didn't mind?'

'No. It's what men do.'

'And Lady Sarah Millard?'

'Yes, I knew about her too. And that was stupid, especially when all that nonsense came out about her old man chasing him out into the street.' Hilda Naylor laughed at the thought. 'I'd loved to have see Royston running down the street holding up his trousers.'

'It attracted some unwelcome publicity,' continued Hardcastle. 'Particularly when the court martial was held.'

'I told Royston that he'd been a bloody fool.' Lady Naylor stubbed out her half-smoked cigarette in the tin lid that did service as an ashtray. 'And I told him that if anything was going to cast doubt on his getting a seat in the House of Lords that would.'

'Major Millard's intention of divorcing his wife would have brought more publicity, too,' commented Hardcastle.

'Of course it would,' snapped Hilda Naylor. 'But it didn't

stop him; he even carried on seeing her when she moved to Artillery Mansions.'

Hardcastle noted that Hilda Naylor had finally acknowledged knowing where Lady Sarah Millard was living after her husband Hugo had left her.

'And you took the key to Lady Sarah's flat from your husband, I suppose.'

'No. Royston gave it to me.'

'And he knew why you wanted it, I suppose?'

'Of course he did,' sneered Hilda Naylor.

'And with Lady Sarah dead, all the obstacles to your husband's chances of a peerage would have been removed,' said Marriott.

'And so you decided to do away with her,' said Hardcastle quietly.

'Yes, I . . . no, I didn't mean to say that.' For the first time since the interview had begun, Lady Naylor became flustered as she realized the damaging admission she had made.

'And Sir Royston knew all about it, I suppose?'

'Of course he did.' It was a lame attempt to shift the blame on to her husband.

'Which is why he told me that you'd been at Kingsley Hall when in fact you were in London murdering Annie Kelly and Lady Sarah.'

'What do you think?' asked Hilda Naylor listlessly; it seemed that she had finally tired of all the pretence.

'How did you lure Annie Kelly to the Washbourne Street house where we found her body, Lady Naylor?' asked Hardcastle.

'Easy. I told her that I was going to give her a thousand pounds to disappear and keep quiet, and that that's where the money was.'

'But you had no intention of paying her anything, did you?' asked Marriott.

'Of course not, the slut. And when the house was bombed, I thought that she'd never be found.'

'You'd better write all that down, Marriott,' said Hardcastle mildly, 'and then take Lady Naylor into the charge room. I'll be there shortly.'

'Very good, sir,' said Marriott.

Hardcastle walked through to the front office. 'Open up Sir Royston's cell for me, Skipper.'

'Yes, sir,' said the station sergeant, and seized a large bunch of keys from a hook near the door to the cell passage.

Sir Royston Naylor stood up as the DDI entered his cell. 'I hope you've come to tell me that I'm being released, Inspector.'

'No, Sir Royston, I haven't. I'm here to tell you that I will shortly charge your wife with two counts of murder.'

Naylor sank down on to the wooden plank that did service as a bed. 'Well, that'll put the kibosh on my peerage if nothing else does,' he said, putting his head in his hands. 'Can I go now?'

'No,' said Hardcastle. 'I am about to charge you with being involved in this murder.'

'*What*?' Naylor leaped to his feet again. 'On what grounds?'

'The alibi you gave Lady Naylor when you told me that she'd been at Kingsley Hall for the whole weekends of both the murders. You knew damned well where she was and what she was doing. What's more, she told me that you gave her the key to Lady Sarah's apartment at Artillery Mansions.'

'You'll have a job proving it,' said Naylor.

Hardcastle just smiled, but said nothing. In the event, Naylor was proved right. The Director of Public Prosecutions pointed out that a husband and wife cannot conspire with each other; in law they are one.

Furthermore, he ruled that, in his view, the provision of an alibi did not amount to an offence in this case, unless it could be proved that Sir Royston Naylor *knew* that his wife was intent upon murder. The same went for Lady Naylor's allegation that Sir Royston had *given* her the key to the Millard girl's apartment at Artillery Mansions, rather than Hilda having *taken* it without her husband's knowledge.

And proving any of that, Hardcastle surmised, would be very difficult, if not downright impossible.

On Friday the third of November 1916, Lady Naylor appeared in the dock at Bow Street police court. As the clerk of the court read out her name, there was an immediate hubbub of chatter in the public gallery, and a babble of renewed conversation in the press box.

Just over six years previously Hawley Harvey Crippen and Ethel le Neve had stood in that same dock charged with the murder of Crippen's wife, Belle Elmore, at 39 Hilldrop Crescent, Camden Town in North London. They had been arrested in Halifax, Nova Scotia, following a dramatic dash across the Atlantic by Detective Chief Inspector Walter Dew of Scotland Yard. But there the similarity ended.

Hardcastle stepped into the witness box and gave brief details of Lady Naylor's arrest and asked for a remand in custody.

'Remanded in custody for eight days,' said the Chief Metropolitan Magistrate, 'to reappear here on . . .' He paused to examine his register. 'Saturday the eleventh.'

'I'm obliged to Your Worship,' said Hardcastle.

'When will you be in a position for depositions to be made, Mr Hardcastle?'

'I would think in about two weeks' time, Your Worship.'

'At the second remand hearing, then.'

'Yes, sir.'

On Saturday morning, a constable appeared in the detectives' office, and crossed to where Marriott was seated at the far end.

'A message for you, Sergeant.'

Marriott looked up. 'Yes?'

'A Mr Gilbert Parfitt telephoned, Sergeant,' said the PC, reading from the message form he was holding. 'He's a jeweller in Victoria Street apparently, and he asked if you'd call on him. He has some information for you.'

'Ah, Mr Marriott.' Parfitt withdrew a sheet of paper from beneath his counter as Marriott entered his shop. 'I circulated details of the platinum and diamond necklet you found, and a colleague of mine with premises in Bond Street has identified it.'

'Has he? Does he know who bought it?'

'Yes, at least he's fairly certain. According to his records, it was purchased by Sir Royston Naylor as a gift for his wife on the twentieth of March this year. Is that of any assistance?'

'Indeed it is, Mr Parfitt,' said Marriott. 'I'm much obliged to you.'

Back at the police station, Marriott told Hardcastle what he had learned from Parfitt.

'And just to make sure, sir, I took the necklace to the Bond Street jeweller and he was adamant that it was the piece he sold to Sir Royston. Apparently Sir Royston mentioned that it was a gift for his wife.'

'There's no doubt whose necklace it was, then, Marriott,' said Hardcastle. 'Not that I thought there would be.'

A fortnight later the laborious business of taking depositions began before the Bow Street magistrate. Each prosecution witness testified to the evidence they would give at the Old Bailey trial and the clerk of the court painstakingly wrote it down in longhand.

Eventually a bill of indictment was placed before the 23 freeholders who constituted the grand jury. After a suitable period of deliberation they returned a true bill.

The trial of Hilda, Lady Naylor, opened at the Central Criminal Court in Old Bailey on Monday the fifth of February 1917.

The press box was full: it appeared that every national newspaper was represented along with reporters from the local press in Buckinghamshire and Westminster.

For the spectators the charge of murder against Lady Naylor was a *cause célèbre* not to be missed. The public gallery in number one court was thronged with men in morning dress, a couple of peers among them. There were even several army officers, and a commander in the Royal Navy. The ladies wore the sort of finery that befitted such an occasion: expensive fur-trimmed hats with eye-level veils and coats of either sealskin or musquash.

For a reason known only to himself the Solicitor-General, Sir Gordon Hewart, KC, had decided to prosecute. Languishing on the front bench, he was seated close to Sir Roland Storey, KC, who was appearing for the defence. Behind these two eminent silks was a group of juniors, each of whom was busily reading through his brief for the umpteenth time.

As the judge entered, the court rose as one and the barristers bowed.

'Put up the prisoner,' said the judge.

Flanked by grim-looking prison wardresses, Lady Naylor

was ushered into the high dock. She was soberly dressed, all in black, with a small straw hat and a veil.

She pleaded Not Guilty to the indictments: the wilful murders of Annie Kelly and Lady Sarah Millard.

The bailiff led twelve severely countenanced men into the jury box. As the law required they were all men of property.

The trial was ready to begin.

Sir Gordon Hewart rose, introduced himself and counsel for the defence, and outlined the case against Hilda Naylor.

But Hardcastle and Marriott saw none of this; together with the other prosecution witnesses they were corralled in the echoing hall outside the courtroom.

An usher appeared. 'Divisional Detective Inspector Ernest Hardcastle,' he cried, peering around at the assembled witnesses.

In a masterful demonstration of how evidence should be given, Hardcastle outlined the salient points of his investigation, including the finding of Lady Naylor's necklace close to where Annie Kelly's body was found, and receiving from Mrs Cartwright the key to Lady Sarah's apartment.

The trial continued prosaically for the next few days with only the occasional highlight to break the monotony of dull testimony.

One such notable exception was the appearance of Bertha Cartwright.

Elegantly attired in a black coat and a wide-brimmed hat with a feather, she took the oath in a confident voice.

Sir Gordon Hewart smiled. It was an attempt to put her at her ease, but it was unnecessary. 'You are Mrs Bertha Cartwright, and you are employed as the station matron at Cannon Row police station. Is that correct, madam?'

'Yes, sir.'

'Please tell My Lord and the gentlemen of the jury what occurred on Wednesday the first of November last.'

'Sergeant Marriott asked me to search Lady Naylor and her belongings, sir.'

'And what did you find, Mrs Cartwright?'

'I found nothing of consequence on her person or her clothing, sir, but then I searched her handbag.'

'And what did you find?' asked Hewart.

'A bunch of keys, a diary, a small account book, a lace-trimmed handkerchief, a pencil in a silver holder, and some visiting cards in a silver case, sir.' Bertha Cartwright spoke without hesitation.

'Was that all?'

'No, sir. I also found a separate key that I handed to Sergeant Marriott.'

'Thank you, Mrs Cartwright. Just stay there in case my learned friend wants to ask you any questions.'

Sir Roland Storey rose to his feet, hitched his gown back on to his left shoulder, and glared at the witness.

'Mrs Cartwright, I put it to you that you made Lady Naylor strip naked in a cold cell.'

'Yes, sir. It was necessary so's I could search her properly. It's the procedure.'

'I also put it to you that at one stage you struck Lady Naylor a blow. In fact, I suggest you slapped her face.'

Mrs Cartwright was not in the slightest discomfited by the accusation, true though it was. 'I did, sir,' she said blandly. 'Lady Naylor was hysterical at the time, and it's the correct treatment for hysteria.'

'You are qualified in such matters, are you?' asked Storey sarcastically.

'I am, sir. I am a state-registered nurse. I also remember Lady Naylor calling me a fat cow. Not the behaviour I'd've expected from a titled lady.'

'Yes, I see. Thank you, Mrs Cartwright.' Storey sat down. Eminent KC he might be, but he had not reckoned on so spirited a response from a police station matron.

The hint of a smile crossed the judge's face as he glanced at Sir Gordon Hewart. 'Mr Solicitor?'

'I have no further questions of this witness, My Lord,' said Hewart.

'Thank you, Mrs Cartwright,' said the judge, 'you may step down, but stay within the precincts of the court.'

The trial lasted three weeks. Among those called to give evidence were Dr Spilsbury, DI Collins, Edward and Gladys Drake, Mrs Hampton, the cook at the Naylors' Grosvenor Place house, Cyril Pearce, the butler who had walked out on the Naylors, and James Charlton, the Wendover cab driver, making his first visit to London.

The jury took ten hours to reach their verdict, but it was damning.

'Hilda Naylor,' began the judge sternly, 'you have been found guilty of the heinous crime of murder, and rightly so in my view. Have you anything to say before sentence of death be passed upon you?'

But Lady Naylor was incapable of a response. She had been so unreasonably confident of an acquittal that the verdict took her by surprise, and she had collapsed when it was returned. Now sobbing hysterically, and supported by the wardresses, she was unable to say anything; just a low moan emerged from her.

The judge donned the black cap and passed sentence. The chaplain appealed to the Almighty to have mercy on Lady Naylor's soul, and within the hour she was in the condemned cell at Holloway prison in north London.

The Home Secretary, Sir Herbert Samuel, carefully considered the sentence, but marked the docket 'Let the law take its course.'

Three weeks later, Hilda Naylor was hanged. The usual collection of morbid sightseers waited outside the gates of the prison until the black flag was raised and a stark, brief notice confirming her execution was placed outside.

'There's an interesting piece on the Court Circular page of *The Times* this morning that might interest you, Ernie.' Superintendent Arthur Hudson stood in the doorway of Hardcastle's office holding the newspaper.

'What's that, sir?' asked the DDI as he stood up.

'It states that the King has commanded that the name of Royston Naylor be struck from the roll of Knights Bachelor.'

'Can't say I'm surprised, sir,' said Hardcastle. 'In my opinion, Naylor was lucky to get away with just losing his knighthood. And it certainly puts paid to his aspirations for a peerage. Their lordships don't much care for sharing a bench with someone whose missus has been topped for murder.'